THE COWGIRL AND THE COLTS

A STORY ABOUT CAROLYN CLARK, DIXIE, AND THE BALTIMORE COLTS

PAUL J. TRAVERS

THE COWGIRL AND THE COLTS

A STORY ABOUT CAROLYN CLARK, DIXIE, AND THE BALTIMORE COLTS

For information address:
Helm Publishing
3923 Seward Ave.
Rockford, IL 61108
815-398-4660
www.publishersdrive.com

ISBN 978-0-9792328-7-9
Printed in the United States of America

DEDICATION

To Carolyn, Willie and Dorothy

Happy trails to you, you've met around the bend,
Happy trails to you, your smiles will never end.

To Frank, Take a walk down memory lane with the Baltimore Colts. Hope you enjoy the trip! Best Wishes!

QUOTES AND COMMENTS

"Over the years I've discovered that there's more to being a cowgirl than punching cows, or winning rodeo trophies, or galloping off into a movie sunset with Roy. Cowgirl is an attitude, really, a pioneer spirit; a special American brand of courage. The cowgirl faces life head on, lives by her lights, and makes no excuses. Cowgirls take stands. They speak up. They defend the things they hold dear. A cowgirl might be a rancher, or a barrel racer, or a bull rider, or an actress. But she's just as likely to be a checker at the local Winn Dixie, a full-time mother, a banker, an attorney, an astronaut.

Children of my generation longed to be movie stars. Today, even movie stars want to be cowgirls. I'm in my golden years, as they say, but I still sometimes find myself thinking about what I'd like to be when I grow up. It's sort of silly, I know, but... I think I'd like to be a cowgirl."

Dale Evans Rogers, "Queen of the West,"
Cowgirl Hall of Fame 1995

"During my rodeo career, I worked with Dale Evans and Gail Davis as Annie Oakley, two cowgirl legends. Like Dale and Gail, Carolyn's life embraced the true spirit of the American cowgirl."

Arlene Kensinger, world champion trick rider and barrel racer,

Cowgirl Hall of Fame 2002

"The "can do" spirit of the cowgirl was evident in Carolyn at a very early age. Cowgirls are pioneers, and Carolyn was a pioneer as a mascot for a professional football team. During her short life, she made her mark as a cowgirl and paved the way for future generations of girls and women who dared to achieve...this giving them fulfillment of their cowgirl attitude and spirit."

Pam Minick, champion calf roper, former Miss Rodeo America,

Cowgirl Hall of Fame 2000

"This is a heart-warming story about a young girl and her wise pony. Let Carolyn's pixie-like twinkle captivate you, but don't let it fool you. She was a passionate girl who exuded "cowgirl" confidence and fortitude. Read the story and you're sure to feel that you've been touched by an angel."

Sharon Camarillo, champion barrel racer, educator and performer,

Cowgirl Hall of Fame 2006

Acknowledgements

The book was originally titled "Ride the Magic Carousel." From proposal to print, the story of Carolyn Clark and Dixie was just that, a ride aboard a magic carousel. My sincerest thanks to all of those who rode with me. Without your unbridled enthusiasm and endless encouragement, I would not have held onto the reins to finish the ride and grab the brass ring.

As with any book, the story of Carolyn and Dixie was a chance to renew old friendships and new friends. I am graciously indebted to the following friends for allowing Carolyn and Dixie to ride again:

To the Sports Legends Museum at Camden Yards, Baltimore, Maryland, who accommodated my every request and opened their archives. Visit their website at www.baberuthmuseum.com. Tour the museum in person to discover a sports treasure chest.

To John Ziemann, band director and sports historian, whose encyclopedic knowledge about the Baltimore Colts and their marching band brought the memories to life.

To the 1959 Baltimore Colts, my childhood heroes, for their support, most notably Raymond

Berry, Hall of Fame football player and Texas gentleman.

To the National Cowgirl Museum and Hall of Fame, Fort Worth, Texas, for their research assistance and Texas hospitality. To learn more about some great cowgirls, visit their website at www.cowgirl.net.

To Sharon Camarillo, Arlene Kensinger, Sherri Mell, and Pam Minick, Hall of Fame Cowgirls and grand ladies of the Old West, who rallied around Carolyn as one of their own. To learn more about these incredible women, visit www.cowgirl.net.

To Cynthia Travers, off-shore editor, mariner, and Artic explorer, whose love of horses rekindled my memory of Carolyn and Dixie.

To Deborah and Catherine Travers, the Belles of the Patapsco, for their technical assistance and emotional support.

To Dianne Helm of Helm Publishing who believed there was nothing ordinary about an extraordinary girl and her pony.

And to Dottie Hicks, the Honorable William Donald Schaefer, Rachel Kassman and the Hornblake Library at the University of Maryland, Shelley Smith and Malinda Armstrong, the Pro Football Hall of Fame, former band members and cheerleaders of the Baltimore Colts Marching Band, and Baltimore Colts fans around the country for fondly remembering a football team and the times of their lives.

Time to saddle-up! I hope you enjoy the ride!

Table of Contents

Chapter 1 – The Pony Express Rides Again

Carolyn shielded her eyes from the stinging sand and gulped hard. Her last chance for a summer job did not look promising. From all appearances, the town of Bitter Creek was going to be a bitter pill to swallow. A red haze shrouded the landscape as swirling clouds of coarse, brown dirt blotted out the sun. Buildings shimmered in the heat like a mirage, their whitewashed exteriors sandblasted to a ghostly pale. Bitter Creek was a dreary place to hang your hat, if only for a few months. The wind blew hard, and the sun burned hot. The blowing heat was like living in a pizza oven, Carolyn thought. She chuckled to herself, but it was no laughing matter. Cowboys always bragged about the majestic view of the world from the saddle. It was obvious they had never laid eyes on Bitter Creek, a place more jest than majestic.

Like many prairie towns, Bitter Creek was clinging to a dream. Any day the railroad was coming. That was the rumor on the lips of the townspeople. When the dirt trails became steel rails, the wilderness would be tamed. Gandy dancers, the nickname given to track workers, would replace cowpunchers. Tourists would sing, and cash registers would ring. Settlers would finally call Bitter Creek their home, and businesses would boom. Sturdy brick buildings would replace the wood structures that swayed in the wind. In a few years, the town would rival the grand city of Denver as the gateway to the West. That was the dream, but for now Bitter Creek was living a nightmare. This part of the country was still the "wild west" where the sheriff and the undertaker did most of the business. It was no surprise that most of the population was either in an iron cell or pine box. But there was a glimmer of hope. The Pony Express, the mail service running from Missouri to California, recently opened a branch office in the center of town. For Carolyn, that's where the trail ended and the dream started.

Carolyn slid out of the saddle and tethered her pony Dixie to a hitching post. A mangy black and white mutt raced from beneath one of the buildings, growled at Carolyn's feet, and quickly retreated. "Welcome to Bitter Creek where bitter is better," she murmured to herself. Wiping her brow with her riding glove, she searched the deserted streets with an icy stare. Most of the storefronts were vacant, their windows covered in a thick dust. Could the Pony Express office be closed before it even opened, she thought dejectedly as she kicked away a prickly coil of tumbleweed lodged at her feet. Three hard days on the trail were going to be a waste of time. Carolyn grimaced and took a deep breath. The only thing to do was saddle up and ride to the next dying town. That was a way of life for cowboys and cowgirls. As Carolyn stepped up in the stirrup, a violent gust of wind slapped her to the ground. The stunning blow left her momentarily paralyzed. An angry buzz filled her head. Seconds later, a soft squeak echoed in her ears. Shading her face with her hand, she looked up, still flat on her back. A soft smile creased her face as she read the weathered sign blowing in the wind. "The Pony Express, Bitter Creek Office," she mumbled with satisfaction. Jumping to her feet, she dusted off her buckskin jacket and hitched up her saddle-worn chaps. A few steps farther, the smile grew wider. A handwritten sign in the window announced *Now Hiring Riders*.

Carolyn stepped inside the office and instantly did a double take. Except for the gun rack that lined the back wall, the room was identical to the post office back home. Peeking over the chest-high counter, she rubbed the trail dust from her eyes and quietly stepped back. The window clerk, hidden from view behind the counter, was a dead ringer for Mr. Harper, her English teacher. Carolyn fretted about her chances of being hired. She had gotten an A in the class, but Mr. Harper didn't seem to like any of his students, including Carolyn. He had the reputation as the toughest teacher in middle school, a title he relished with delight.

Raising her hand to her mouth, Carolyn politely cleared her throat. "Be right with you. Got some real important business to attend here," the clerk said impatiently. After frantically scrawling some squiggly lines across a piece of paper, he dropped his pen and looked up. "Why, yes ma'am, what can I do for you?" he said curtly.

Carolyn fished a handbill out of her pocket and laid the crumpled piece of paper on the counter. "I came for a job," she announced in a husky voice, hoping to sound older than what she appeared.

The clerk glanced at the flyer and swept it off the top of the counter with the back of his hand. "I know what is says, but aren't you a little young for this kind of work?" he grumbled.

"Your flyer says expert riders, young and skinny, not over 18. That's me," Carolyn said boldly.

"It also says fellows willing to risk death daily, and I don't see where you're a fellow," the clerk shot back, spitting a flume of tobacco into a spittoon at his feet.

"Heck, I can ride as good as any man," Carolyn bragged, her hands folded across her chest.

The clerk scratched his head as he sized up the young cowgirl. He was in a bind. He desperately needed a rider, and right now, any warm body would do. Who knows, this cowgirl might be worth a chance. She was certainly sassy enough for the job. After all, he did hire Bronco Charlie. Only eleven years old at the time, he turned out to be one of the company's best riders. "Here's the deal. I need a rider to deliver medicine to Sweetwater about a hundred miles from here. Some kind of plague is killing off every living creature. People are dropping like flies. Deliver the medicine, and I'll give you a hundred dollar bonus plus a regular job when you return."

Carolyn blinked and raised her eyebrows, startled by the sudden offer. It was a strange way of doing business, but she had no reason to be suspicious. Every day people went to job interviews and were hired on the spot. "I'm the girl you're looking for," she crowed, tipping her hat. "When do I start?"

"Just as soon as I finish filling out your job application," the clerk answered eagerly as he thumbed through a pile of papers. Pulling out a crisp company form, he dabbed his pen into the inkwell. "Let's see," he mumbled as he wrote. "You look to be a little over five feet tall and a little over a hundred pounds with blue eyes and blonde hair."

"That's just about a bull's-eye," Carolyn replied with a Texas twang, hoping to sound like a genuine cowgirl.

"Name?"

"Carolyn Clark."

"Age?"

"About twelve, almost thirteen."

"Birthplace?"

"The jockey's room, in Charlestown, West Virginia."

"Riding experience?"

"Ten years."

"Trouble with the law?"

"No, sir, I'm a straight-shooter."

"Any bad habits?"

"No, sir. don't cuss, smoke or gamble. I spit every once in a while."

"Next of kin?"

"Dorothy and Willie Clark."

"Mailing address?"

"The Jolly Jockey Farm, way back east in Maryland."

The clerk placed the form and his pen on the counter. "Just sign on the dotted line, ma'am."

"I'll do your company proud," Carolyn boasted as she hurriedly signed her name in case the clerk had a sudden change of mind. She didn't bother to read the fine print about the company's policy for accidents on the job. At this point in time, it didn't matter. She had the summer job of her dreams. It was time to stop reading and start riding. This wasn't school; this was work.

"Congratulations Miss Clark! You are now an official employee of the Pony Express," the clerk declared elatedly. "Head across the street to the livery stable, and Jake will get you saddled up." The clerk smiled and crossed his fingers for good luck as Carolyn turned for the door. He conveniently had forgotten to tell her about the bad food, bad weather, bad outlaws, bad Indians, and the "biggest and baddest" horse west of the Mississippi. No sense in scaring off the tenderfoot who might be another Bronco Charlie, he reasoned. The young whippersnapper had a lot of spunk. She just might be able to save the town of Sweetwater. If not, she'd disappear in the wilderness like the others, never to be found. Staring at the sign in the window, the clerk was tempted to turn it around to read "Not Hiring Riders." No use in bothering, he finally decided. He might need a new rider by daybreak.

Carolyn walked into the stable and stopped dead in her tracks. In town for only an hour, she had seen some strange sights, but this was the strangest. Jack, the stable boy, was busy shoveling coal into a wheelbarrow from one of the horse stalls. Every stall had been turned into a coal bin.

"Just hired for the ride to Sweetwater," Carolyn announced after she caught Jake's attention by waving her hat.

"Just in time to feed the beast," Jake replied wearily as he looked over his shoulder. "Follow me. Your ride is out back." With a loud grunt, he lifted the wheelbarrow and wobbled out the back door.

Carolyn almost fainted when she eyed the beast. The mammoth creature was tall as a giraffe, wide as an elephant, and black as coal. "Why, that's not a horse. It's a… It's a…" she gasped in shock.

"It's a machine!' Jake shouted with glee, taking obvious delight in finishing Carolyn's sentence. "Can you believe it? The original iron horse is right here in Bitter Creek," he added proudly. Without another word, Jake went right to work. The beast was hungry and thirsty. Jake opened up a trap door on the side of the machine and shoveled in the coal. When the iron plates warmed, he grabbed a fire hose and ran to the front. Using a crowbar, he pried open the jaws and shoved the hose down the beast's throat. The beast hissed and gurgled as waves of heat radiated from its body.

Carolyn nervously stepped forward for a closer look at her ride. Sweat started to bead on her forehead.

"It's nothing but a fancy steam engine made to look like a horse," Jake explained as he walked around the beast and checked gauges that were mounted on the sides. "About a month ago, a stranger rode into town with a wagon full of parts. He said that since we weren't getting a railroad

8

anytime soon, he was giving us an iron horse. Told us we wouldn't need any rails. Just fire up the machine and watch it go. I was his helper. After the stranger disappeared into the night with all of our horses, I got the job as caretaker." Just as Jake finished talking, the beast roared to life. Flumes of scalding steam spurted from its mouth and nose. When a low rumble stirred from deep inside its belly, Jake placed his ear next to the beast and made a sour face. The beast was always moody, but this was not normal behavior. Lightly touching one of the iron plates, he jerked back his finger and stuck it in his mouth. The iron was red hot and starting to glow. Suddenly, the machine started to rattle and rock. When it began to sway violently from side to side, Jake had seen enough. "Run for cover! It's going to blow!" he yelled at the top of his lungs.

Carolyn scrambled a few steps and dove behind a bale of hay. With her hands tightly around her head, she trembled as the beast continued to roar. Finally, the bellowing ceased, and Carolyn summoned the courage to peek. The beast had stopped moving, but it was still very much alive. Rivets popped like corks from a bottle and dropped to the ground. Iron plates groaned as they buckled from the intense heat. Black oil oozed from the ruptured seams. With its dying breath, the beast expelled a stream of liquid flame that started a small grass fire. Carolyn stuck her fingers in her ears and waited for the explosion that would blast the beast into outer space. A thick cloud of white smoke shrouded the beast as she began the countdown. "Five, four, three, two, one, lift-off!" she shouted. With a thunderous, metallic bang, the beast rocketed two feet in the air and collapsed with a loud clang into a pile of smoldering junk.

Wiping soot and sweat from their faces, Carolyn and Jake cautiously emerged from their hiding places for a closer look. As the steam cloud faded, a lone figure in a black top hat and black overcoat hovered over the wreck. "It's the stranger! He's come back for this machine. I'm in big trouble," Jake wailed, fearing for his life.

The stranger took a step forward with two horseshoes in each hand, his face hidden in a veil of darkness. "You will need these for your trip," he said in a ghostly voice that echoed from the grave. He extended his arms towards Carolyn and dropped the smoking horseshoes. Instantly, the sod beneath his feet ripped apart. As a thick, cold fog seeped from the fissure, the stranger raised his hands to the sky. "Ride for the care of your soul," he howled madly, or at least that's what is sounded like to Carolyn. Suddenly, a wild and wicked wind blew from the west and formed a tornado around the remains of the beast. With a deafening clang, the funnel lifted the junk pile to the sky. Seconds later, it spiraled downward with lightning speed and slammed into the earth like a thunderbolt. When the smoke cleared, the crack in the earth had disappeared. Not a blade of grass was scorched or a clump of dirt dislodged. All that remained were the horseshoes. The iron horse and its owner had vanished without a trace as if they had never existed.

Wide-eyed and shaking, Carolyn and Jake looked at each other in disbelief and shrugged. "That's strange," said Jake, clumsily picking up the shoes. "They're ice cold."

"Strange is the normal for this town," Carolyn replied smugly. "Maybe they should change the name of the town to Strange Creek or Bitter Strange."

"Either one would suit me just fine. But right now, we have to get you on the trail. And these shoes might be your ticket out of here," Jake gushed before running to the barn to fetch his farrier's tools.

Dixie held steady as Jake's large, meaty hands nimbly replaced her old shoes. When Jake dropped the last hoof, Dixie pranced about the paddock like a frisky filly, bouncing on air. The new shoes were a perfect fit. "I think your horse is ready to ride, how about you?" asked Jake with a proud grin as he admired his handiwork.

"I was ready to leave this town the second I entered it," Carolyn replied tersely as she threw the medicine bag over her saddle and stepped in the stirrup. Taking hold of the reins, she gently squeezed her heels. Dixie raced around the paddock in a large oval, gradually gaining speed. When Dixie's mane started flying in her face, Carolyn headed for the fence. "Yee- ha!" she shouted as she slapped her hat against the saddle. With a giant leap, Dixie soared through the air, high over the top rail. Touching ground, Carolyn turned and waved at Jake. She chuckled as she finally remembered where she had seen him. He looked just like the boy who pumped gas at the local filling station. Carolyn just chalked it up to another strange coincidence.

Dixie streaked across the prairie like a steam locomotive. Ten miles out of town, she was still at a full gallop, trailing a cloud of red dust with sparks flying from her hooves. Carolyn had never seen her pony run so fast and so far. She had no doubt the stranger was a wizard, and his horseshoes were magical. After all, they had transformed Dixie into an iron horse.

The ride was so smooth that Carolyn dosed off after about an hour in the saddle. Snapping back her head, she awoke just in time to pull hard on the reins. The noon stagecoach from Bitter Creek was blocking the road. Dixie slowed to a walk. A disabled stagecoach was a common sight in this part of the country. The overland trail was hard on everything and everyone. The problem could be a busted wheel, a broken axle, an injured animal, or a sick passenger. Whatever it was, Carolyn was bound by the cowgirl creed and her Pony Express oath to render assistance. She stopped short of the coach and waited. Things didn't look or feel right. The air was still, and nobody was in sight. A chill ran up Carolyn's spine. She had seen the same situation in a hundred TV westerns. The stagecoach was being robbed. She had to hightail back to town and fetch the sheriff.

As Carolyn turned Dixie around, a masked gunman, dressed in black with a mask over his face, blocked her path. Two other gang members quietly emerged from the brush, herding along the driver and the passengers at gunpoint.

"Now be calm, young lady, and no one gets hurt," the leader warned as he pointed his six-shooter at Carolyn. "Just throw down the saddlebag. That medicine is worth its weight in gold. I'm sure the people of Sweetwater will be more than glad to meet our price."

Carolyn did as instructed. As she slowly reached around to unfasten the saddlebag, she suddenly jerked back the reins. "Up, girl," she hollered. Dixie reared high in the air and let out a menacing whinny. The gunmen immediately opened fired. Smoke and flame spewed from their gun barrels. Dixie jabbed the air with her legs, knocking away the bullets with her hooves. Sparks filled the air as the bullets ricocheted harmlessly to the ground. With their pistols empty, the outlaws dropped their weapons and froze, too scared to move, too stunned to speak, and too stupid to think about their next move. The passengers applauded as the driver and his assistant quickly lassoed the bandits and tied them to the back of the stagecoach.

"Mighty grateful ma'am, but we can take care of things from here," the driver said in a gruff voice as the passengers climbed in the coach. "You best be headin' to Sweetwater before the weather moves in."

"Just doing what a Pony Express rider gets paid to do," Carolyn said with a smile and a tip of her hat. "Hi-yo, Dixie! Away!" she shouted. Once again, Dixie reared up and whinnied before disappearing in a cloud of dust. Within a few strides, Dixie was back on her pace. If there weren't any more glitches along the trail, Carolyn figured to be riding into Sweetwater at sunrise. Hopefully, she wouldn't be too late.

About fifteen minutes later, the stagecoach driver's prediction came true. Dark gray clouds rolled in from the north and blotted out the sun, turning day into night. A light, cold rain began to fall on the parched prairie. Carolyn lifted her hat to splash her face and then stuck out her tongue for a cool drink. But a minute later, the delightful drizzle turned to dreadful downpour. Raindrops as big as water balloons exploded on the ground, turning the dusty trail into an oozing mud pit.

Carolyn was worried about Dixie. Some horses loved to run in the mud, but others hated to even walk in it. Careful not to slide out of the slippery saddle, Carolyn leaned over for a glance at the ground to see if Dixie was having any problems. Mud was flying in every direction, but Dixie's churning white legs were spotless. Charging along at a breakneck speed, her horseshoes were splashing the puddles dry. If only the stranger had made a pair of magic shoes for me, Carolyn thought. Rainwater was running down her jacket and filling her boots to the brim.

Seconds later, lightning cracked the sky and stabbed the earth with blades of fire. Electrical explosions sent clouds of dirt flying in the air. Sitting high in the saddle, Carolyn was the tallest object on the prairie for a hundred miles, a human lightning rod. Instinctively, she lowered her body and leaned forward until her head brushed Dixie's cheek. With her body pressed hard against Dixie, she held on tight, hoping that her pony could outrun the storm.

When a blinding bolt of lightning split the distant horizon and faded with a muffled round of thunder, Carolyn knew the storm was over. But as she leaned back in the saddle to relax, she felt the earth shudder as if the thunder was rolling up behind her. "What in the Sam Hill is going on?" she yelled in surprise as she looked back. A buffalo stampede was hard on her heels and rapidly gaining ground. Earlier in the day, she had seen the large herd grazing on a grassy plateau. Now they were running for their lives in a line that stretched for miles. In a blur, hundreds of panicked animals raced past her with their massive dark brown heads lowered, ready to trample anything that stood in the way. Globs of white, bubbling foam dripped from their mouths as their bright red tongues wagged from side to side. Carolyn could only watch in horror as one by one they vanished from view, swallowed up by pools of quicksand.

The relentless rain had turned the prairie into a swamp, hiding the trail beneath a layer of brown slime. Carolyn feared that she was lost, but couldn't risk stopping to look at the map that was tucked in her jacket. Her first step out of the saddle might be her last, and she could easily end up like the buffalo. All she could do was trust her pony. With Dixie still running hard and fast, there was no reason to panic just yet. She was still in the saddle and hopefully still headed toward Sweetwater.

When Dixie passed the black, bowl-shaped rock known as the Witch's Cauldron, Carolyn breathed a short-lived sigh of relief. According to Jake's directions, she was headed in the right direction but on a collision course with the El Mucho Grande, the biggest river west of the Mississippi. With the heavy rain, the river would be spilling its banks. Her only option would be to camp on high ground and wait for the river to recede. By then, the town of Sweetwater might be down to a few citizens, but every life was precious.

Carolyn heard the angry roar from a mile away. When the swollen river finally came into view, she was terrified. Towering white-capped waves pounded the riverbanks and tore away huge chunks of earth. Giant tree limbs, spinning wildly in the current, splintered apart as they smashed into house-sized boulders that were being dragged along by the undertow.

The river was widening with each passing second. Any attempt to cross it would be suicide. Carolyn pulled hard on the reins to stop, but Dixie didn't flinch. "Woe-ah, girl! Woe-ah, Dixie!" she screamed as she pulled harder. But Dixie didn't falter. Carolyn was sure that Dixie had been spooked by the river, and nothing was going to slow her down until she was safely on the opposite riverbank or on the bottom of the river. With only seconds until Dixie plunged into the raging floodwaters, Carolyn prepared to jump out of the saddle.

Reaching back, she grabbed the medicine bag and slipped her feet from the stirrups. As she loosened the reins in her hands, a deep and dark voice whispered in her ear. "Trust your horse. She has the power," it commanded. To Carolyn's surprise, it sounded like the stranger from Bitter Creek, but there wasn't soul in sight.

"Just a case of prairie fever," Carolyn mumbled, reassuring herself that she wasn't going crazy. The loneliness of the wilderness often played tricks on the senses. Every pioneer and prospector had a hair-raising story about seeing and hearing things that didn't exist. Carolyn had to decide in a hurry if the voice was real or imagined. The river was dead ahead, and Dixie was closing fast.

Carolyn squeezed her legs and whipped the reins against Dixie's shoulders for more speed. "Jump, Dixie!" she shouted. With a tremendous leap, Dixie splashed the edge of the river and soared high in the air as if she had wings. But halfway across the river, she started to quickly lose altitude. Carolyn stretched forward and looked down. The crumbling riverbank on the other side was getting closer but so was the swirling water.

"Lay out, girl," she barked as she flattened her body against Dixie's taunt neck to decrease wind resistance. Dixie immediately lowered her head and stretched her legs until they were straight out. If she could glide for a few more seconds, she might safely reach the other side.

Carolyn hoped to land in the mud, but Dixie was headed for a head-on collision with a large tree. When tree branches brushed her body, she grimaced and braced for the impact. But Dixie had other plans. Turning and twisting in mid-air, she squeezed in an opening between two trees and landed just beyond the riverbank. Her hooves barely touched the ground before she bounded away in full gallop.

"Yee-ha!" Carolyn shouted joyously as she twirled her hat over her head and slapped it against her thigh. It was a smooth take-off and a soft landing. Not bad for a pony that couldn't jump anymore, Carolyn thought.

A few miles down the road, the sun broke through the dark clouds with an intense, baking heat. Within minutes, the prairie was bone-dry. Carolyn unbuttoned her buckskin jacket to dry out her shirt and leaned back to watch the clouds drift overhead. Next to watching horses, sky gazing was one of her favorite pastimes. The funny shapes never failed to stir the imagination. Back on the farm, she often sketched the different cloud formations in her notebook, giving them silly titles, such as Kissing Crabs, Talking Turtles, or Dancing Dixies.

When puffy circles started chasing the fluffy cotton balls, Carolyn reached for her spyglass to take a closer look. Trouble was on the horizon, and that wasn't a figment of her imagination. The white circles were man-made smoke rings. Somewhere in a far corner of the prairie, an Indian war party was announcing the arrival of an intruder. Carolyn had seen it all before on the TV westerns and knew exactly what to do. She chucked the reins and squeezed her heels, hoping that Dixie could outrun the attack.

The warriors waited along the ledge that rimmed the steep canyon walls. When Carolyn passed underneath, they pulled back their bows and fired. Arrows rained down, blotting out the few rays of sunlight that reached the canyon floor. Once again, Carolyn had no idea how she would survive this latest calamity. All she could do was trust her horse. Any second, she expected Dixie to rear up and swat away the arrows with her hooves. But instead, Dixie sprinted through the rugged rock formation at breakneck speed. One by one, the arrows whizzed by Carolyn's head and struck Dixie with a loud metallic ping, falling harmlessly to the ground with flattened heads. Dixie's hide had turned to iron.

When the last arrow had been flung, the warriors raised their arms and threw their bows into the canyon. Rubbing their eyes, they whooped in frustration and pointed to the streaking pony. Their weapons were no match for the powerful medicine of the Pony Express girl and her iron horse. Back at their village, the warriors told their strange story to the chief. Scratching his wrinkled chin, the wise, old Indian knew exactly what to do. For years to come, he would gather the young braves around the campfire and tell them about the magic of the two, white ponytails. The tale was destined to become a Wild West legend.

Carolyn didn't take her eyes off the trail until she reached the forest at the base of the mountain. The less she saw, the less she worried, but that didn't stop her from thinking about the job interview. She had been hornswaggled, plain and simple. Now she knew why the clerk had been eager to offer her a job, and now she knew why they called this part of the country The Badlands. There wasn't anything good about it. On her next contract, if she lived long enough to see it, she vowed to read every word of the fine print before signing on the dotted line.

Taking a break, Carolyn stood in the stirrups to stretch her aching arms and legs. The ride was taking a physical toll. Her fingers were beginning to cramp, and her stomach was knotted in hunger pains. At this point, all she wanted was a home-cooked meal and a good night's sleep. She didn't how much longer she could last without either one. All she knew was that she couldn't stop.

Straight ahead was the Devil's Horn, the pyramid of ancient black rock that sent a shiver down Carolyn's spine. She pulled up her collar against the chilly air. The mountain was more than cold; it was evil. She felt it in her aching bones. It was time to start worrying once again.

Carolyn didn't hesitate when she reached a fork in the road. To save time, she heeded Jake's advice and veered onto the Gold Mine Trail. It would be a difficult ride--almost three miles straight up the side of the mountain, but Sweetwater didn't have any hours to spare.

Dixie chugged along the rocky trail at a steady but slower pace, her horseshoes clinging to the mountain like magnets. About halfway up the trail, snow started to fall as expected. The flakes were small and light and Carolyn easily brushed them off with a flick of her wrist. But as Dixie climbed higher, the snow fell harder. Large flakes, the size of loose-leaf paper, filled the air and covered the ground. Even though Dixie was a Welsh pony whose ancestors were bred to survive in the mountains of Wales, the deep snow would eventually become an icy quicksand if she didn't soon climb the summit.

Carolyn decided against heading down the mountain to wait out the storm. The peak was just

21

ahead. As long as Dixie was making progress, the journey would continue. After the stagecoach robbery, the monsoon, the buffalo stampede, the river jump, and the Indian attack, Carolyn was confident that Dixie could meet the challenge. In a few hours, she would be riding down the other side of the mountain in the bright sunshine.

Passing the last stand of scraggly pine trees, the weather worsened. The wind howled around the peak with the fury of a hurricane and cut through Carolyn's clothes like a cold knife. As the wind increased and the temperature dropped below zero, the snowstorm became a full-blown blizzard. In the whiteout conditions, Carolyn didn't know if the top of the mountain was a few feet ahead or a few miles away. Dixie was still moving, but Carolyn couldn't tell if it was up, down or sideways. It was now impossible to turn back.

"Trust your horse. Always trust your horse. She has the power," Carolyn muttered incoherently as her head drooped. She was freezing to death in the saddle. Her clothes were frozen stiff, and her hands and feet were numb from frostbite. Even her mind was beginning to feel the ill effects of the cold as her thoughts returned to the encounter with the stranger. "Ride for the care of your soul," she mumbled sadly, trying to make sense of the words. "What have I done?" she called out in vain. But the howling wind was her only answer. Did I make a deal with the devil to ride for Pony Express, she wondered. There was no other way to explain the stranger and the crazy events of the day. Dixie's shoes were cursed with black magic. That was the only explanation.

Carolyn lifted her head and peered through the blinding snow at the dark silhouette directly in front of her. The crest of the mountain was within reach. Safety was minutes away, but she had only seconds to live at the rate Dixie was plowing through the deep snow. She needed one more jump from her pony. That was her only chance of survival.

Digging in her heels with all waning strength, Carolyn leaned forward in the saddle. "Jump, Dixie! Jump, girl!" she shouted in the wind, her voice a raspy whisper. Dixie came to a dead halt. Carolyn was stunned. Had the horseshoes fallen off, she wondered as she looked to the ground in despair. There was nothing to see. The snow was above Dixie's legs and touching her boots. She didn't have to worry about freezing to death because shortly she would be buried alive. Maybe, just maybe, Dixie didn't hear her command, she prayed.

"Jump, girl! You've got to jump, girl!" Carolyn pleaded in a choked voice. Dixie remained motionless. It's too late, Carolyn thought. Dixie was also freezing to death. Carolyn painfully wiggled off one of her gloves and reached out to stroke her pony's neck. Dixie's coat was covered in a thick layer of ice. "I'm so sorry, girl," Carolyn said faintly. "I didn't mean for it to end this way." Tears streamed down her face and formed icicles that hung from her chin. She knew the struggle would soon be over. She had seen it before on the TV westerns. The dying cowboy, caught in a raging blizzard, simply drifted off to a peaceful sleep. If she was lucky, a search party might find her and Dixie during the spring thaw, frozen in place like a statue. Then the Indian chief would have another tale to tell the young braves around the campfire, the day the iron horse and her rider turned to cold stone.

Carolyn dropped the reins and slumped forward until her limp body rested against Dixie's mane. Closing her eyes, she felt warm and sleepy as the falling snow quickly covered her body in a white sheet. The aching pain from the bitter cold was gone.

Dixie instantly sensed that her rider was in trouble. To save them both, she had to get off the mountain. She tried to step, but couldn't move her legs. Walking down the mountain would be impossible. She was frozen in the snow that was now up to her shoulders. Lifting her head, she sniffed the air. Riding the wind was a faint but familiar scent. She sniffed deeply a few more times and neighed. Now there was a voice in the wind, calling her home to the other side of the mountain, the dwelling place of her ancestors. She had to answer the call at all costs.

Careful not to tumble Carolyn out of the saddle, Dixie leaned back slowly and burrowed her rump in the snow until it touched the ground. She then gently rocked back and forth, gradually tightening her legs muscles until they were ready to snap. Filling her lungs to the bursting point, she raised her forelegs high over head and then pushed off with thrust of a rocket engine. Exhaling a deafening whinny that echoed down the valley, she vanished like a ghost into the snowy sky high above the peak.

The sudden jolt awakened the slumbering Carolyn. Through sleepy eyes, she spotted a pulsating white orb directly ahead. "We're going to heaven, girl," she whispered softly in Dixie's ear. Any second, her guardian angel would appear at her side, grab the reins, and lead Dixie home. As Dixie drifted closer, the light grew brighter. When Carolyn reached out to touch the orb, it exploded into a million diamonds of dazzling white light.

A loud swoosh was the last sound that Carolyn heard before passing out. With her mind spinning out of control, she imagined herself snuggled in her bed with a fuzzy blanket pulled tight under her chin. She was not going to die on the mountain. The journey to Sweetwater was only a dream, a figment of her imagination. When she awoke, she would be safe and sound in her bedroom.

Carolyn slowly lifted her eyelids to greet the new day. "Oh my gosh! It's real. It's not a dream," she shrieked in horror. Instead of leaning over the side of her bed, she was leaning over the side of her saddle. Far below on the valley floor, the town of Sweetwater basked in the summer sun. Meadows of wildflowers carpeted the slopes, and waterfalls cascaded down the cliffs that rimmed the valley.

Carolyn sat upright and looked over her shoulder at the mountain. The parallel tracks in the snow told her what had happened. Incredibly, Dixie had jumped the rocky peak and skied down the side of the mountain on her hooves. And the white orb was no diamond, only the winter sun hidden behind the storm. Shaking her head with a tight smile, Carolyn wondered how much magic was left in the shoes and hoped that she didn't have to find out.

While Carolyn pondered her fate and enjoyed the scenery, Dixie stood perfectly still with her head pointed towards town. As currents of warm, fragrant air drifted up, she sniffed the air, took a deep breath, and then exhaled with a soft whinny that sounded like a smug laugh. Carolyn couldn't smell the problem, but could see it right under her nose. Apple orchards and hay fields surrounded the town. From high above, Sweetwater looked like an all-you-can-eat horse buffet. Carolyn chuckled as she remembered the sniffing episode in the blizzard. As strange as it seemed, Dixie's hunger pangs had saved her life. Strange events were already occurring on the other side of the mountain.

The more Dixie sniffed; the more she fidgeted. "Not so fast, girl. We still have work to do before we dine," Carolyn said as she stroked Dixie's neck. "No one deserves a good meal more than you." Dixie nodded her head in agreement and galloped down the mountain. Dinner was an hour away.

The lookout in the church steeple was the first to spot Carolyn. "Rider on the road! Heading this way," he shouted excitedly to the empty streets below. Since the town was quarantined days ago, the approaching cloud of dust could only be the Pony Express.

Carolyn pulled hard on the reins, and Dixie skidded to a stop in the center of the town. Doors slammed and feet pounded the ground as the mayor, the sheriff, and the town doctor rushed out to greet her.

"Ma'am, you don't know how glad we are to see you," the mayor gushed, grabbing Carolyn's hand and shaking it repeatedly.

"Mr. Mayor, the feeling is mutual. I'd thought I might never see this day, much less your town," Carolyn replied wearily as Doc grabbed the saddlebag. He immediately pulled out a couple of vials and held them to the light.

"Medicine looks good, mayor. Let's get started," he said with a grim smile. The mayor looked up at the steeple and gave the signal. As the bell tolled, gaunt faces with yellow skin filled the streets.

Carolyn watched helplessly as a long line formed outside Doc's office. She wanted to do more but knew her job was done. Turning away, she walked Dixie to the stable at the edge of town, wondering if she would ever get another chance to be a hero. Finding a fresh pile of straw, she collapsed in a deep sleep while Dixie stood guard.

After a few minutes, Dixie grew bored and walked away, sniffing the air. There was an apple orchard next to the stable, waiting to be sampled.

The medicine was a miracle cure. Minutes after receiving the vaccine, people were back on their feet, smiling and talking. Life was once again sweet in Sweetwater. The town had been saved, and now it was time to celebrate. That evening, a banquet was held to honor the new heroes. Tables were set up in the street. Blue and white banners were hung from the buildings. The town band serenaded the citizens with an evening concert.

Carolyn and Dixie sat side by side at the center of the head table. The main course was spaghetti and meatballs, Carolyn's favorite meal. Meanwhile Dixie ate non-stop from a bucket of honey oats, a barrel of sugared apples, and a bale of sweet hay.

After dinner, the mayor delivered a long-winded speech about the heroic exploits of Carolyn and Dixie, comparing their trip to the midnight ride of Paul Revere. Carolyn didn't see the connection but was flattered to be mentioned in the same breath with an American legend. As the mayor droned on, she leaned back in her chair and daydreamed. Years from now, old-timers would sit around a woodstove and recall the famous ride of Carolyn and Dixie, the princesses of the Pony Express. History books would have a whole page dedicated to the event with action photos of Carolyn and Dixie.

"And now a few words from one of our heroes," the mayor proudly announced to cheers from the audience.

Carolyn nearly choked on her final bit of apple pie. The mayor certainly wasn't talking about Dixie. At that moment, Carolyn almost wished that she was back on the trail. She had trouble speaking to a class of twenty students. How in the world was she going to speak to a crowd of two-hundred people? With her knees shaking, she haltingly stepped to the podium and cleared her throat.

"Aw, shucks, I'm just a cowgirl doing what a cowgirl's got to do," she drawled shyly as the crowd roared their approval. "But I was just along for the ride. The real hero is Dixie. She saved all of our lives." Carolyn stepped down to hug Dixie. When Dixie responded with a loud whinny, the crowd erupted into another round of thunderous applause. As children rushed forward to meet their four-legged hero, Carolyn beamed proudly and scanned the crowd. Far in the back, she saw him, a man dressed in a white top hat and a white overcoat. Carolyn blinked hard, and the man, who resembled the stranger from Bitter Creek, vanished into thin air.

The town celebrated late into the night with music and dancing. Carolyn mingled briefly with the crowd before hitting the hay. She asked everyone about the stranger, but no one could recall such a person.

The following morning townspeople filled the streets to say farewell to their heroes.

The mayor read a proclamation, declaring Carolyn and Dixie honorary citizens of Sweetwater with lifetime benefits and privileges. "Young lady, you are always welcome in our fair town," he clamored as he handed her an action-packed travel brochure of Sweetwater County. "We would consider it an honor if you stopped by to visit us again. Sweetwater would be the perfect place for your next family vacation."

"Mr. Mayor, I'll be back someday, but until that time, your town will always be close to my heart," Carolyn said sincerely. She knew that Dixie wouldn't mind returning for another visit to the buffet table. But before they could return, they first had to travel back to Bitter Creek where a reward and a full-time job were waiting.

Carolyn grabbed the medicine bag, now filled with letters, and slung it over the saddle. "Cowgirl, up!" the sheriff shouted with a grin as he stooped down to give her a boast. "Cowgirl, up! Cowgirl up!" The words echoed in Carolyn's ears. A second later, she heard another familiar voice. "Cowgirl! Get up," her mother called out. "You're running late. Your student will be here soon."

Carolyn bolted upright and rubbed her eyes. The morning sun flooded the room with a brilliant white light. "I've got to stop watching all of those TV westerns," she muttered as she pinched her arm to make sure she wasn't dreaming. It had been her strangest dream. Even stranger was the fact that she could remember every detail about it. Scratching her head, she thought about the stranger in black and her deal with the devil. Then she thought about the stranger in white and smiled. She had made a deal with her guardian angel, or at least, she hoped so.

Chapter 2 - Welcome to the Jolly Jockey

Maggie Farnsworth slumped in the back seat of the black sedan and stared at her wristwatch. There was still an hour before her first riding lesson. Even though she had been waiting for this day all of her life, she just couldn't wait a minute longer. Time had become a slow torture, moving like an old plow horse when it should be racing like a wild stallion. Looking at the watch every few seconds only made the time pass slower. When Mrs. Farnsworth leaned forward to speak with Walter the chauffeur, Maggie discreetly removed the watch and stuffed it in the pocket of her riding blouse. After checking his map a final time, Walter turned the ignition key and stepped lightly on the gas pedal. Maggie craned her neck to look in the rear view mirror. An easy smile creased her face as the mansion grew smaller and eventually disappeared from view. The countdown to the Jolly Jockey Farm had officially begun. Now she had to decide what to count.

Counting mailboxes seemed a little foolish, but it made perfect sense to Maggie. Today she was a package to be delivered on the doorstep of her summer dream. But that good idea soon soured after she quickly lost count. She closed her eyes to relax, but that was worse than counting. Every time Walter slowed down, her heart fluttered and her eyes sprang open. Had they finally arrived or were they lost, she wondered. To her disappointment, it was only Walter shifting gears on the hilly road. "Pedal to the metal, Walter," Maggie whispered under her breath. She was in a hurry for good reason. At the age of eleven, she faced the challenge of salvaging her career as a kid. And today, the wheels of change were in motion, even if they were only the four tires on the family sedan.

Maggie squirmed in her seat and pressed her face against the window. She had been down this road many times but never remembered seeing the Jolly Jockey. Of course, she was always busy looking for horses to notice any of the stately manors. This region in Maryland was the heart of horse country where every address was a horse farm with a wealthy owner who kept horses as a business or hobby.

Another mile down the road, Maggie bit her lip in frustration. Still no Jolly Jockey. It could have passed in the blink of an eye. Now she was sure that Walter was lost. To non-horse people like Walter and her mother, one horse farm looked like another, just a bunch of pastures, stables and horses. Hopefully, the Jolly Jockey was tucked away in a hidden valley off the main road.

The thought of being lost was terrifying. Maggie knew the possible consequences. "Walter, I believe we should turn around and head to the girls' camp instead of the farm," she could hear her mother say. One wrong turn would end her dream. If that happened, Maggie vowed never speak to Walter again. If he only drove faster, she would already be in the saddle. For some reason, the normally heavy-footed chauffeur was driving like a grandmother. Silently, she again begged him to step on the gas and pressed her feet hard to the floor. So close and yet so far away, that's the way it was with dreams. And no one knew that better than Maggie. She was ready to jump out of the sedan and run the rest of the way. But with her bad leg, it would take days for her to hobble to the farm. Instead, she had to suffer in silence. As the sedan slowly rambled past another pasture, she vividly remembered the recent events that led to this momentous day in her life.

The decision was made last summer after the last day of summer camp. Maggie vowed the upcoming summer would be an adventure on horseback. The adventure called for a major change in lifestyle, and that change started with trading her Camp Pocahontas t-shirt for a western riding blouse. The thought of not attending summer camp didn't seem like a big deal, but to her mother it would be breaking a sacred family tradition. Her mother simply would not understand why Maggie would not want to attend Camp Pocahontas, an academy of fine arts and athletics for girls of distinction. There was no better place on the planet to learn new skills and meet new friends. Maggie's mother and grandmother had attended camp every year until they were sixteen and then volunteered as counselors while in college. After all of those years, Camp Pocahontas was more than a tradition; it was a family heritage to be passed down to future generations of Farnsworth women.

Every year on the first day of camp, Maggie and her mother visited the Wall of Fame in the lobby of the gymnasium. Mrs. Farnsworth always beamed with pride when she spotted her name on the plaque for camper of the year. She had won the award for three consecutive years, a record that remained unbroken. Decades later, she still cherished the genuine Indian necklaces that she received for the honor. The fragile strands of brightly colored beads were carefully stored in a cedar chest at the foot of her bed with her other awards. In her younger days, Mrs. Farnsworth had been an outstanding student in classical literature and an accomplished athlete in cross-country and lacrosse. The chest was crammed with certificates, pins, ribbons, and medals, but no award was more prized than the necklaces. They were revered as if Princess Pocahontas had hand-crafted them.

On one occasion, Maggie spied her mother modeling one of the necklaces in front of a mirror. Her mother sighed and then smiled softly as her fingers gently caressed the beads. Maggie smiled also, realizing that she finally had a common bond with her mother, even if her mother didn't know it. The necklaces symbolized the dreams of two women, one past and one present. To Maggie, the precious beads should be handed down to future generations of Farnsworth women, not the privilege of attending Camp Pocahontas. One day, she hoped to tell her mother exactly how she felt about the necklaces, but first she had to prove that she was a worthy recipient of the treasures. And to do that, she had to collect her own heirlooms. Presently, her hope chest was an old cigar box filled with two medals for music, a first place pin for a spelling bee, and a picture of her riding a pony. It was more of a hopeless chest with plenty of room for awards.

While Maggie could argue with her mom about attending camp, she couldn't argue about the camp. It was one of the finest on the East Coast that offered the best activities, counselors, facilities, and, most importantly, food. The cost was high, but there were plenty of parents willing to pay the price to ensure that their princesses were properly pampered. And Mrs. Farnsworth, camper of the year, was always ready with an open checkbook.

Since her first camp, Maggie decided that if she had to spend the summer in her mother's shadow, she would do it in the sunshine. A virtual shut-in for most of the year, outdoor sports became a passion. Swimming and archery were her favorite events. In the pool, she swam like a fish, but at the range her arrows were slightly off target. Counselors joked that she couldn't hit the broad side of a barn with a bulldozer, and they were probably right. But she liked the sport anyhow because it was a pioneer sport like shooting a buffalo gun. Plus her mother would have a heart attack if she knew that her frail daughter was training to become a warrior princess.

Camp wasn't all that bad, but it had become a bore because Maggie could not take riding lessons even though the camp had a first-class stable. Riding was the only thing she wanted to do, but camp regulations prohibited handicapped children from participating in any equestrian events. In the Farnsworth house, camp policy was ranked with the Ten Commandments. There was never any debate or argument about the wisdom of the camp elders. Mrs. Farnsworth firmly believed that camp directors knew what was best for each camper. No exceptions should be allowed, even for her own daughter. She often told Maggie that one change in the rules would lead to another, and before too long no rules would exist. Camp Pocahontas would be plunged into chaos as wild gangs of uncivilized young ladies stalked the campgrounds in a rampage. But despite the rule, Maggie found a safety deposit box for her dream. That box was the stable where she spent all of her free time, imagining the day when she could finally saddle up.

Maggie painted and played music when she wasn't swimming, shooting or sightseeing at the stable; exactly what she did during the school year and exactly what her mother preferred. But the violin and the paintbrushes were becoming crutches on the road of life, and she already wore a leg brace. She had to stand on her own two feet. It was time to walk down a different path without the help of anybody or anything. It was time for a season of change.

Maggie clearly remembered that morning during Easter vacation when the seed of change was planted. It happened while watching a television talk show. A lady author was brashly plugging her book about women "coming of age" in the new decade. "In the 1960's, women will pioneer advances in sports, medicine and business. We will take charge of our lives and change the course of history. The revolution has begun," she boldly proclaimed. Maggie loved to hear that kind of talk. The words struck her like a thunderbolt, forever seared into her memory. At that moment, Maggie decided to become a pioneer and begin her own revolution of change. But her revolution would be a cavalry charge. What else could it be for a girl who loved horses! Now was the time to prepare a battle plan that would ensure victory. Realizing that her mother was a formidable foe, Maggie knew the plan had to be foolproof.

Mrs. Florence Farnsworth wasn't old, just old school. The daughter of a Baltimore blueblood family and wife of a successful businessman, she traced her roots back to Maryland's first colonists. She was a rock-solid pillar of the community who was set in her ways like reinforced concrete. To her, tradition was a national treasure, not a trend. Talk about women changing their lives was dismissed as utter nonsense. Change pertained to nickels and dimes in a purse, not the role of women in society. She was a benevolent dictator who must be overthrown for at least one summer.

Maggie knew that her plan was a long shot and she had to act soon. If she didn't, she faced the prospect of another summer at Camp Pocahontas. She had no desire to break her mother's record as camper of the year. And she certainly didn't want to be camp director before she could drive a car, but that's where she was headed. Every summer camp counselors pointed to the trophy case and joked about Maggie's camp career. She didn't think it was funny. Such talk made her sick to her stomach. No doubt, her mom would beam with pride when Maggie's portrait was hung on the "Wall of Fame" next to the old biddies who had served as camp directors. Future generations of campers would know Miss Maggie Farnsworth as the "oldest youngest" or the "youngest oldest" director in the camp's glorious history. Someday the place might be named Camp Farnsworth in her honor. Maggie cringed at the thought. She could easily picture the smile of her mother's face when it came time to write out the check for the new entrance sign. That simply was not going to happen this year, next year, or any year.

By the end of Easter vacation, Maggie's constant nagging about riding lessons finally paid off. Her mother made a half-hearted promise to "explore options" for summer camp. That was the phrase used in the Farnsworth house when it came to change. The young Ms. Farnsworth never changed but explored options. Either way, Maggie was encouraged by the response. At least her mother was listening.

Riding lessons were the answer to her dream, but Maggie quickly realized that the solution was also the problem. Not only did she have to deal with her mother, but she also had to deal with real horses. About the only thing the "girl who loved horses" hadn't done with a horse was ride one by herself. She painted, sketched, and collected them in paper and plastic. Her collection of plastic horses and riders was the envy of her friends. Every birthday was another horse and rider, and every Christmas was at least two more horses and riders. That was just fine with Maggie. She didn't want dolls; she wanted horses. They were the gifts that kept giving. She loved to trace her fingers along the plastic, feeling each intricate detail. One morning, she expected to see her plastic herd grazing on the front lawn. Plastic was an amazing invention, so life-like, yet so lifeless. Maggie only wished that she could breathe life into her collection, and on the weekends, she did her best to make that wish come true.

Every Saturday, Maggie transformed her bedroom into the Maggie's Flying Horse Circus, featuring Maggie as the ringmaster. "Ladies and gentlemen, step right up to the greatest show on horse! It's razzling! It's dazzling! It's death-defying and mystifying! You won't believe your eyes," she barked at the opening of every show. Daredevil feats that defied the laws of gravity were the featured acts. Horses and riders vaulted into space, soared gracefully through the air, and landed gently as a feather. It was a show where horses never went lame, and riders never limped away in pain. No one broke a bone or even a sweat. On the surface, the circus looked to be a perfect world for horses and humans.

But in reality, it was a very dangerous place, especially for a young girl with ambition. It was a shadowy land where fiction became fact, fantasy became reality, and the impossible became possible. There were no limits to what you could do or what you could be. All you needed was imagination, and Maggie had plenty of that. Show after show, she imagined herself in the center ring, riding one of her plastic horses. And above the applause of the crowd, she could hear the lady author shouting at her to follow her dream.

In her horse life, Maggie did have some flesh and blood experience. Every spring when the volunteer fire department held a carnival, she'd pester her parents for a pony ride. And being good parents, they readily obliged. Before getting in line with the other kids, she would carefully count horses and riders to ensure that she rode Brownie. The light brown pony with the blond mane was her favorite. If the numbers didn't work out, she would step aside and adjust her brace while someone else moved ahead. She had to ride Brownie, no matter what it took. They were a team with a special bond. When kids laughed at Brownie because of his limp, he'd hang his head and drag his bad leg.

Maggie saw the hurt in his eyes and felt his pain. She remembered the many times that she was taunted because of her bad leg. After her ride was finished, she'd wait near the fence until he made the final turn. She'd call out his name, and Brownie would lift his head. Their eyes would meet for a brief second, and he would nicker softly. Until recently, Maggie kept a picture of her and Brownie on her dresser. No girl in the world had a bigger smile. It used to be her favorite picture, but now she hated it. It was a fake just like her plastic horses. Real pioneer women didn't ride a pony that was being walked by a volunteer fireman.

At this year's carnival, the ritual had ended. Maggie was too embarrassed to stand in line with the little kids. They squealed like it was Christmas morning, jumping up and down and pointing to the ponies. So instead of riding, she stood near the pony pen and talked. "Brownie, you will always be my friend," she whispered softly as she reached out to touch his neck. "But I've got to ride on my own."

Brownie nodded his head and snorted in response. He knew how she felt and forgave her for not wanting to ride. Maggie's heart ached as she walked away. She wanted to ride so badly, but she couldn't ask her parents for a ride, not today, not tomorrow, and not ever. This was a season of change, and for the first time she realized that change could hurt the heart. Her stomach knotted and her eyes grew misty as Brownie was led around the oval with other riders. She promised herself that she wouldn't cry. That was for little kids. Today she was going to be brave. But when Brownie turned his head towards Maggie and blinked, Maggie had to wipe the tears with the back of her hand. She said a silent prayer that someday they would meet again.

Maggie had fretted for weeks about when to make her move from camper to rider. The first shot of the revolution had to be a warning to get her mother's attention, not a great explosion to rock her world to its foundation. Since Easter vacation, Maggie had waited patiently for the opportunity to strike, but time was running out. Finally, in the first week of summer vacation, she fired her cannon.

The flyer had been hanging on the bulletin board at the grocery store for a couple of weeks. When only two tabs with a name and phone number remained, Maggie swung into action. She knew that when the tabs disappeared, so did her last chance. At the checkout counter, she casually pointed to the flyer and gently reminded her mother about their Easter conversation and summer options. Mrs. Farnsworth, knowing that she was obligated to make an effort, reached up and grabbed one of the tabs. "The Jolly Jockey - Specializing in Young Riders," she said flatly as she read the ad. Maggie said nothing, not wanting to look overly eager. She was just glad that her mom had taken the bait. When they got home, she hoped to finally reel in her dream.

But Mrs. Farnsworth tried to wiggle off the hook as soon as the front door closed. "I don't know anything about horses. Maybe it's not such a good idea," she said nervously. She was returning Maggie's opening shot with a volley of her own. The battle of words had officially begun.

"But you have friends who own horses. Maybe they know something about the Jolly Jockey Farm," Maggie chirped. She knew what to expect from her mother. Many a sleepless night, she had silently rehearsed a similar conversation. She had prepared a mental script to counter every one of her mother's comments. The challenge was to respond quickly

44

and keep attacking with suggestions. If she forgot her lines, she had to effectively improvise. If she ran out of verbal ammunition, the battle for her dream would be lost.

"I suppose I could, but I'm just worried that you'll get hurt. This horse business can be very rough, and some of those horse people are very rough themselves. You always see those rodeo riders wearing a cast," Mrs. Farnsworth said solemnly.

Maggie was ready for her mother's casualty report. "But the doctor said I should try something else besides swimming to build my stamina. If I spend another year in a pool, I'll grow gills," Maggie joked, trying to lighten her mother's serious mood.

Mrs. Farnsworth bit her lip and tilted her head to the ceiling. After a few deep breaths, she lowered her head and pursed her lips. Maggie held her breath. "Well, I suppose if Doctor Warner said it was alright then we can give it a try. The good doctor seems to know what's best," she said, trying to convince herself that she was making the right decision.

"Thanks, Mom! It really means a lot to me," Maggie replied excitedly as she hugged her mother. She was stunned by the announcement. Her mother had surrendered this time, but Maggie knew there were many battles ahead.

That afternoon, Mrs. Farnsworth finally called her "horse" friends. They had nothing but praise for the Jolly Jockey and its trainer, Dorothy Clark. Some knew her personally but didn't know that she was offering riding lessons. They agreed that she was a topnotch trainer who would be an excellent instructor for a new rider.

After hearing their recommendations, Mrs. Farnsworth finally summoned the courage to call the Jolly Jockey Farm. Maggie anxiously paced her bedroom as snippets of conversation drifted up the stairwell. From the tone of her mother's voice, she couldn't tell if it was good or bad news. Finally, she heard footsteps on the stairs. The bedroom door squeaked open. "Congratulations!" Mrs. Farnsworth declared. "You're officially enrolled as a student in the Clark Riding Academy."

Walter's booming voice jolted Maggie back to reality. "Ma'am, I believe the farm is just on the right,' he announced. Maggie pressed her face hard against the window. Mrs. Farnsworth dropped her appointment book and leaned over Maggie for a better look.

"Oh, my goodness, what a dreadful looking place," Mrs. Farnsworth exclaimed. "Everything looks so shabby. I believe…"

The alarm had been sounded. Red lights flashed in Maggie's head. She had anticipated smooth sailing once the sedan pulled out of the driveway, but now there was an iceberg dead ahead. Disaster suddenly loomed on the calm seas. She braced herself for the collision of opinions. Instead of staying the course, her mother would utter the command to return home. This was one scenario that Maggie had not rehearsed. To her, a horse farm was a place where people lived and worked with horses. It wasn't supposed to be neat and tidy. Obviously, her mother was expecting something a little more upscale and elegant. Maggie had to think fast, faster than her mother. She knew that she couldn't let her mother finish the sentence. "I believe this is what they call a working farm," she said hurriedly.

Mrs. Farnsworth paused, "Yes, I believe you're right," she replied hesitantly. "But it certainly looks like they could use some hired help." Maggie breathed a sigh of relief. The collision had been avoided. All engines full speed ahead, she silently ordered.

Maggie winced when she saw the entrance sign that proudly proclaimed "Welcome to the Jolly Jockey." It was a good thing her mother was looking the other way. The oval-shaped slab of weathered wood, dangling from two rusted chains, was not a good omen. Underneath the arched letters, a jockey leaned far over his horse, his green and white silks bubbled and cracked. It was obvious that he had been riding for a long time, possibly years. His horse fared no better, sporting a coat of brown blotches and sooty white stains. Posed in full stride, the once noble steed looked ready to leap off the sign and, hopefully, into a bucket of fresh paint.

Maggie bit her tongue. She would never admit it to her mother, but the place looked a little rundown. The farmhouse needed painting, and the porch needed fixing. With farm machinery strewn about the front of the property, the farm looked like a working junkyard instead of a working horse farm. Knowing how finicky her mother was when it came to appearances, Maggie dreaded seeing the stable behind the farmhouse. Walter probably wouldn't even stop. On orders from Mrs. Farnsworth, he would step on the gas and spin his tires in a cloud of dust. It would be one quick lap around the Jolly Jockey and out the front gate. Maggie closed her eyes as Walter made the final turn.

"Oh, my goodness, it's unbelievable!" Mrs. Farnsworth gasped. At the sound of those dreaded words, Maggie panicked and sprang open her eyes. Her mother was right. It was an unbelievable sight that had Maggie gawking with her mouth wide open. Without stepping in the building, she instantly knew the Jolly Jockey was the right place for her. The stable looked practically brand new. Fresh paint covered every inch of the structure. The white walls and red roof glistened in the morning sun. Even the copper weather vane atop the stable was polished to a shine. Everything outside was neatly stored and stacked. As far as Maggie was concerned, the Clark Riding Academy had its priorities in the right order. These were horse people who put the comfort of their horses above their own.

"Well, you sure can't judge a book by its cover," Maggie exclaimed with feigned delight. Nobody knew that more than she did. But one thing was certain. If the flyer in the grocery store had featured a picture of the farmhouse, Mrs. Farnsworth would have dialed the other number. "Hello, Camp Pocahontas. I would like to register my daughter Margaret for the summer session," Maggie could hear her saying.

Mrs. Farnsworth grunted in agreement with Maggie's comment. The stable certainly wasn't what she had expected, but she still wasn't fully convinced it was the right place for Maggie. Looks could be deceiving. This first view of the Jolly Jockey was only the cover. There were many pages in the book to be turned before the ending.

Chapter 3 - Don't Fence Me In

"What a fantastic dream!" Carolyn muttered to herself as she headed out the kitchen door. It was a shame that it ended so soon. She had been looking forward to the ride back to Bitter Creek. But as her mother politely reminded her, there were stable chores to be done before her new student arrived.

The more Carolyn dwelled on her dream, the faster she walked. By the time she remembered the stranger and the magic horseshoes, she was in a full sprint. "Sorry, girl, but I've got to make sure," Carolyn said as she barged into Dixie's stall. She gently lifted the pony's front leg and cleaned the shoe with her hand. It was just the standard metal plate. "That's okay, girl. You'll always be magical to me," she cooed as she kissed Dixie on the cheek and offered her a treat. Dixie didn't know what to make of Carolyn's odd behavior but quickly snapped the carrot from her hand.

After the last stall had been mucked out, it was time for some fun. Carolyn grabbed the top of the pitchfork for a microphone and belted out one of her favorite tunes. "Oh, give me land, lots of land under starry skies above. Don't fence me in," she crooned, tilting her head back. The words rose with the heat of the summer day, fluttered in the air with the loose hay, and fell to the floor like rocks. Carolyn's voice was flat and uninspired. Baltimore's own singing cowgirl was no competition for any singing cowgirls from the Old West, the New West, or anything west of the Chesapeake Bay. After a couple of verses, she stopped and sighed, realizing that she was howlin' at the moon for the sake of making noise. Any noise except her singing would be welcomed. Things were just too quiet. The farm was like a ghost town. All of the horses were out to pasture except for Dixie. Paddy O'Brien, part-time trainer, part-time groom, and full-time friend, had gone to the racetrack with Mr. Clark to check on a lame horse, and Mrs. Clark was working a horse in the riding ring. What Carolyn really wanted to do was talk to someone. On this morning, any ear would be fine.

"If I could only yodel, that would chase away the cowgirl blues. It's as simple as that," Carolyn said to Inky Dink, her faithful canine companion who was resting comfortably at her feet. "Dink, I saw Roy, Dale, and the Sons of the Pioneers yodeling last night on television. It looked like they were having fun. Not a sad face in the crowd. Even more fun than pitching hay." Inky Dink's response was a soft snore. The heat had claimed its first casualty of the day.

Carolyn leaned on the pitchfork and checked her wristwatch. There were still twenty minutes before her student arrived. She stared at the dial and watched thirty seconds tick away. Dale Evans and her horse Buttermilk stared back from the face of the watch. At least Dale was smiling, Carolyn thought wistfully. She desperately needed a smile of her own, and counting seconds was not a pursuit of happiness.

To pass the time more quickly, Carolyn thought about watching her mother train Bojangles. So far this summer, the black stallion was the most exciting thing to happen at the farm. He was well muscled, moody, and always a challenge in the ring. Too slow for the racetrack, he finally found a career as a show jumper. He was a natural sprinter who vaulted over fences with an explosive stride. Carolyn liked him, but Paddy was leery of the big horse. "He's got a look of evil in his eye," Paddy always said, spitting at the ground. "In all my years, I've never seen a horse that didn't like other horses. He's got a disorder of the mind. That's why he can't race. He needs a shrink, not a trainer." Carolyn couldn't understand Paddy's disgust and was afraid to ask. No one ever questioned Paddy's opinion when he got emotional about a horse. He had his reasons, and that was a good enough reason for everybody else.

In addition to his bad personality, Bojangles had developed some bad riding habits. That's how he ended up at the Jolly Jockey. Miss Roberts, owner and rider, was hoping that Mrs. Clark could fix the hitch in his stride. He was losing height on his jumps and losing points in competition. As a result, Miss Roberts was losing any hope of making the United States Equestrian Team for next summer's Olympic Games in Italy. One point could be the difference between riding in Rome and sitting at home. If anybody could help, it was Dorothy Clark.

Dot, as she was known in horse circles, was a horse mechanic. If your horse didn't run smoothly, you took it to Dot for a tune-up. She didn't just work her horses; she studied them inside and out, often seeing things that were invisible to their owners.

Carolyn had a special interest in rooting for Miss Roberts. Not only was she an excellent rider and a fellow jumper, but she was also a classy lady, a real cowgirl in her own right. She was always willing to give Carolyn free jumping lessons or offer advice. On one visit, she even gave Carolyn a t-shirt from the equestrian team. Watching her work Bojangles around the course fueled Carolyn's own dream. If she kept jumping, one day she could be standing on the awards platform, clutching a gold medal and waving the American flag. That would be the sweetest dream ever, even better than riding for the Pony Express. A chance to compete against the best riders and the best horses from around the world would be something special; a huge step up from her pony club rodeos.

Carolyn glanced at her watch. Fifteen minutes to the hour. Dale was still smiling, but Carolyn hadn't even started. Her daydreaming had wasted precious seconds. There wasn't enough time to watch Bojangles but plenty of time for another verse of song, only this time with gusto. "Just turn me loose, let me straddle my old saddle underneath the western skies," Carolyn wailed. Seconds later her voice cracked and her patience snapped as she tossed the microphone aside. The pitchfork hit the ground with a loud clang. Inky Dink looked up and growled, irritated that his nap had been so rudely interrupted.

"Sweaty and stinky, that's what I am," Carolyn grumbled loudly. "No cowgirl should be sweaty and stinky. Sounds like names for a mule team, not for a cowgirl." Carolyn knew it had been a mistake to change into her riding clothes so early, but she was anxious to start the day. Now with only minutes remaining until her student's arrival, she worried about her appearance. Flecks of hay clung to her jodhpurs and dark blotches of perspiration spotted the front of her riding blouse. The spit-shine on her black riding boots was melting into a murky sludge. "Dink, I know just what I need," she said enthusiastically. "Give me some fence and some sky, the perfect place to get away from it all." Carolyn kicked up her heels and headed out the door. Inky Dink looked up, barked weakly, and fell back to sleep.

Carolyn's hideaway was a section of corral fence behind the stable that enclosed about five acres of rolling pasture. The fence wasn't anything fancy, just three oak planks between two oak posts. But the spot offered a stunning panoramic view of the Jolly Jockey and the neighboring farms, and that's what made it special to Carolyn. Like a pair of old blue jeans and a flannel shirt, the place was comfortable on any occasion and in all kinds of weather. Carolyn's favorite time to visit was at sundown when the first stars blinked in the heavens. That's when she connected with the generations of cowgirls who went before her. She pictured them leaning on a fence, gazing at the starry sky and wishing upon the brightest star to make their dreams come true. In her own backyard, she had a small parcel of the Old West. That thought always brought a smile to her face.

But the fence was more than a hideaway. It was a personal hitching post, a place where a cowgirl could tie up her thoughts and sort out her problems. Carolyn had been coming to the fence since she could walk, as if this one spot on earth had been reserved exclusively for her. At first, she couldn't figure out her attraction to the spot, but as she grew older, the reason became clearer. The fence was her connection to the cosmic energy of the universe. To tap its power, all she had to do was touch it. It was like plugging a lamp into a wall socket, but instead of lighting a room, you were enlightening a mind. She tried to explain the theory to her friends, but they always looked at her as if she was speaking a foreign language.

Carolyn leaned forward on the middle plank and rested her chin on top of her hands. There was still enough time for some serious thinking about the summer that had started with so much promise. Only a month ago, she was certain that her riding academy would be an instant success. Now, she was getting ready to restart the summer and wondering how things went so wrong.

Two weeks before school ended, Carolyn had placed her homemade flyer on the bulletin board at the local grocery store. Advertisements were layered like roofing shingles. Everybody in the county was trying to sell a car, a lawnmower, a desk, a guitar, or a puppy. Carolyn didn't mind the clutter. What bothered her was the large number of advertisements for riding lessons. In horse country, competition for students was keen. There wasn't much room for a twelve-year old instructor, either on the bulletin board or in the riding ring. For a second, she was tempted to trash some of the other horse ads to limit the competition, but such thievery, not to mention downright meanness, was against the cowgirl code. Carolyn lived and breathed the cowgirl code. If caught breaking it, she knew the harsh consequences. The Roy Rogers and Dale Evans Fan Club would permanently revoke her membership. That wouldn't look good on her application for the United States Equestrian Team.

The initial response to the flyer was encouraging. There were five phone calls the first week alone, but the pool of students dried up quicker than chicken spit in a frying pan. "Well, perhaps, I should look for someone just a little older," was the typical response when callers discovered Carolyn's age. Carolyn wondered what people were expecting. Maybe next year, the flyer should read "Young Instructor Specializing in Young Riders." But truth in advertising was no guarantee for success. Despite her experience, no one was willing to give her a chance.

Next year, Carolyn vowed to have a flashy flyer in bright colors that would catch the eye of every customer in the store. It would feature a cowgirl on horseback, racing underneath a rainbow with one hand holding the reins and the other twirling a lasso that spelled out her name. However, Carolyn wasn't even good enough to be a bad artist. For two days, she tried her hand at sketching the flyer, but her drawings always looked like a stick girl waving a hula-hoop while riding a plow horse. The flyer would surely attract attention for all the wrong reasons. But there was plenty of time to get ready for next summer. By then, she hoped to find a real artist.

When the telephone fell silent after the first week so did Carolyn. She moped around the farm and waited for the phone to ring again, but nothing happened, not even a wrong number. Finally, at the end of the second week, she received the long-awaited call. Mrs. Helen Tuttle wanted riding lessons for her nine-year-old twin boys. She didn't care about the age of the instructor or the price of a lesson. What mattered most were the day of the week and the time of the day. Carolyn should have known it was a trap. Mrs. Tuttle was really looking for a babysitter so she could play bridge at her social club.

At the first lesson, Carolyn learned more than she taught. Harold and Lawrence, or Harry and Larry as they liked to be called, weren't bad kids. They just weren't interested in learning to ride horses. All they wanted was a ten-minute pony ride and then time to play for the rest of the afternoon. The Tuttle Gang, as Carolyn liked to call them, were outlaws on the run. They ran up and down, inside and outside, and all around the stable. They finished the first day by racing each other around the practice track. Too bad they weren't horses, Carolyn thought. They would have made fine steeplechasers.

To her credit, Carolyn was a quick learner. The second week she shadowed the boys at a safe distance. Ten dollars an hour for baby-sitting was going to be easy money. But to Carolyn's surprise, the boys were no longer interested in chasing. This time they brought a football for entertainment. After the mandatory pony ride, they were content to kick and throw the ball, pretending to play for the Baltimore Colts, Baltimore's professional football team. They ran up and down their imaginary field, shouting out the names of the most popular players. Carolyn politely declined their requests to be the quarterback. She stood quietly to the side with hands on hips until an errant kick bounced over the fence and landed in the pasture.

"Time out, guys!" Carolyn shouted, holding up her hands to form a T. "I'll get the ball for you. The last thing you need is to get stampeded." But before Carolyn could say another word, Dixie appeared from nowhere and charged across the field toward the ball. Tha-wack! Her hoof struck the leather ball like a whip. Carolyn and the boys watched in stunned silence as the ball exploded off the ground. End over end, it sailed higher and higher until it disappeared over the stable roof.

"That was truly awesome! One of the greatest kicks in football!" shouted Larry.

"Unbelievable! Dixie should be playing for the Colts," Harry howled with laughter.

Carolyn shook her head from side to side and exhaled sharply. "Guys, let's just get the ball and

59

get ready to go home," she groaned. She was counting down the minutes until Mrs. Tuttle arrived.

Harry charged around the building, elbowing his brother out of the way. Carolyn jogged slowly behind them, still shaking her head. After a few minutes of frantic searching, the trio was puzzled. There wasn't a ball in sight. It seemed to have disappeared into thin air.

"Maybe it got stuck on the roof," suggested Harry.

"Maybe Inky Dink ran off with it," countered Larry.

Carolyn had her own ideas. Without a word, she walked to the sludge pit behind the stable. "Guys, I found your ball," she teased. Harry and Larry ran over and peered into the shallow pit. To their delight, the brown ball had landed right on top of the manure pile, making it almost impossible to see. Carolyn gingerly plucked the ball from its resting place and handed it to Harry, who rubbed it clean against the front of his shirt and passed it to his brother. With their heads touching, the boys peered down and methodically fingered every inch of the ball. The force of the kick had split the leather stitches on the top of the ball and punctured the rubber bladder inside.

"What a souvenir!" Larry exclaimed as he held the deflated chunk of leather above his head.

"Wait until Dad sees this! He won't believe it. Heck, I don't believe it myself," Harry said excitedly.

"That was a neat trick. You and your horse should join the circus and be like Circus Boy," Larry said to Carolyn, referring to his favorite TV show about an orphan who joins the circus.

"Yeah, Carolyn, that would be really cool. You might even get your own TV show. They could call it Circus Girl," Harry added.

"I'm sorry guys, but it wasn't a trick, just an accident. Dixie hit the ball just as it bounced off the ground. She just bumped into it. That's all it was," Carolyn replied flatly.

"That's not the way we saw it," they responded in unison.

Harry and Larry spent the rest of the afternoon talking about the kick and inspecting the ball. Their only regret was that they didn't have another football. They wanted to see Dixie kick again. When Mrs. Tuttle finally arrived, the boys thanked Carolyn for one of the greatest days of their lives. They couldn't wait to get home and spread the word about Dixie the football pony. Carolyn watched from a distance as the boys excitedly told the story to their mother. Mrs. Tuttle made a sour face and refused to touch the ball, stepping back as if it was radioactive. She gave Harry the car keys and had him place it in the trunk. Carolyn laughed at the scene but had to admit the ball had a peculiar odor.

"Boys will be boys and cowboys will be cowboys, and those boys will never be cowboys," she whispered under her breath as she waved good-bye. Good riddance was her only thought. She wasn't heartbroken when Mrs. Tuttle called the next day with the news. The boys had decided to spend the rest of the summer at a camp. No doubt, Mrs. Tuttle was delighted with the decision. Her calendar was clear to shuffle the deck and deal the cards. After only two lessons, the Tuttle Gang rode the bus out of town to the mountains of upstate New York. They were the first official dropouts from the Carolyn Clark Riding Academy.

But out of sight was not out of mind for the twins. A week later, they delivered on their promise to keep in touch. In the mail, Carolyn received a multi-colored, glossy brochure from Viking Mountain, the adventure camp where young warriors learn the arts, crafts, and sports of their ancestors. Carolyn skipped the sales pitch and studied the action photos. She didn't know how the boys would survive. Life was rough for these young recruits in the army of Valhalla. A hard day of swimming, climbing, or hiking was followed by a fast-paced game of ping-pong or billiards. Hungry? Don't forget to stop at a fully stocked snack bar for an appetizer. After an all-you-can-eat buffet dinner, enjoy the evening movie and then retire to your log cabin in the pines.

Carolyn scanned the list of activities. The twins were safe from harm. There was no horseback riding, but there was football. She was certain that one of the boys had slipped the football into his suitcase when Mrs. Tuttle wasn't looking. At this very moment, the ball was being passed around to legions of young warriors. The legend of Dixie was spreading up and down the mountain like a wildfire. In a year or two, school kids around the country would solemnly recite the legend by heart. With each telling, the story would become bigger and bolder. Dixie would be renowned for kicking a football through the center towers of the Chesapeake Bay Bridge.

Carolyn once again glanced at her watch. There were five minutes to the hour, still plenty of time to think. Perhaps, Harry and Larry had the right idea. What kid in their right mind would want to spend the summer learning to ride a sweaty horse on a stinky horse farm in the middle of a hot and humid Maryland summer? Other than Carolyn, obviously, not too many. The idea of a summer vacation away from the farm sounded appealing.

But forget Viking Mountain. The beach at Ocean City was Carolyn's first choice for a vacation. She had been there only once a few years ago, but the sweet memories lingered. Closing her eyes, she imagined a whole summer of riding the big waves on an inflatable raft, building sand castles, collecting seashells, and walking up and down the boardwalk in search of caramel popcorn. She could hear the waves crashing on the beach and smell the salty air. While shopping for souvenirs, she'd buy the biggest postcard that she could find and send it to the twins.

As the ocean faded from view, Carolyn opened her eyes and faced reality. The thought of a salty ocean was rubbing salt into the wound of failure. The only waves she saw were shimmering plumes of heat rising from the fields. The only breeze she felt was a blast of hot air from the stable's exhaust fan.

Carolyn lifted her head and scanned the blue horizon. "Summer vacation might as well be over," she sighed. "Nothing to show for it. Not even a saddle sore." All she could do was chalk up the Tuttle Gang to experience and wait for the next student.

Since the twins had departed, thoughts about summer vacation raced wildly in her head, and she was losing the race. Right now, she needed an ice-cold root beer to settle her nerves, but there wasn't enough time. There was only enough to take to the airwaves and vent her frustration, only this time as Carolyn the announcer.

"And they're coming around the far pole and heading down the stretch," Carolyn shouted madly, holding her fist to her mouth for a microphone. "Summer Vacation is in the lead, followed by Tuttle Boys, running a length behind. Bringing up the rear is the favorite, Carolyn Clark. There's still a chance but time is running out. Carolyn is slowly fading down the stretch." She slowly dropped her hand and sighed.

But win or lose, today was another chance. As Mrs. Clark had predicted, Carolyn was back in the race. Last week's phone call from Mrs. Farnsworth was another ride in the saddle. The only things Carolyn knew about her new student was that she was eleven years old and had no riding experience. With the present enrollment at the academy down to zero, those qualifications moved her to the front of the class. "Who would want to spend a summer vacation learning to ride a sweaty horse on a stinky horse farm?" she asked herself quietly. The answer was heading her way.

Chapter 4 - Born to Ride

"Rider on the road! Heading this way," Mrs. Clark shouted in Carolyn's direction.

Startled by her mother's voice, Carolyn jumped up and banged her head against the top rail of the fence. "Dag gum it!" she yelped as she scrunched her face in pain and gently rubbed her scalp. Bumps and bruises were a way of life for a cowgirl on the range and the ranch. Hopefully, this little misfortune wasn't an omen for the rest of the day. Carolyn shrugged her shoulders and faced the driveway, her mother's words echoing in her ears. She thought about it for a few seconds and then dropped her hand, slapping it sharply against her thigh. A slight smile creased her face. "Well, if that ain't a hoot," she declared. Those were the exact words of the lookout in the bell tower when Dixie galloped into the town of Sweetwater.

The black sedan sped along the gravel road like a stagecoach highballin' across the plains. A billowing curtain of white dust dragged in its wake. Carolyn peeked at her wristwatch. It was exactly ten o'clock. The stagecoach was right on time. In a few seconds, the latest city slicker would try her hand as a cowgirl. Carolyn wondered how long she would last. Would this tenderfoot be sproutin' roots or blowin' through town like tumbleweed?

Carolyn bolted from the fence and sprinted through the stable. "Slow down! You're not a race horse," Mrs. Clark shouted. Carolyn skidded to a stop and joined her mother. Together they walked briskly to the parking lot to greet their guests. Carolyn sucked in a few gulps of air to calm the butterflies that fluttered in her stomach. "Now don't start hyperventilating. You sound like a sick pony," her mother chided playfully. Carolyn held her breath for as long as she could. It worked for hiccups. It just might work for butterflies.

The sedan stopped a few feet in front of Mrs. Clark. Once the road dust had settled on the hood, the chauffer pounced from his seat and shuffled around the back of the vehicle to the opposite side. Bending at the waist, he grabbed hold of the door handle and slowly pulled it open. Cold air gushed from the darkened interior. Mrs. Florence Mildred Farnsworth was the first to exit. Grasping a small white purse, she took hold of the chauffeur's hand and steadied herself to a standing position. She was a tall and attractive woman with the fluid movement of a professional model. Wearing a light blue summer dress with white high heels and a strand of white pearls, she proudly reflected the glamour and wealth of Baltimore's high society. After brushing the brim of her over-sized white straw hat with her fingers, she strutted towards Mrs. Clark.

"Florence Farnsworth at your service and you must be Carolyn Clark?" she asked in a haughty tone.

"A pleasure to meet you, Mrs. Farnsworth," replied Mrs. Clark. "But you're only half right. I'm Dorothy and this is my daughter Carolyn. She's the riding instructor."

The reply caught Mrs. Farnsworth by surprise. She looked down at Carolyn, searching for something to say. "Oh, my goodness, I was expecting someone a little older, someone, perhaps, with a little more experience." Mrs. Farnsworth raised her head and paused, this time searching for the right thing to say. "Mrs. Clark, you came highly recommended as a trainer. It would follow that your daughter has the same skills but I have concerns about her…"

Before she could finish the sentence, Mrs. Clark politely interrupted. "Mrs. Farnsworth, I may be an excellent trainer but not an excellent rider.

That title belongs to Carolyn. She is more than qualified to instruct your daughter."

Carolyn clenched her teeth in anger. The annoying comments made her temperature skyrocket on an already hot day. And suddenly, the butterflies in her stomach disappeared, boiled to a crisp in a churning cauldron of fiery blood.

"Oh, yes, I almost forgot" Mrs. Farnsworth chuckled awkwardly and reached around her side. "That brings us to my daughter, and the reason why we're here."

The girl, partially hidden behind her mother, stepped forward and introduced herself in a nervous whisper. "I'm Margaret Farnsworth, but you can call me Maggie. I want to learn to ride a horse." Maggie shook hands limply and stepped back, hoping the ground would open up and swallow her whole. How dumb can I be? Of course, she wanted to ride a horse. That's why she signed up for riding lessons. Her introduction was just downright embarrassing. What a greenhorn! Mrs. Clark and her daughter had to be biting their tongues to keep from laughing. Next Mrs. Clark would ask her if she used a right or left handed saddle. Maggie knew from her own experiences that first impressions were lasting impressions. She lowered her head and stared at the ground. Things could only get better, or so she hoped.

"I'm sure that Margaret will do just fine under your supervision," Mrs. Farnsworth stated in a firm voice that sounded more like a command than a compliment. "Now that introductions have been made, I will leave Margaret to your care. I shall return at noon. That should be more than enough time for Margaret to get acquainted with this horse business. Please see to it that Margaret is properly outfitted for today. If we pursue further lessons, I will see that she obtains the proper costume." Mrs. Farnsworth walked back to the sedan. Just as Walter was ready to open the door, she turned to face Mrs. Clark. "And one more thing, Mrs. Clark, please don't forget our conversation."

"You can rest assured I will not forget our conversation. We are all professionals here. We know our business and take it quite seriously," Mrs. Clark replied politely but sternly. From the tone of her voice, she was obviously annoyed with Mrs. Farnsworth's attitude.

Maggie waved weakly at the sedan as it disappeared in another cloud of dust. Instead of being energized by the start of her summer adventure, she was already emotionally exhausted. From the looks on the faces of Mrs. Clark and Carolyn, her mother did not make a very favorable impression. An empty feeling settled in the pit of her stomach. Maybe she wasn't cut out to be a horsewoman. Perhaps her summer dream was just a pipe dream. There were other ways to be a pioneer woman, even if they had to be found at Camp Pocahontas.

Carolyn looked at her mother with raised eyebrows. "Don't worry, I'll tell you about it later,"

Mrs. Clark said. "You'd better get going. You and Maggie have a lot to do. If you need me, I'll be in the kitchen."

"That's one woman who sure kicks up a lot of trail dust when she rides into town," Carolyn replied with relief. Mrs. Farnsworth had spooked her like a sidewinder slithering across the trail. The comment about the riding "costume" had her in a real dander. It was downright slanderous to talk like that in horse country. The only times that real cowgirls wore costumes were at rodeos and Halloween. Even more disturbing was the comment about the "conversation." That had Carolyn scratching her head. She didn't have a clue or time to worry about girl talk between mothers. With Mrs. Farnsworth out of the way, it was time to start teaching and preaching about horses.

"Come on, Maggie, let's get started. Just follow me. I'll give you a quick tour and then we'll get you some riding boots and a helmet." Carolyn stepped inside the stable and began a lively non-stop banter. "The stable was built five years ago. It's the newest building on the farm. We've got twelve stalls, a tack room and an office. There's plenty of space to work indoors. We could even add more stalls if we want. And over here, we have..." Before she could finish the sentence, Carolyn stopped dead in her tracks and listened for the echo of a footstep. The building was silent. Wondering what happened to her student, she spun around hard on her heels.

71

Maggie stood in the entrance to the stable with her arms crossed and lips pressed tightly together. "I know what the conversation is about," she shouted angrily.

"The conversation?" asked a befuddled Carolyn.

"You don't have to play dumb to avoid hurting my feelings. My mother was talking about the brace." Maggie looked down at the leather and steel contraption that encased her right leg. "I've learned to live with it and I hope you can do the same. I don't want any special treatment. I just want to be treated like any of your other students, not like some cripple."

Carolyn walked over to Maggie, looked her square in the eyes, and placed a hand on her shoulder. "I'll be honest with you. I couldn't help but notice the brace, but I really don't see it. When I look at you, I see a girl who loves horses and wants to learn to ride. That's what I see."

"I appreciate that a lot," Maggie said, wiping a tear from her eye. "If you only knew how hard I worked to get here. I dreamed of this place all winter long, and this is the first time that I've seen it. I want to ride more than anything in the world."

"I think you'd be surprised to find out how hard I dreamed to get you here," Carolyn replied softly. Her words had a calming effect. Maggie dropped her arms to her side and grinned. Suddenly, Carolyn began to laugh.

"And what's so funny about that?" Maggie demanded, now smiling.

"It's what you said," Carolyn replied. "By all means, I'll treat you like the rest of my riding students. The problem is that I don't have any other students. My only students quit after two weeks. Right now, you are the Carolyn Clark Riding Academy." She howled with laughter.

"You promise?" Maggie asked anxiously.

"I promise."

"A pinky promise?"

"As long as you promise not to quit after one lesson. Then, yes, a pinky promise," Carolyn said triumphantly as she extended the little finger on her right hand and locked it around Maggie's. "Now, let's get on with the tour. Before you know it, your mother will be here to pick you up. Remember, you came here to ride and ride you will."

"You know, my mother means well. It's just that she's too protective," Maggie apologized. "I'm eleven years old and my mom treats me like a baby. It probably has something to do with the brace."

"I know exactly what you mean," Carolyn replied in agreement. "I'm twelve and sometimes my mother is the same way, especially when I'm around certain horses. She thinks they might be too much for me to handle." Carolyn started to walk down the aisle, and then abruptly stopped. "And one more thing, you can walk next to me and not behind me."

"But you're all sweaty and stinky," Maggie blurted out, making a sour face. Carolyn knew the joke was on her. Her own words from earlier in the morning had come back to haunt her.

"Well, I may smell like a horse but at least I'm not a greenhorn. You'd better give those new jeans a good scrubbing. They look like blue cardboard. The way you walk I can't tell if it's your brace or your pants standing you up," Carolyn fired back cheerfully, trying to even the score. Maggie bit her tongue. She wanted to squeeze in the last word like she usually did with her mother. But she knew better if she wanted to make a favorable impression on her teacher. She didn't want to known as a smart-aleck or smarty-pants. Right now Carolyn Clark was the only person in the world who could make her dream come true.

Their first stop was the tack room. Carolyn explained every piece of leather that touched a horse and then handed Maggie a riding helmet and a pair of her old riding boots. "Give me a hand here and we'll get started," Carolyn said as she started to clear a space in the center of the room.

Maggie didn't hear Carolyn's request for help. She was too busy staring at the ribbons on the wall to notice the wood horse tucked in the corner. The horse was a life-size rocking horse, outfitted with an old saddle, bridle, and reins. "It's been here for years. I used to ride it when I was a kid. At least you won't get stepped on if you fall off," Carolyn said after she had dragged it into the open area.

Maggie listened intently as Carolyn explained the basic skills for the beginning rider. In a half hour, she learned how to mount and dismount, sit in the saddle, and hold the reins. After a few questions, she was ready for her first solo ride. Placing her foot in the stirrup, she pushed up with all of her might. Reaching up, she grabbed the saddle and then hung limply until her arms gave out. A few more tries produced the same results. Maggie was frustrated but determined. She gritted her teeth and breathed hard. Nothing seemed to work until Carolyn grabbed her by the waist and threw her on top of the saddle.

"It ain't pretty, but it gets the job done," Carolyn stated as she made a few adjustments to the routine.

"I think I've got the hang of it," Maggie replied after a few more successful mounts.

"Then I guess it's time we find a real horse," Carolyn declared as they headed down the center of the building. No matter how hard she tried, she couldn't wipe the smile from her face. Maggie was a quick learner who showed a keen interest in horses. Unlike the Tuttle Gang, it looked like Maggie was going to be an outstanding student. Maybe this was going to be a great day after all, she thought.

At the last stall, Carolyn turned to face Maggie. "With great pleasure, I give you the pride and joy of the Jolly Jockey, Dixie the Wonder Pony!" she proudly proclaimed. Suddenly, a large white head shot forward and hit Carolyn in the back. Stumbling forward, she regained her balance and faced her assailant. "Now that wasn't very ladylike, Miss Dixie," she scolded playfully. At the sound of her name, Dixie perked her ears and swished her tail. She was always glad to see Carolyn and always eager to make friends. And today, she was anxious to meet the new kid in town.

"Dixie, I'd like you to meet my new friend Maggie. We'll be teaching her to ride this summer. I want her to be your friend too," Carolyn cooed, gently stroking Dixie's neck. Reaching into her pocket, she pulled out a carrot and handed it to Maggie. "Since you and Dixie are going to be riding partners, I'll give you the honors."

Maggie nervously shuffled her feet. "I've never done this," she stammered. "What if she bites my hand?"

"Then bite her back," Carolyn fired back.

"Is that a training method?" Maggie asked in shock.

"Only kidding, kid," Carolyn wisecracked. "First, hold out your hand in front of her mouth so she can learn your scent. After she nuzzles your hand, pull it back, place the carrot in your palm, and offer her your hand. It's as simple as that." Maggie carefully positioned the carrot in her trembling hand and slowly moved it toward Dixie's mouth.

"Oh, no, no, no!" Carolyn chided playfully. "She's a proper lady with plenty of manners. Don't be nervous. If she senses you're afraid, she'll get nervous and think something is wrong."

Maggie did as instructed, and Dixie gently snatched the carrot from her hand. "She likes you. I can tell," Carolyn said. "Now, gently rub your hand along her neck and introduce yourself. Horses recognize voices, especially friendly voices."

"You want me to talk to a horse? What if she talks back?" giggled Maggie.

"Then I'll be rich and famous as the owner of the world's only talking horse. Who knows, they might put us on television just like Mister Ed," Carolyn chuckled.

"Hello, Miss Dixie," Maggie whispered softly as she gently stroked Dixie's neck.

"My name is Maggie, and I'm looking forward to being your friend. I can't wait until we ride." When Maggie finished, Dixie shook her head up and down and whinnied softly.

"I think you and Dixie are going to be fine. Always remember that horses are people, too. Well, more like babies most of the time. You just have to know how to treat them. Now let's get ready to ride," Carolyn declared enthusiastically. She opened the stall and led Dixie to the outdoor riding ring.

As Carolyn saddled Dixie, Maggie stood quietly, nervously rubbing her forearms with her hands. An intense cold had instantly spread throughout her body until her fingers and toes were numb. On the hottest day of the year, fear had turned her into a human icicle. All week she had looked forward to putting her foot in a stirrup on a real horse, but now she wasn't so sure. She had trouble mounting a rocking horse. How in the world would she be able to mount and ride the real thing? If she asked politely, maybe Carolyn would ease her into the saddle and walk Dixie around the ring, just like the pony rides at the firemen's carnival. That would be enough riding for one day.

"Rider, up," Carolyn barked. The words boomed in Maggie's ears. She gulped hard and raised her eyebrows. It was time for the wannabe pioneer woman to face her first test.

"Rider is ready… I think," Maggie responded weakly as she bent down to unbuckle the leather straps on her brace. Carefully placing it on the ground, she limped over to Dixie's side and placed her hands on top of the saddle.

"Are you sure you can do this without the brace?" Carolyn asked with a worried look etched across her face.

"My doctor said that it's okay. It will work my muscles and make my legs stronger," Maggie said calmly, sensing Carolyn's uneasiness. But her confident voice masked her true feelings. This was a real horse that she was riding. She was scared past the point of being nervous.

"Okay, up we go," said Carolyn. She cupped her hands under Maggie's boot and gently lifted her to the stirrups. Maggie slid across the smooth leather and settled comfortably in the saddle.

Carolyn grabbed the lead line and walked Dixie in a large circle. Maggie was relieved. Everything was going as planned. A pioneer woman had to learn to walk before she could run. She could wait until next week to solo.

While circling the ring, Carolyn stopped at various times to give Maggie the feel of a horse and offer pointers on saddle posture. Gradually, the pace was increased until Dixie was in a light trot. After the fifth lap, Carolyn stopped and adjusted the reins in Maggie's hands. "Now remember what I told you. It's all in the hands and legs," she said as she double-checked all of the straps and buckles. "Relax and stay calm. Sit straight with your weight on your rear. At first, it's going to feel bouncy, but after a few minutes, you'll start to feel the rhythm. It's just like learning to waltz except you have a horse for a partner. Your hands and feet will tell your partner where you want to go."

Maggie looked down at the reins and panicked. "But I don't know how to waltz," she pleaded, wondering what happened to next week's solo attempt.

"I don't either, but I know how to ride a horse," Carolyn replied playfully. With a gentle smack on her rump, Dixie was off to a brisk walk. Maggie stared straight ahead, afraid to even blink or breathe. She held the reins as tight as she could and prayed that Dixie didn't gallop over the fence.

For the first few minutes, horse and rider moved awkwardly like two dancers with four left feet. Maggie pulled one way; Dixie pushed the other. Dixie lurched forward; Maggie leaned back. Dixie stepped down; Maggie bounced up. "Hang in there, Maggie. You're getting the feel of it. Just relax your body and let Dixie take the lead," Carolyn shouted. Maggie nodded her head in agreement with a fierce look of determination.

"Ride the magic carousel. Ride the magic carousel," Maggie whispered to herself. The chant worked. After a couple of laps, the ride became smoother. She and Dixie were finding found their rhythm as a dance team and moving in unison. Dixie's flexing muscles were her muscles. Maggie saw herself whirling and twirling with her partner across a ballroom floor of dirt. Gradually, a wave of exhilaration swept over her Maggie. For the first time in her life, she was totally free from the leg brace. Dixie's strong and steady legs had become her legs. For the first time in her life, she was like every other girl that ever rode a horse. There were no curious looks or hushed remarks about the brace. She felt as light as a feather. Sitting tall in the saddle, she was floating on her dream.

Standing in the center of the ring, Carolyn barked instructions like a drill sergeant. "Don't slouch! Steady hands! Thumbs up! Feather the reins!" Maggie heard every word and responded instantly. She glanced down at the reins in her hands and smiled. She couldn't believe that she was finally riding a horse by herself. Brownie would be proud to see her now. With that thought, she vowed that next year they would ride again, the two of them alone in the field next to the fire hall.

After thirty minutes in the saddle, Maggie decided to quit for the day. "I'm sorry I stopped so soon. My legs are really tired, but I'll be ready to ride next week," she said wearily. "But you're right about Dixie. She's quite a lady, actually a princess. You have such a wonderful horse. She really is special."

"Sorry about what?" Carolyn wisecracked. "You were great in the saddle. Stay with me, and you'll be running a steeplechase before you know it."

Maggie grinned and nodded. She didn't want to jump or race. She just wanted to dance with Dixie.

"Just one thing, what were you mumbling there? Something about why do I carry and sell," asked a puzzled Carolyn.

"Ride the magic carousel," replied a somewhat embarrassed Maggie with a blush. "Riding Dixie in the ring was like riding on a carousel. Collecting carousels is one of my hobbies. Someday, I'll show you my collection. It's truly magical."

"A carousel," Carolyn mused as she scratched her chin. "Never thought of the riding ring like that before."

"As a matter of fact, my friends call me the Queen of the Carousels," Maggie stated proudly.

"Imagine that, will you? Move over Dale Evans, Queen of the West, and make room for

Maggie Farnsworth, Queen of the Carousels," Carolyn kidded. "I like the sound of that. Guess I'll have to find me a highfalutin' title to go along with yours."

"But you already have one," Maggie replied earnestly.

"And what might that be?" Carolyn asked.

"Why, you're Carolyn Clark, Queen of the Cowgirls."

Carolyn was flattered by the comment. "You know, tenderfoot, I like you more with each passing minute."

After Dixie was cooled down and put out to graze, Carolyn and Maggie headed back to the house. It was time to celebrate the day with an ice-cold glass of lemonade. Back in her brace, Maggie hobbled alongside Carolyn. "If there's one good thing about this stupid contraption," she blurted out. "It makes you slow down and enjoy the view. And speaking of view, what's that over there?" she asked, pointing a finger beyond the riding ring.

"That's the oval where my mother trains race horses. I was going to give you the grand tour next week, but we still have a few minutes until your mother arrives. Want to take a look?" Carolyn asked. Maggie didn't answer. She turned and headed for the white rails that circled the track.

"Why, it's a real racetrack. It even has a starting gate," Maggie marveled, standing in the middle of the track. "My father goes to the Preakness every year with his business partners.

The race is all that he talks about for the whole week. It sounds so exciting. I always wondered what it would be like to ride in a real race."

"Well, you can find out today," Carolyn said as she squatted until her palms touched the ground. "Climb aboard, jockey, and I'll give you a ride. Just hold on tight. And don't worry, I'm no faster than Dixie."

Maggie didn't think twice and immediately climbed on Carolyn's back. Carolyn slowly rose to her feet and leaned forward to balance the load. Stumbling for the first couple of steps, she quickly regained her balance and headed to the starting gate. To keep from sliding off, Maggie tightened her grip around Carolyn's neck.

Once inside a chute, Maggie knew why some horses refused to enter the gate. It was a jail cell with steel bars and flaking green paint. Horses were trapped like wild stallions that had been herded into a box canyon. When the gates finally sprang open, they instinctively bolted for their freedom. Maggie knew the feeling. She had been standing in her mother's starting gate for years, waiting for the bell to sound and the gate to open.

"Whenever you're ready, just ring the bell," Carolyn groaned, feeling her jockey getting heavier with every second.

Maggie gulped hard. "Reee-iiing!" she shouted, doing her best impression of a doorbell.

"And they're off!" Carolyn shouted as she sprinted down the track. "Coming down the stretch, it's Carolyn and Maggie neck and neck." Running on the sandy track was like running at the beach. With each step, Carolyn was slipping and sliding on the grainy surface. "Coming to the wire, it's Carolyn, the winner by a nose," she yelled after a dash of about ten yards. Swaying violently, she tripped and tumbled, spilling horse and rider onto the track. Both girls rolled over and slowly sat upright. Only a few feet apart, they stared at each other with furrowed brows and waited. When they were sure no one was hurt, they roared with laughter and brushed the sand from their sweaty arms.

"A magnificent race! Now it's off to the winner's circle for a victory toast!" Carolyn shouted with delight. She walked over and helped Maggie to her feet. Arm in arm they walked back to the house, chattering about the race. Neither girl had seen the black sedan pull up into the driveway minutes earlier.

Mrs. Farnsworth had been impatiently checking her watch and fretting. Maggie was nowhere in sight. "I don't know how many times I've told Margaret that a young lady is never late for her appointments," she huffed loudly.

"They'll be here in a few minutes," Mrs. Clark said calmly. "Would you like to come in the house for something cold to drink?"

Mrs. Farnsworth ignored the offer. Her eyes were busy searching the property. "My goodness! I believe I see Margaret over there... and I believe she's racing on a horse," Mrs. Farnsworth said frantically. "Just what kind of riding school are you running here, Mrs. Clark?" she then demanded angrily. "Having a crippled girl on a race horse for her first lesson is outrageous!"

Mrs. Clark looked toward the oval. She couldn't argue with Mrs. Farnsworth. Maggie's head was moving along the rail, but much too slow to be on a horse. "I believe the girls are just..." she started to say when Mrs. Farnsworth spooked.

"She's down! My baby is down!" Mrs. Farnsworth cried out in horror as Maggie's head disappeared from view. In a flash, she dashed across the parking lot with quick but unsteady steps. Mrs. Clark immediately gave chase, knowing that a runaway was always in danger. She just wished she had her lasso by her side. That would make the job much easier.

Florence Farnsworth hit the grass in full stride, her arms pumping furiously. Looking straight ahead, she didn't see the hole in the high grass. Snap! The heel broke off her shoe. Crackle! The cartilage in her ankle crunched like cereal. Pop! The ankle joint slipped from its socket. The fall was hard and quick. Mrs. Farnsworth rolled over twice and came to rest in a crumpled heap. "I broke my ankle! I broke my ankle!" she screamed in agony, clutching her left leg.

Mrs. Clark dropped to her knees next to Mrs. Farnsworth. The ankle was already swollen and turning purple. A grotesque lump protruded just above the anklebone.

"It looks like a bad sprain. I don't think anything is broken. We need to get some ice on that right away to reduce the swelling," she said urgently.

"Just what I need, a horse doctor," Mrs. Farnsworth said angrily, her face contorted in pain.

"Well, it's a good thing you're not a horse or else I'd shoot you to put you out of your misery," Mrs. Clark replied sharply to the insulting remark.

"But what about Margaret?" Mrs. Farnsworth asked in a panicked voice. "She could be seriously hurt."

"I'm right here," Maggie replied, hovering over her mother as Mrs. Clark continued to treat the ankle.

"You scared the daylights out of me, young lady! When I saw you fall from the horse, I ran to help."

"That was no horse. That was only Carolyn. And we were just playing at the track," Maggie said sadly, turning her head away.

"Well, this predicament is your fault. If you had been on time, this never would have happened. Why, look at you! You're covered in dirt. Not just dirt, horse filth. Why, you even smell like a horse." The scolding ended with a painful grunt as Mrs. Clark and Walter lifted Mrs. Farnsworth to her feet.

"Honey, help your mother to the car while I go get some ice," Mrs. Clark said to Maggie. A minute later, she returned with an ice pack and secured it to the ankle. Mrs. Farnsworth winced as the elastic bandage was tightened. Beads of sweat formed on her forehead and trickled down the sides of her face.

"I sincerely thank you for your assistance, Mrs. Clark," Mrs. Farnsworth said curtly once inside the car. Although in great pain, she wasn't going to humble herself to a bunch of barbaric horse people. "But in all honesty, I must tell you that I am reconsidering my decision to allow Margaret to participate in this style of training. Your methods of instruction seem ill suited for our needs. Someone will call you later about my decision."

Mrs. Farnsworth quickly rolled up the window. As the sedan sped down the road and disappeared from view, Carolyn bit her bottom lip and frowned. The bump on the head that morning had been a bad omen. Her latest student lasted only one lesson, even shorter than the Tuttle brothers. Once again, Carolyn wondered how things went so wrong so quickly. After two hours, Maggie seemed like a friend. She pictured the smile on Maggie's face as she rode Dixie, knowing she might never see that smile again.

"Did we do anything wrong, Mom?" asked a dejected Carolyn.

"No, honey, sometimes girls just need to be girls, and sometimes mothers just need to stop being mothers, at least for a minute or two. It's always hard to let go," Mrs. Clark said. She wrapped an arm around Carolyn's shoulder and pressed her close to her side. "When it rains, you look for rainbows. When you get lemons, you make lemonade. Let's go in the house and have that cold drink. We can talk girl to girl, woman to woman."

Carolyn nodded in agreement. "I hope she comes back, for her sake more than mine. She really had a knack for riding. I know she had a good time."

In the back of the sedan, mother and daughter sat in silence. Maggie was anxious to tell her mother about her day at the Jolly Jockey but knew that her mother was in no mood to talk about anything. The only thing on her mother's mind was the imprudent behavior of Miss Margaret Farnsworth.

Knowing the lecture was coming sooner or later, Maggie summoned the courage to break the silence. "I hope you're alright, Mom. I'm sorry the day had to end so badly, but I just wanted you to know that I had a great day with Carolyn. She showed me a lot about horses, and riding Dixie was just…"

Before Maggie could utter another word, her mother interrupted. "A fine day, indeed! You come running up hill like a wild child, covered in horse filth, and scare me to death. You were supposed to be taking horse lessons, not lessons in horseplay. And look at the results of your tomfoolery! As for your friend Carolyn, she's quite the ruffian. Rough around the edges like a tomboy.

I would dare to say she's a modern day Huckleberry Finn."

"I think she sees herself as an Annie Oakley more than a Huckleberry Finn," Maggie replied meekly, hoping to salvage her friend's reputation.

"Hah! More like a Calamity Jane than an Annie Oakley," her mother thundered. "She doesn't need a riding school. She needs a finishing school."

Maggie clenched her teeth to keep from laughing at her mother's unintended joke. Carolyn would be flattered with the comparison, no matter how it was intended. If she couldn't be Annie Oakley, she would gladly settle for Calamity Jane.

Instead of home, Walter headed to the doctor's office. The diagnosis was a severe sprain. There were no broken bones or torn ligaments, but Mrs. Farnsworth was required to stay off the ankle for at least two weeks. She was given a prescription for pain medicine and a pair of crutches.

The ride home continued in silence. Maggie saw it as a bad sign. Next week, there would be two phone calls, one to the Jolly Jockey and one to Camp Pocahontas. If the camp had a class for remedial social graces for truant debutantes, Maggie was sure to be enrolled. "Yuk! Another summer with a bunch of snobs who look at me like a lame horse," she muttered quietly. But there was a bright side to the ordeal. She had lived her dream, even if only for a day. Now the challenge was to make that memory last a lifetime. What she needed was a memento to put in her cigar box. She was now sorry that she didn't bring along her camera. There would have been some great pictures of her, Carolyn, and Dixie. But who, other than her mother, could have imagined that riding lessons would have ended so abruptly?

After a minute of deep thought, a sly grin creased Maggie's face. The answer to her problem was waiting at home with her horse collection. All it required was some artistic ability, and she had plenty of that. With a fresh coat of paint, she could have her own plastic versions of Dixie and Carolyn. Then she would have the pair enshrined in Maggie's Flying Horse Circus Hall of Fame. Seconds later, Maggie grinned again. One great idea had led to another. Why stop with Carolyn and Dixie? With a little more paint, she could have a plastic Maggie and Brownie. Then her horse collection would be complete. She could relive this day and her other horse days forever.

As Maggie replayed the day in her head, there was more good news from the great horse disaster. This was a headline guaranteed to bring a smile to her mother's face. Maggie couldn't wait until school started. For the first time, she had a real-life, action-packed story to tell her classmates. Instead of the usual, woeful tale about a crippled girl who spent the summer painting pictures and shooting arrows, she would recall the day she met Calamity Jane and her horse Dixie. Maggie chuckled quietly at the thought. This year's essay on how I spent my summer vacation would be about one day, one lesson, one girl, and one pony. To Maggie's calculations, the numbers added up to the adventure of a lifetime. But the painting and writing would have to wait for a couple of weeks. Mom needed some tender loving care, and Maggie wanted to be her caregiver.

For two days, Mrs. Farnsworth seemed content to have her husband and daughter tend to her needs. She spent all of her time in the family room, reading, sewing, and listening to classical music. A hospital bed was set up in the library so she wouldn't have to climb stairs.

On the third day, the patient's condition took a turn for the worst. Maggie had seen it coming since the first day. Mrs. Farnsworth was a fiercely independent woman who loved to be in control. In her eyes, having to depend on others for your daily needs was more than a sign of weakness; it was a character flaw. On Sunday, she was overly frustrated because she wasn't able to attend church. With a scowl on her face, she spent the day in the recliner, watching television. Phone calls from her friends at the social club went unanswered. That evening, she ate dinner alone.

"I'll get that for you, Mom," Maggie said as she reached down to pick up the dining tray after her mother had finished.

"If you want to help, hand me one of those crutches," Mrs. Farnsworth snapped. Maggie did as instructed and then stepped back, ready to spring

91

into action.   Standing on her good foot, Mrs. Farnsworth propped the crutch under her arm and leaned forward to pick up the tray. She gripped the edge of the tray in her hand and started to lift, but the weight was too much for her wrist. In slow motion, the plate and the glass slid off the other end and crashed to the floor.

"Don't worry. I'll clean it up," Maggie said calmly as she stooped to pick up the broken pieces.

Mrs. Farnsworth exploded with anger. "I'm perfectly capable of doing it myself!" she yelled. "It's not like I'm a cripple." Instantly, she covered her mouth with her hand, but it was too late. The words were already gone from her lips. "Oh, honey, I'm so sorry. That's not what I meant. People get angry and say mean things that they don't really mean. Please forgive me," she begged with tears streaming down her face. How in the world could she have broken the heart of a loved one so easily?

With her head slightly bowed, Maggie glanced at her mother with sad eyes. She was disappointed more than hurt by the outburst. In her heart, she knew her mother didn't mean it, but it still stung.

"It's alright, Mom. I know how you feel," Maggie said tenderly. "You're no more a cripple than I am. There are plenty of things in life that you can't do, but that doesn't make you a cripple."

"You're right, dear. It's something I believe, but never really thought about," Mrs. Farnsworth said honestly. "From now on, I promise to give it more thought. It's just that I love you so much and don't want to see you hurt in any way."

"Just remember, I feel the same way about you," Maggie replied as she hugged her mother. "Now enough of this girl talk. I'll get this mess cleaned up, and you'll do what the doctor told you to do."

Mother and daughter smiled at each other and wiped the tears that trickled from their eyes. When Maggie went to get a broom, Mrs. Farnsworth fell back into her chair and closed her eyes. For the first time, she viewed life though the eyes of her daughter. It was challenging to say the least. She realized that a crutch or a brace was not a handicap but a helping hand. Instead of being angry about it, she should be proud. Her daughter was blossoming into a fine young lady. She was standing tall on her own two legs and ready to step into the world of young adults. She didn't need someone to hold her hand; she needed someone to point the way. And that someone was her mother.

It was lunchtime on Monday when the phone rang in the kitchen of the Jolly Jockey.

Carolyn ran to pick it up, hoping it might be a potential student. "The Jolly Jockey Farm and Riding Academy. Carolyn Clark speaking. How may I help you?"

"I would like to sign up my daughter for riding lessons," replied the husky voice on the other end of the line.

"And when would she like to start?" Carolyn asked, reaching for a pen and a piece of paper.

"I've already started. I just need to finish," the voice squealed with joy. "It's me, you silly! It's Maggie. I'm back. Can you believe it? I'll be riding again!"

"Wow! That's super," Carolyn replied excitedly. "What happened?"

"My mother finally realized that her daughter is no longer a sickly little girl but a budding pioneer woman. I'll give you the details at our lesson."

Carolyn hung up the phone and looked at her mother. "Maggie's back in the saddle," she said with a wide smile.

That evening, Mrs. Clark received her own call. "Mrs. Clark, I would like to apologize for my actions last week and thank you for your assistance," Mrs. Farnsworth said sincerely. "My doctor said that your quick action reduced the extent of the injury. But more than that, I would like to thank you for allowing Margaret to continue her lessons."

"Your apology is accepted," Mrs. Clark replied graciously. "And rest assured, your daughter is in good hands at the Jolly Jockey." After the phone call, Mrs. Clark walked out to the front porch to clear her thoughts. She was glad to see that Mrs. Farnsworth was finally loosening her grip on Maggie. Letting go was the hardest thing in the world for a mother. In the distance, she spied Carolyn leaning on the fence and remembered when she had to let go for the very first time. She was in the backyard when Carolyn pulled away and sprinted to the small field of wildflowers. In her heart, she could still feel the warmth and softness of her daughter's hand as it slipped from her grasp.

Chapter 5 – A New Kid in Town

For the next two weeks, riding lessons went as planned when Carolyn first posted the flyer. Maggie was an honor roll student who was willing to work overtime to become a good rider, and there was not better place to work than the Jolly Jockey. At first, she arrived fifteen minutes before the start of her lesson, and then thirty. Today it was a full hour. Hanging around a horse farm was fun for Maggie. Nobody seemed to notice the early arrivals, and if they did, nothing was said.

Every visit, Maggie walked the length of the stable, peering into every nook and cranny. Along the way, she'd strike up a friendly conversation with the horses still in their stalls. Her hurried footsteps always alerted Inky Dink. The black and white mutt would give a quick bark, race to her side, and follow her until Carolyn arrived.

Maggie's destination was always the tack room or the trophy room as she called it, at the far end of the building. Normally, she spent time there cleaning and polishing leather gear with Carolyn, but Carolyn never wanted to talk about the awards hanging on the wall. She'd blush and mumble something about "later on." The Queen of the Cowgirls was too modest to toot her own saddle horn.

Once inside, Maggie stood in front of the wall and gazed at the rows of ribbons and medals. Even though Carolyn was only twelve, there were hundreds of awards. Blue ribbons and gold medals draped the wall like a curtain. Maggie gently stroked each ribbon with her fingers and clutched every medal in the palm of her hand. If only these awards could speak, she wished. What wonderful stories they would tell about an amazing rider and her horse. To Maggie, the tack room was more than a storage area for saddles, bridles, and blankets. It was a vault that held a priceless collection of golden moments on horseback. Someday, she hoped to have her own ribbon. One would be plenty, and any color of the rainbow would do just fine. Tilting back her head, Maggie breathed deeply. The scented air energized her body like a magic elixir.

It was more than the smell of leather and polish; it was the sweet smell of success.

But today, Maggie arrived early to play music, not to sightsee. When she strolled into the stable with a violin case dangling from her fingers, the building was empty as planned. Dragging a bale of hay into the open area for a seat, she quickly unfolded her music stand, opened the case, and gently lifted the violin to her chin. "If they don't know I'm here yet, they will now," she whispered as she tuned the strings. She had already decided that if her practice sessions became a hit, she would write a symphony for the Jolly Jockey. While she didn't have a note of music, she already had the title, "Concerto for the Classical Cowgirl."

The practice session was a deal with her mother. To keep riding, Maggie had to keep playing. Much to Maggie's dismay, her mother still saw her more as a classical violinist than a classical cowgirl. But a deal was a deal, and nothing in the deal said that she had to practice at home. In Maggie's mind, the stable would be the perfect place to practice. Mrs. Clark agreed as long as Maggie didn't mind the smell. If nothing else, it was another good excuse for spending more time at the farm.

"Maestro, strike up the band," Maggie shouted. Taking a deep breath, she exhaled and pulled the bow across the strings. Sweet melodic notes swirled to the beams and evaporated into the fragrant air. Maggie stopped and listened. Nothing but silence, the exact response that she wanted. The last thing she wanted was an audience. Again, she drew the bow across the strings and stopped. This time the notes lingered in the air before fading. Quite odd for a note to echo so long, she thought. The sound seemed to be coming from the back of the building near the office. It sounded like her violin, but then it didn't. To be sure her ears weren't playing tricks, she played a few more notes. Once again, the notes lingered, louder and longer. This time Maggie wasn't fooled. That wasn't the sound of her instrument. Someone must have snuck into the stable and was playing a practical joke. Carolyn came immediately to mind, but she could barely strum a guitar. Nevertheless, it was time to flush out the prankster.

Maggie stood and faced the rear of the stable. She began to play, her hands racing across the strings as if she was trying to saw the violin in half. Then abruptly, she flicked her wrist upward and listened. There was only the buzz of a few horseflies. Once again, she lowered the bow. Before she could draw it across the strings, a tidal wave of notes flooded the stable with a deafening screech. From behind the center post, Paddy O'Brien leaped into the aisle with a violin tucked loosely under his chin. Swaying from side to side and wearing a mischievous grin, he kicked up his heels and danced circles around Maggie. Maggie immediately took her cue and matched the crazed fiddler note for note. Together, they whirled like musical tops until Paddy dropped to a knee directly in front of Maggie.

"Paddy O'Brien, at your service" he panted in his squeaky voice as he tipped his cap. "Saw you carrying your case. Didn't think you would mind a fiddlin' with me."

Maggie doubled over in laughter. She should have guessed that Paddy was the merry prankster. "I love to fiddle, but my mom said that's not what the violin was made to do."

"Aye, lassie, Irish fiddlin' is my heart and soul. Makes you happy when you're sad, and happier when you're happy," Paddy remarked in jest. "I like all kinds of music, even that Elvis Presley fellow who sings rock and roll. He's a very good crooner. Must have some Irish in him."

"I like all kinds of music too, but do you think that horses like music?" Maggie asked seriously, afraid that she might frighten them.

"They don't like it; they love it. I play music for them all the time on the radio," Paddy replied. "Can't find too much Irish music on the dial, so it's mostly classical music and baseball games. For some reason, baseball helps them relax. I think it's the announcer's voice. He's kind of an Irish baritone"

"Music helps me relax too," Maggie said. "But I really like that rock and roll stuff. It gets my feet moving, and I need all the help I can get there."

"Are you thinking about playing a concert for the horses?" Paddy asked, continuing the conversation with small talk.

The question caught Maggie off guard. Did Paddy know about the Concerto for the Classical Cowgirl, she wondered. But since he had asked about thinking, now was a good time to ask for an opinion about a nagging thought. "To be honest, Paddy, I have been thinking about horses," Maggie stammered as she lowered her eyes. "I was thinking that, maybe, you could use another farmhand. Maybe, somebody like me."

"So you want to work here?" Paddy responded eagerly, not a bit surprised at the request.

"And for free. You don't have to pay me or anything like that," Maggie quickly added.

Paddy walked over and sat down next to Maggie. "To tell you the truth, lassie, I think you'd make a fine stable girl. I've seen you around the horses. You have some horse blood in your veins. There's no better place for a young girl than a horse farm, but Mrs. Clark has to decide. She's the boss. But I'll give you my highest recommendation."

Before Maggie could respond, the sound of running feet burst into the stable. "What in tarnation is going on here? I didn't know Saint Patrick's Day was in July," Carolyn bellowed. Maggie and Paddy didn't say a word. They just held up their violins and smiled.

"I think your student has some Irish horse blood in her," Paddy joked. He winked at Maggie and danced back to the office with the violin in his hand.

"Sorry about the commotion, but I thought your mother told you about the violin," Maggie said contritely.

"No problem. You're more than welcome to play any time between sunup and sundown. I'm sure Paddy told you how much the horses like the fiddle. Though, it's been quite a while since I've heard him play," Carolyn replied.

"I swear Paddy is part leprechaun. He just popped out of thin air," Maggie declared.

"Just stick around here long enough and you'll think he's all leprechaun," Carolyn joked. Maggie nodded in agreement for more than one reason. Carolyn's words were encouraging. She would like nothing more than to stick around the Jolly Jockey, permanently.

In the riding ring, Maggie worked on saddle posture and changing directions. Lessons were fun but hard work. She was a quick learner, but she had never realized how much there was to learn about horses. On the TV westerns, cowboys made it look easy. All you had to do was casually climb in the saddle, yank on the reins, and off you went in a cloud of dust. But Maggie was glad that riding wasn't that easy. Learning the proper techniques required time, and she wanted to spend more time with Carolyn and Dixie. After knowing Carolyn for about a month, Maggie considered her a close friend. Now it was time to find out if Carolyn felt the same way.

"Pull gently with your left hand. Slight pressure on the outside leg," Carolyn barked from the center of the ring. Maggie smoothly walked Dixie through a series of turns with only the slightest of body movements. "You're a natural. I wish I had more students like you."

"You really mean that?" Maggie asked seriously, sensing her chance was at hand.

"Of course! You know a cowgirl sworn to the cowgirl creed couldn't lie to a tenderfoot," Carolyn kidded.

Maggie winced at the comment. Hopefully, Carolyn didn't really think she was a tenderfoot. But it really didn't matter. The opportunity had arrived. "If you could use more of me, do you think you could use more of me around the farm?" she asked hoarsely, the words sticking in her throat.

Carolyn blinked her eyes and gave Maggie a puzzled look. "I'm not sure I know exactly what you're asking, buckaroo."

"I want to work on the farm. I want to be a stable girl," Maggie blurted out. "Don't need to be paid or anything like that. I just love being around the farm, around horses, and around you." Maggie flashed a bashful smile and blushed, her pale white cheeks turning crimson. Now that it was said, she felt relieved. Regardless of the answer, Carolyn had to know exactly how she felt about the Jolly Jockey.

103

Carolyn raised her eyebrows with a look of mock surprise and rubbed her forehead. The question really didn't come as a surprise. With more horses boarded in the summer, the farm could always use help. Mrs. Clark usually hired an apprentice jockey from the racetrack who needed a few extra bucks. As far as Carolyn was concerned, the only job requirement was a love of horses, and Maggie certainly had that.

"I've been thinking the same thing," Carolyn replied. "Lately, we've been pretty busy. It's hard work, but you do love horses. I don't see why not. If you keep arriving any earlier, you might as well work here if not live here." Carolyn paused to collect her thoughts. There was only one nagging question to be answered. "But what about your mother?"

"She's all for it, as long as I practice my music lessons," Maggie fired back.

"Oh, brother, a whole summer of you, Paddy, and fiddle music. I don't know if I can take that," Carolyn moaned playfully.

Maggie breathed a sigh of relief. Now that Carolyn was enthusiastic about the idea, she had to sweeten the pot to seal the deal. "Maybe we can work out some kind of deal where I help you if you help me," she suggested casually.

Carolyn automatically nodded in agreement, but she didn't have the slightest idea about what Maggie could do for her. Who knows, maybe Maggie could teach her to play the fiddle. That and yodeling were two things that she had always wanted to learn. "It's a deal with me, buckaroo, but first I have to run it by the trail boss," Carolyn said as she shook hands with Maggie.

Mrs. Clark liked the idea with one condition. Maggie had to audition for the job. She would serve a week's apprenticeship before a final decision was made. That way, if things didn't work out, there would be no hard feelings, and she could continue her riding lessons. Mrs. Clark was candid with the job offer. Horse work was hard work, and not everybody was cut out to be a farmhand. If Maggie couldn't keep up with the work, she would be put out to pasture.

Maggie readily agreed to every condition, no matter how imposing. All she wanted was a chance to show the world that she wasn't really handicapped. Walking out of the office, she was pleased that Mrs. Clark didn't mention the bad leg. Mentally, she was ready for the challenge. Physically, she had some doubt if her body could hold up under the strain.

By mid-morning on the following Monday, Mrs. Clark's words proved to be true. Horses were not only a labor of love, but also a love of labor. Maggie's arms were ready to fall off. It seemed that in only a few hours she had lifted everything that wasn't tied down or tethered. Buckets and bags always needed to be filled or emptied. Around every corner was a pile of hay to be moved or a mound of manure to be removed. A wheelbarrow and a pitchfork were the farmhand's best friends.

One chore led to another in an endless cycle of hard work. Maggie often helped her mother clean around the house but never pushed anything larger than a broom or lifted anything heavier than a dustpan. And when she finished cleaning, she didn't immediately repeat the process. She quickly discovered that horse work was a lot more demanding than housework. Now she knew why farmhouses had that rundown look. Farm people were too tired to do anything but eat and sleep. Maybe being a housewife instead of a horsewoman wasn't such a bad career choice after all. Maggie was sure that her mother would agree with her on that.

The endless routine continued day after day. In the morning, Maggie pitched hay, shoveled manure, and tended buckets. In the afternoon, she groomed horses and cleaned tack. In between, she ran errands for Paddy and Mrs. Clark, everything from answering the telephone to fetching cold drinks. "The bottom rung on the ladder for an apprentice stable girl is only a few inches above the manure pile," was the first thing Carolyn said to her on her first day. After mucking out every stall in the stable, Maggie knew that no truer words were spoken.

Carolyn was the perfect partner for a wannabe stable girl. After explaining each chore, she rolled up her sleeves and pitched in with a helping hand.

106

Her strength and stamina were amazing. Only slightly taller and not much heavier than Maggie, she was as strong as an ox. Carolyn was literally a farm machine.

Maggie learned the hard way that looks could be deceiving. Of all people, she should have known better than to judge a book by its cover. One morning, she made the mistake of challenging Carolyn to an arm wrestling contest. At the time, it seemed like a good way to show Carolyn how tough a city slicker could be. Maggie didn't think she'd win, but she thought she could give the cowgirl a run for her money. Seconds later, her arm was pinned to the table with a dull thud. Of course, Carolyn, the gracious winner, giggled and offered a rematch at a later date. There wasn't any point in kicking a cowgirl when she was down. Maggie just shook her head and shrugged her shoulders. Now she was an official tenderfoot. At least she had moved up from being a greenhorn.

Carolyn always joked that if she were a horse, she'd want to be a Clydesdale. That statement came as no surprise to Maggie, who was certain that more than a few drops of horse blood coursed through Carolyn's veins. If Carolyn had a harness to fit, she could have pulled a covered wagon all the way from Missouri to California. A pioneer family wouldn't need a team of horses. All they'd have to do was hitch up Carolyn. She'd huff and puff, but she'd pull from sunup to sundown with a smile on her face and a song on her lips. If it wasn't a song, then

107

it was some other verbal exercise to keep those lips flapping. Maggie found it hard to believe, but the cowgirl talked harder than she worked. The day was an endless stream of campfire songs, corny horse jokes, and cowboy stories. Carolyn was a walking encyclopedia of TV westerns. She knew every show, every star, and, of course, every horse that ever appeared in front of a camera.

At first, Maggie found the chatter annoying but she realized it smoothed out the rough spots in the day and helped pass the time. Listening to Carolyn was better than thinking about her aching arms and legs. Maggie had a few stories of her own, but her adventures at Camp Pocahontas didn't exactly get the heart pumping. Besides, it was much more fun listening to Carolyn. Her enthusiasm for the work was highly contagious. Maggie was just thankful that she caught it.

One day at a time was Maggie's attitude for surviving the week. When she started feeling sorry for herself, she bit her lip, gritted her teeth, and muscled up. Every time she thought about quitting, she pictured her mother sitting by the telephone, waiting for her to call. "Now, you just rest until Walter gets there. I'll have him take you directly to Camp Pocahontas," she could hear her mother say.

"Mother, say no more," Maggie would reply. "This cowpoke isn't quitting until she's fired, retired or expired."

On Friday morning, Maggie had to admit that being fired might be a good career move. She was bone-tired and plum worn-out. Every morning had been an exhausting effort just to roll out of bed. On Tuesday, only the muscles in her arms had been sore. Today, every inch of her body burned with pain. She spent afternoons daydreaming about a long soak in a bubble bath. But before she could turn on the spigot to fill the tub, there was one more day. Today had to be her best day. It was her last chance to impress Carolyn and Mrs. Clark.

Maggie matched Carolyn word for word, bucket for bucket, and shovel for shovel. Today she was the nonstop chatterbox. Today she was the machine. She grunted and groaned with every breath. Sweat flowed down her face in little rivers as she summoned every ounce of strength remaining in her body.

Fearing that Maggie would collapse from exhaustion, Carolyn deliberately took extra breaks, telling her to slow down and take it easy. But Maggie wasn't paying any attention. She continued to work fast and furious. Her father always preached that success in any job was ten percent inspiration and ninety percent perspiration. And from the wet blotches on her t-shirt and baseball cap, Maggie was ninety percent sure of success. It was the other ten percent that had her worried. In her case, that percentage was limitation, not inspiration. The bad leg slowed her down at times. She just hoped it wouldn't bring her job to a screeching stop.

At noon, Mrs. Clark called for a meeting in her office. Maggie took a deep breath and marched through the doorway with a grim look of determination. She stood at attention in front of the large oak desk, her stomach churning and knees wobbling. "Ma'am, you wanted to see me," she announced cheerfully, knowing that it never hurt to be nice to the boss.

Mrs. Clark lowered the paper that she was reading and looked up to make eye contact. "You know why you're here, Maggie. I have given it a lot of thought, but..." Mrs. Clark said solemnly with a pause. Maggie quietly exhaled a shallow breath. The corners of her mouth flattened and turned down. She wanted to scream in anger like a wild stallion that had been lassoed. The word "but" was nothing but bad news. It meant that she didn't get the job. Maggie heard the same news at school and at camp. She could finish the sentence for Mrs. Clark. "But you're not strong enough, but you're not fast, but you're a cripple," she said silently. If only Mrs. Clark had said "if "or "and." That would have been a ray of hope. That could have meant that Mrs. Clark had another job in mind. Maggie was willing to do anything to work at the Jolly Jockey. Desperate to plead her case, she decided to just start talking and hope that it made sense. As she opened her mouth to speak, Mrs. Clark continued.

"But I wanted to hear your thoughts before I offer you the job," Mrs. Clark said with a smile.

110

Maggie snapped her jaw shut, stunned by the words. A second ago, she was ready to get down on her knees and beg for a job. Now she was ready to jump on top of the desk and dance a jig. "I think this is the best place in the world to work. Thank you so much. I'll be the best stable girl you ever hired," she stuttered humbly with a proud smile. The job was hers, no "but" about it.

"And don't forget, I pay every hand a decent wage based on their experience. You'll start at two dollars a day, ten dollars a week. Any raises are based on performance. Free lunch is included," Mrs. Clark added as she stood and leaned forward. A quick handshake sealed the deal. That's all that was needed between cowgirls.

"Welcome aboard," Carolyn said warmly as she walked into the room and hugged Maggie. "And don't worry about being the best. Just worry about being the best you can be."

Mrs. Clark saw Maggie staring at the telephone on the desk. "By all means, give your mother a call and give her the good news. I know she's waiting anxiously by the phone."

After the call, Maggie smiled bashfully and replayed the conversation. Her mother sounded genuinely excited. To celebrate the occasion, dinner was going to be Maggie's favorite, macaroni and cheese. At that point, Maggie knew that today was special. Her mother hated macaroni and cheese. Then again, Maggie remembered that her mother didn't like horses either.

111

Later that afternoon, Maggie and Carolyn headed outside to wait for Walter. When the black sedan turned into the driveway and began rumbling up the hill, Carolyn made her announcement. "Now that you're a full-time stable girl, I think a promotion party is in order," she declared. "How about an overnight trail ride next Friday with all the fixins'?"

"Sounds great! I can't wait to saddle up,' Maggie replied excitedly.

"We'll ride the range and then sleep under the stars," Carolyn said, pointing to the ridge behind the farmhouse. "It's not the Rocky Mountains, but it's the tallest peak around these parts. No matter what, it will be lots of fun."

"Count me in, pardner," Maggie replied. "And thanks for all of your help. I couldn't have done it without you."

"Aw, shucks," Carolyn said meekly. "I'd do the same for any saddle pal."

Maggie climbed into the back of the sedan still wearing the broad smile that had creased her face since noon. As Walter pulled away, Carolyn's last words echoed in her mind. A saddle pal was someone special among cowgirls. That could only mean that she and Carolyn were friends after all. She loved the idea of being a saddle pal, especially Carolyn's saddle pal. Who wouldn't want to be saddle pals with the Queen of the Cowgirls? It was an honor for any buckaroo.

Chapter 6 – Home on the Range

After the successful audition, Maggie finally had a chance to enjoy life at the Jolly Jockey. As she had discovered in the tack room, farm life was a magic elixir. She never felt or looked healthier. In only a week, her pale skin tanned to a light brown. By the end of the summer, she hoped to be as tan and tough as old saddle leather. There was some added muscle in her arm, but she wasn't ready for a rematch with Carolyn just yet. Even the leg brace felt lighter with each passing day. The bulky contraption was cumbersome at times, but it didn't stop her from doing her chores. The combination of work and riding was making her bad leg stronger. Now that her summer dream had come true, maybe one day, her other dream would come true. She tried not to think about it too much, but it always crept into her mind. Someday, she would do what doctors said couldn't be done. One day, she would remove the brace and walk on her own. For a pioneer woman, such as herself, the impossible would just take a little extra time.

During the second week, the job schedule changed due to the weather. In the heat of the early afternoon, work slowed to a steady crawl and then stopped. When Carolyn removed her bandana, wiped her brow, and called for a break, the end of the workday had arrived. As much as Carolyn liked to work around horses, there was also time to "horse around" the work as she liked to say. It was time to be a genuine cowpoke. She and Maggie usually spent the rest of the afternoon walking around the farm and talking about horses. Pole sittin' became the favorite afternoon pastime. After one session, Maggie understood why Carolyn liked fences. The view from the top rail was almost as good as the view from a saddle. Located in a narrow valley, the farm offered rolling fields, hilltop forests, and horses in every direction. When Carolyn got bored in one spot, she simply moved to another section of fence. With miles of fences on the property, there was always a good seat waiting for a seasoned sitter.

Next to pole sittin', lunch was the other highlight of the day. Hard work and hearty appetites went hand in hand on a horse farm. A hired hand might leave with aches and pains but not hunger pains. Mrs. Clark made sure of that. The kitchen table was always crowded with plates of sandwiches and homemade desserts, such as apple pies and oatmeal cookies. And of course, there was always a pitcher of lemonade in the refrigerator and a pot of freshly brewed coffee on the stove.

On Tuesdays and Thursdays, the lunch menu was expanded to include a generous helping of Mr. Willie Clark, professional jockey, co-owner of the farm, and Carolyn's father. For Maggie, he was a spice of life that added flavor to any meal. He turned a peanut butter and jelly sandwich into a gourmet dinner.

During the summer racing season, Mr. Clark spent almost every waking hour at the racetrack so Maggie rarely saw him. But when she did, he always smiled and chatted. From what she saw and heard, he was an American version of Paddy, a suspicion confirmed by Carolyn. She wasn't sure if their shared traits were unique to jockeys, short people or leprechauns, but they had so much in common that people thought they were brothers. They walked, talked, and even dressed alike. The only obvious differences were birthplaces and accents. Paddy was born in Dublin, Ireland, and Mr. Clark in Philadelphia, Pennsylvania. To

Maggie, they were a pair of matched bookends from opposite sides of the Atlantic Ocean.

After her first lunch with Mr. Clark, Maggie knew why the farm was named the Jolly Jockey. If Paddy had a million stories about Ireland, Willie Clark had a million and one stories about his most memorable races. And they were all funny. Carolyn and Mrs. Clark groaned every time Mr. Clark opened his mouth, but Maggie perked her ears. Mr. Clark had a captive audience of one, and the King of the Oval was not going to disappoint any of his fans. It didn't matter if they were sitting in his kitchen or in the grandstand. The stories were always lively and animated, usually requiring kitchen chairs and Maggie as props. If pressed for space, drinking glasses, salt and peppershakers, and bottles of condiments were used to replay the action. The background was always different, but the plot was always the same, Willie Cark matching wits with horses and jockeys. "And wiry Willie wins by a wink and a whisker," Willie would shout in victory at the end of each tale.

A rousing good story usually resulted in a round of questions from Maggie. Her thirst for "horse" knowledge only prolonged the agony for Carolyn and Mrs. Clark. Willie Clark may not have won every race he ran, but every story he told was a winner. He had the gift of gab to make the ordinary sound extraordinary and the natural seem supernatural. Maggie clapped and cheered as each story raced down the backstretch to the finish line that was more often the punch line. Racing was a part of the horse business that she had never seen. It sounded so exciting, especially when Mr. Clark called the race in his unique style. When he invited Maggie to visit the racetrack, she immediately accepted.

On Friday, Carolyn was chomping at the bit to hit the trail. All week she had blabbered endlessly about the ride. A cowgirl's "dream come true" she called it, especially for a budding pioneer woman like Maggie. Even though she had made the ride many times with her pony club, it was always a special treat. The trail transported her back to the Old West. In the saddle, she was a Pony Express rider, streaking along the Oregon Trail. To play the part, she always wore a western blouse with rolled up sleeves, red silk scarf, and a floppy leather hat.

From the start, Maggie was a little leery about her first trail ride. She didn't want to get her hopes up too high if it didn't go as advertised. She had to constantly remind herself that the sales pitch was coming from a girl who made mucking out stalls sound like a day at the beach. If Carolyn's career as a horsewoman ever fizzled out, she could get a job selling used horses. Every time Carolyn opened her mouth to talk about the ride, Maggie pictured her on a late night TV commercial. "Now right over here, I have a real beauty in black and white. Driven only on Sundays by a little old cowgirl. No dents. No dings. No spur marks. Real leather seat with a new horn. Low mileage. Ready to ride off the lot. Buy

117

now and I'll throw in a year's supply of hay and oats," she could her Carolyn say. Maggie always chuckled at the private joke. When that happened, Carolyn would give her a quick glance, whistle, and shake her head from side to side. There must have been some locoweed in the girl's breakfast feed was all that she could figure.

That afternoon, Maggie and Carolyn finally saddled up for the First Annual Carolyn Clark Summer Trail Ride. Maggie rode Dixie, and Carolyn rode Cherokee, a beautiful Palomino that was used as a track pony. Their destination was Sagamore Farm, a neighboring horse farm about four miles away. Maggie had never heard of the place, but Carolyn praised it as a shrine to horses and horseman.

Carolyn led the way along a wooded ridge that started behind the Jolly Jockey. After a refreshing ride on a shaded trail, the girls exited the hilltop forest and slowly descended into the valley. The view was breathtaking. Pastures and cornfields stretched to the horizon. Patches of wildflowers dotted the landscape like exclamation marks. Once again, Mother Nature proved why she was the world's greatest painter. The rolling canvas of the valley floor was brushed with shades of green and dabbed with dazzling bursts of yellow, blue, red and purple. In Carolyn's mind, it was the same painting that settlers saw when they crossed the Great Plains in the 1800's. For the next two miles, she and Maggie joined the wagon train of America's past as they rode across the prairie in the searing heat. Carolyn the trail boss quickly pointed out the historical markers on her personal frontier. A cloud of dust on a distant hillside could be an Indian hunting party or horse soldiers from the United States Cavalry. Cows became buffalo; cars became covered wagons; and houses became outposts. And everyday people were just fellow pioneers heading west. After listening to Carolyn, Maggie was nearly convinced that it was 1859 instead of 1959.

Halfway across the valley, the girls stopped at a spring-fed stream to water the horses. Carolyn broke out her saddlebag rations for a snack of gooey cupcakes washed down with hot lemonade from a canteen. There were no fancy meals for these pioneer women. They would rough it like their ancestors. Before climbing back in the saddle, they soaked their bandanas in the cold water and tied them loosely around their necks.

Minutes later, they crested a gently sloping ridge and finally glimpsed their destination. "There's our Sweetwater. It doesn't look like much, but wait until we get there. You're in for a real treat," Carolyn eagerly announced as she pointed to a cluster of white buildings with red roofs. At the far end of the valley, Sagamore Farm shimmered like a desert mirage.

"Okay, sheriff, your posse is right behind you as long as they have a soda machine," Maggie responded with a half-hearted smile as she leaned over the saddle. The trip had been fun and lived up

119

to Carolyn's hype, but she was tired, thirsty, and ready to head for home. Her body was sagging as much as her spirit. She was about to suggest a change in direction when she remembered the sedan ride to her first riding lesson. Hardship was part of the dream package. Sometimes a pioneer woman had to tough it out to the end. Plus she didn't want to disappoint Carolyn after all of her hard work in preparing for the trip. So for Carolyn's sake, she trudged along with no complaints.

A half-hour later, the girls rode into Sagamore Farm. They quickly tethered their horses to one of the many hitching posts and began the tour. Carolyn grabbed Maggie by the hand and led her from building to building. Facts and figures about the farm rolled off Carolyn's tongue as if she had swallowed a tour book. Maggie was impressed. Millionaire Alfred Vanderbilt Jr. didn't pinch pennies in building his horse palace. There was a main barn with ninety stalls, an enclosed track, an outdoor track with a two-story timer's stand, and a dormitory for workers. A small army of jockeys, grooms, trainers, and stable hands scurried about their business. The farm was really a small town. The Jolly Jockey and all of its workers could easily fit into the hay barn with room to spare.

Carolyn knew who and what was behind every door. Workers greeted her cheerfully by her first name as if she was an employee. After a quick chat at each stop, she eagerly introduced Maggie as the new stable girl at the Jolly Jockey. In response,

Maggie just blushed and smiled softly. She didn't know what else to do. Being dragged along from room to room was like visiting long-lost relatives during the holidays. The people were nice and friendly, but it was difficult to strike up a conversation with strangers, especially if they were grown-ups.

"One more stop, then we can head back home. It's time to meet the ghost," Carolyn announced excitedly as they dashed from the last building. She had mentioned the ghost to Maggie when talking about the trail ride but deliberately did not provide any details. She wanted it to be a surprise. Maggie doggedly nodded her head and straightened up. The thought of a ghost story gave her a jolt of energy. A good ghost story was almost as good as a good horse story.

They walked over to the paddock fence and waited. Carolyn's eyes darted nervously from side to side. Maggie gazed at her with a puzzled look. All she saw was an empty pasture. The idea of spotting a ghost in the brilliant sunshine seemed ridiculous.

"Time to summon the ghost," Carolyn announced nervously. She raised her fingers to her lips and blasted two loud whistles. No ghost appeared. Any second, Maggie expected to see Paddy jump from behind a fence post or Dixie charge from behind the barn. She was convinced the ghost story was a prank on the new kid in town, but in this case she was more than willing to play along with the pranksters.

Suddenly, out of thin air, the ghost appeared along the fence, first as a dark speck in the distance and then as a massive gray stallion looming larger than life. Thundering hooves, a cloud of dust, and a bellowing whinny announced the arrival of Native Dancer, the star of Sagamore Farm.

"The Gray Ghost, one of the greatest horses ever! His only loss was by a nose at the Kentucky Derby. Twenty-one wins in twenty-two races," Carolyn proudly gushed as if the horse was her brother.

"Have you ever ridden him?" Maggie asked curiously. The Gray Ghost wasn't the surprise that she had in mind, but at least it wasn't a prank. Other than Bojangles, she had never seen a racing horse up close. Most of the horses at the Jolly Jockey were ponies. With his size and speed, Native Dancer was an imposing animal with a spirited attitude. Maggie saw why horses and jockeys feared him. She wondered if Mr. Clark had ever ridden the Gray Ghost. If not, then she was sure he had a good adventure story about him.

"He's still warming up to me. I sneak him a snack whenever I visit, but I don't know if I'll ever ride a horse like that. He bites, kicks and throws riders. He's got a lot of hot racing blood in him," Carolyn replied as she stepped towards the fence. The stallion stood his ground a few steps away, his eyes fixed on Carolyn's every move. "You have to be careful with thoroughbreds. Some of them are mean and nasty. As long as you're on the opposite side of the fence, you're safe. For some reason, racehorses don't like fences. Normally, they tend to shy away from them. If spooked, they try to jump them. If you're ever in trouble with a horse, a fence could be your escape route," Carolyn cautioned. She fished a carrot out of her pocket and carefully slipped it to the Gray Ghost. When finished chewing, he snorted softly and than galloped away. In the blink of an eye, the ghost had vanished.

The girls arrived home in the cool of the early evening, tired but still buzzing about their journey. The trail ride had been an overwhelming success. On a scale of 1 to 10, they rated it a 10+. In the end, they agreed that Sagamore Farm was a nice place to visit, but they didn't want to live there. Bigger didn't always mean better. Be it ever so humble, there was no place like the Jolly Jockey.

After the horses were cooled down and cleaned up, Carolyn and Maggie hiked up the steep hill behind the farmhouse. To find the campsite, they simply followed their noses. In a small clearing of pine trees that overlooked the valley, they found Paddy tending a large black pot over a crackling fire. "You're just in time for the chuck wagon. Tonight's main course is cowboy... I mean, cowgirl stew," he proudly announced. "Well, the truth be known, it's my own recipe for Irish stew with some extra spices," he added with a wink.

Paddy had already set up camp with the creature comforts of home on the range. No bedrolls and saddles for these trail hands. Tonight they had sleeping bags and pillows. Carolyn and Maggie immediately kicked off their riding boots and leaned back in the folding chairs that faced the fire. A few minutes later, Paddy served steaming bowls of cowgirl stew and mounds of homemade biscuits, all of it washed down with an endless supply of ice-cold root beer. The girls devoured their dinners like a couple of hungry mountain lions, soaking up the last globs of gravy with biscuit crumbs. A hard day in the saddle had been rewarded with a hearty meal. A cowgirl couldn't ask for anything more.

When dinner was finished, the trio sat around the fire and talked about the day. After a few minutes of small talk, Carolyn looked at her watch and then glanced at Paddy with a nod. It was time for the awards ceremony. Walking over to the folding table, she picked up a brightly wrapped package that had been hidden under the cooking gear.

"Ladies and gentlemen, tonight we come together to recognize the newest member of the Jolly Jockey. Miss Farnsworth, please stand up,' Carolyn announced in her TV game show voice. Maggie slowly stood and stepped toward Carolyn with a sheepish look. After some good-natured ribbing from Carolyn, she tore open the package and gently lifted the hat from the box. Her eyes widened as she methodically inspected it from side to side, holding it at various heights and angles. She ran her fingers along the smooth edges, and then with a twirl of her hand artfully placed the white straw hat on her head. At that moment, she felt ten-feet tall. So that's what a hat can do for you, she thought. No wonder all the ladies in her mother's social club wore outlandish hats to the spring ball. But Maggie knew those wide-brimmed hats with feathers and bright colors were as phony as the people who wore them. Her hat was different. She had the real deal, a genuine cowgirl hat right off the shelf of the general store. The "Classic Cowgirl - Ranch Model" sported a wide and rolled brim, a peaked crown with side and top pleats, and a pink and black horsehair band. Although it was only a straw hat without diamonds or emeralds, it was the only crown a real cowgirl would ever wear.

"You can always spot a real cowgirl by her horse and her hat. Since you can't always be ridin' a horse, we figured you could always be wearin' a hat," Carolyn joked.

"This is so neat. Thank you," Maggie whispered humbly, a little confused by the ceremony. Carolyn was referring to her as a cowgirl when she was only a stable girl. Either way, she took no offense. She was just glad to be a saddle pal. "I don't know what else to say. This has been the best day of my life."

"Yes sir, let's hear it for that cowgirl! Never at a loss for words," Carolyn proclaimed as Paddy loudly applauded. She then paused and reached into her pocket for a piece of paper. "But before we let her go back to the bunkhouse, there is one more thing she has to say. Since Miss Farnsworth is being officially promoted from stable girl to cowgirl, it's time for her to take the cowgirl oath. Now raise your right hand, and repeat after me."

"I, Maggie Farnsworth, do hereby pledge to respect all horses and cowgirls, to be honest in all my dealings, to repay my debts, to work hard at home and in school, to help others in need, and to be a patriotic American," Maggie declared boldly, now that she understood Carolyn's comments.

"And one more thing," Carolyn added. "From this day forward, Maggie Farnsworth will be known as Maggie Montana among fellow cowgirls across the land."

"Hear ye! Hear ye! That's a real cowgirl name," Paddy bellowed in laughter. "Next thing you know, you'll be signing on with Buffalo Bill's Wild West Show!" Maggie just grinned from ear to ear. Maggie Montana was the perfect name for a cowgirl. It conjured up images of wild horses and wagon trains. A cowgirl couldn't ask for anything more. Maggie wondered if Carolyn would consider changing her name to Carolyn Colorado. Now that was another great name for a cowgirl.

For the rest of the evening, the group sat around the campfire and swapped stories about their favorite things and funniest moments. Everyone agreed the best vacation would be out west. When

Maggie mentioned that she had relatives in Colorado, they decided the Rocky Mountains would be the place to visit. Even Paddy, who longed to see the rolling hills of the Emerald Isle, said he would like to see the view from Pike's Peak before heading home to Ireland.

The highlight of the evening bull session was the tallest tale contest. The rules were simple. Everyone from youngest to oldest took a turn spinning a yarn. The others had to decide how much of the story was fact or fiction, or as Paddy put it, "horsemeat or horse manure." First, Maggie told about the time that she and Brownie, the carnival pony, rode in the center ring for the Ringling Brothers circus as stars of the show. Next, Carolyn told about her summer job with the Pony Express and the ride to Sweetwater. Finally, Paddy told about the time he won the Grand National, the greatest steeplechase in the world, on the back of a mule.

"Me and the mule crossed the finish line in England, and then I crossed the Atlantic to come to America," he remembered triumphantly in his thickest Irish accent. Puffing hard on his pipe, he crossed his legs and then leaned back in his chair. A swirling cloud of white smoke masked his face. When the girls leaned forward in anticipation, Paddy abruptly fell silent. The greatest storyteller ever to set eyes on a horse had them bewildered.

127

"You mean that you won a lot of money and came to America to train horses?" Maggie asked hesitantly.

"I think he means that he lost all of his money and came to the Jolly Jockey," Carolyn joked, hoping to cajole Paddy into finishing his story. This was one tale that she had never heard, and she thought that she had heard them all at least a dozen times.

Paddy paused long enough for the smoke to clear and then continued. "Well, that's partly right, lassies," he said, taking the pipe from his mouth and stroking his chin. "After the race was over, the judges called for a ruling. It seems that a lot of Brits were upset because their horses were beaten by an Irish mule. Hundreds of reporters and thousands of fans gathered around the grandstand in a frenzy. A riot was waiting to happen. After a few minutes, the head judge told me that I was disqualified because my entry was only half a horse." Paddy paused and switched legs. The girls leaned even closer, their eyes riveted on Paddy's wrinkled face as they waited for the punch line. "He said that my ass was only an Irish half-ass and laughed at me. I stared at him cold and hard, and told him that he was right. Then I told him the only thing worse than an Irish half-ass was an English total ass, and I was looking one right in the eye." The punch line was a knockout punch. The girls roared with laughter and toppled out of their chairs. With a smug look of satisfaction, Paddy calmly drew a long breath on his pipe and blew a cloud of smoke into the air. Carolyn and Maggie scratched their heads with puzzled looks. Knowing Paddy, they wondered how much was horsemeat and how much was horse manure. Tomorrow, they would have to check the record books.

As the fire burned down to a mound of glowing embers, the conversation dwindled to a few yawns. When it came time for the last round of small talk, Maggie pounced on the opportunity to ask Paddy about his past. His mysterious life had been in the back of her mind since their first meeting.

"Paddy, what about you and your family?" she asked sincerely. "You always talk about your adventures, but you never say too much about your family."

Paddy hesitated. The usual grin slowly turned into a painful grimace. For a few seconds, he gazed into the night as if trying to remember. He snuffed out his pipe and cleared his throat. He knew that he had to be careful with his answer. He didn't want to lie, but he didn't want to tell the truth. A working horseman didn't want to be known as someone with a troubled past, although the truth was that most drifters in the horse business carried some kind of troubles. The bags varied in size and weight, but they all contained stories of love, life, and liquor in various combinations and quantities. Among themselves, horsemen joked about it. A good horseman was measured not by broken horses, but by broken hearts, including his own.

"Why, that's a very good question, lassie," Paddy replied with a forced smile. "I do appreciate your interest in ole' Paddy, but the tale about young Paddy is a special story for a special time. Someday when that time is right, I'll be more than glad to tell you, and I think you'll be more than glad to hear it," he lamented. The girls glanced at each other with raised eyebrows and nodded their heads in agreement.

To end the evening, the trio sang a song at Carolyn's request. They really didn't have a choice. It was either sing or have Carolyn yodel. Her earlier attempt at yodeling sounded like a cross between a sick hoot owl and a tone-deaf coyote. To save wear and tear on their ears, Paddy and Maggie gladly harmonized on a moonlight serenade of "Happy Trails."

Paddy retreated to his folding cot. Minutes later, a soft snore signaled that he was riding his mule or visiting his mysterious past. Carolyn and Maggie climbed into their sleeping bags and stared at the millions of twinkling stars in the black sky. In the dwindling hours of the day, there were still a few minutes for some girl talk.

"Well, Maggie Montana, what did you think of the day?" Carolyn asked casually. She was dying to find out how Maggie really felt, but she didn't want to seem pushy.

"You promised the sun, the moon and the stars, and delivered on all three. You were true to the cowgirl code," Maggie responded without

130

hesitation. "But what do you make of Paddy and his family?" she whispered to avoid waking him.

"All the years that I've known him, I've never heard him say a word about his family. It's a real mystery, but there are a lot of mysterious people in the horse business," Carolyn replied softly.

"My mom says horse people are like carnival workers. They drift from place to place. You don't really know where they came from and don't know where they're going. I guess that's what makes them mysterious," Maggie added.

"And speaking about mysteries, I have one that you should able to solve," Carolyn said.

"Go ahead and shoot," Maggie replied, thinking the question was about the trail ride.

"When you were begging me for a chance to work on the farm, you said we could arrange some kind of deal that might benefit both of us. Just exactly what did you have in mind?" Carolyn asked hesitantly.

Maggie swallowed hard. She knew exactly what she had in mind that day. At the time, that part of the deal didn't seem important. It was just part of the sales pitch. For a second, she thought about telling a white lie, but then she remembered that she had just taken the cowgirl oath. If Carolyn took her answer the wrong way, her saddle pal would be saddle sore. But a deal is a deal, Maggie decided. She had to tell her. It was time to open mouth and insert boot. "I was thinking that if you taught me to be a stable girl," Maggie stuttered and stopped.

"And, and?" Carolyn implored impatiently.

"And then, I'd teach you how to be a teenager,' Maggie mumbled rapidly. An uneasy silence filled the campground. Maggie was sure that Carolyn heard every word. She held her breath and waited for a reply.

"Hmmm! Let me get this straight. You want to teach me how to become a teenager," Carolyn stated amusingly, not at all insulted by the comment. She knew exactly what Maggie was talking about. Since the beginning of summer vacation, her mother had frequently reminded her in a polite way that soon she was going to be a teenager. It was important for her to start expanding her horizons. Carolyn wasn't sure what those horizons included, but she was sure that it included something other than horses.

"Did my mom put you up to this?" Carolyn demanded, hoping to catch Maggie in a white lie.

"Oh, no, absolutely not. This was my own idea," Maggie fired back sincerely. "I was just trying to return a favor the best way I could. I thought you might need help in learning about teenage things. Stuff like clothes, hair, makeup, boys, music and dancing."

"And just what do you know about being a teenager. You're not twelve years old yourself."

"I have a baby-sitter, kind of like a nanny, who watches me when my parents are away on business.

She's fifteen and really into all these teenage things. She shows me teenage stuff all the time."

"Well, let me sleep on it for awhile. It might not be such a bad idea," Carolyn replied with a yawn. She turned over and closed her eyes. Becoming a teenager was a scary thought. Mothers talked about it in hushed tones as if it was a disease. To Carolyn's way of thinking, there was nothing to it. It was something that just happened when you got older. But being a teenager was way too much to think about tonight. Tonight was for thinking about cowgirls and horses. The ride to Sweetwater was waiting for its heroine. "Good night, Maggie Montana, and thanks for thinking about your saddle pal," she whispered kindly.

"Sweet dreams, Queen of the Cowgirls," Maggie replied softly as she breathed a sigh of relief now that a disaster had been avoided. Weary but still too excited to sleep, she stared at the stars and replayed the day in her mind. It was a dream-come-true, and there was no good reason to fall asleep and chance another dream that might not have such a happy ending. With the fire doused, the smell of pine trees scented the air. Carolyn was right about the campsite being a touch of Christmas in the middle of summer. Today was a Christmas wish that became a Christmas gift, one that Maggie had on her list for years. As Maggie finally closed her eyes and drifted off to sleep, she heard the howl of a lonesome coyote in the distance. Could the fading symbol of the Old West be calling her name, she wondered. It was highly unlikely, but anything around the Jolly Jockey was possible.

Chapter 7 – Dancing with Mr. Bojangles

By the time the Carolyn and Maggie crawled out of their sleeping bags the next morning, Paddy had already packed up the campsite. "Head on down to the kitchen after you get those bags rolled up. Mrs. Clark is serving flapjacks and maple syrup. I'm going down to the stable," he announced cheerfully as if the gloom from last night was a passing dark cloud on a sunny day.

Maggie was the first to finish breakfast. She wolfed down two pancakes, gulped down a glass of milk, and then excused herself from the table. There were still a few clean-up chores from yesterday's ride. The sooner she started; the sooner she finished. And today, she was in a hurry to get home and tell her mother about the trail ride. She couldn't wait to burst through the front door wearing her new hat.

"Take Dixie out to the corner pasture. Check in with Paddy first. Then I'll meet you in the tack room to clean up the rest of the gear," Carolyn mumbled with a mouthful of food. She was in no hurry to leave the table. Pancakes with maple syrup were her favorite breakfast, and not a drop of batter was going to waste.

"You got it, pardner," Maggie replied as she bolted out the door.

A few minutes later, Carolyn casually strolled into the stable. Peeking into to each stall, she slowly made her way to the office. Everything appeared normal with one exception. "Paddy, where's Bojangles?" she asked.

"In the far grass," Paddy yelled from the end of the building, using his term for the corner pasture.

"Are you sure?" Carolyn asked nervously.

"As sure as I'm standing here. Turned him out myself," Paddy replied as he walked towards Carolyn. "He seemed a little irritated lately. Thought I'd give him a chance to run it out of his system."

"Did Maggie check with you this morning?" Carolyn asked worriedly.

"Not that I know of. I've been out back setting up the ring for your mother," Paddy replied.

A look of terror came over Carolyn's face. "That's where I told her to graze Dixie. We've got to hurry. She could be in trouble," she said in a frightened voice.

"You'd better hightail it over there. I'll get the lasso and be right behind you," Paddy said urgently. It could be a serious situation or nothing at all, but it couldn't be chanced. Two high-strung horses and one frightened cowgirl in the same paddock could be a disaster waiting to happen.

Carolyn turned on her heels and sprinted out the stable. A minute later, she crested the hilly field and saw Maggie standing in the middle of the pasture with Dixie. Frantically, she waved her hands over her head and kept on running. "Maggie, get out of there!" she shouted. But Maggie was too far away to be heard. Carolyn furiously pumped her arms and legs until gasping for air. Every second counted. Danger could be lurking just out of sight. Carolyn's eyes darted from side to side. And then in the corner of her eye, she saw it on the move. It was only a black speck, but growing larger as it gained speed. Her worst fear was realized. "Run, Maggie! Run," she screamed at the top of her lungs. Maggie looked up and waved back with a smile. "Behind you!" Carolyn screamed again, stabbing her finger in the air. Maggie saw the fear in Carolyn's face and instantly turned around. Her jaw dropped and quivered. A cold shock jolted her body. Bojangles was bearing down on her like a runaway locomotive. She felt the ground tremble underneath his pounding hooves. With each massive stride, the black stallion closed the gap. The small black speck was becoming a bold exclamation point. In a few seconds, there would be a catastrophic collision. There was no way Maggie would survive the accident.

Maggie pressed her lips and breathed rapidly through her nose to keep her composure. "No time to panic. Have to think quickly," she hurriedly reminded herself. Dixie was her biggest concern; she was the target. Bojangles, threatened by another horse on his turf, was taking dead aim at the four-legged intruder. There was only one thing for Maggie to do. She had to act like a horse. Flight was the basic survival instinct for horses and humans. "The fence! The fence!" she shouted at Dixie as Carolyn's advice about the Gray Ghost blared in her head. She had to reach the fence to slow down his charge.

Maggie yanked hard on the lead rope that was still attached to the halter. "Come on girl! Got to hurry!" she commanded firmly as she turned towards the fence about fifty feet away. With her first steps, she wobbled forward, veering from side to the side. Have to go faster, she thought, but speed was limited with the leg brace. Taking a long stride, she pulled hard, but the rope slipped through her fingers and tore at the flesh. Unable to clench the end knot, she did a full turn and fell forward. Face down in the grass, she heard the thundering hooves grow louder and covered her head with her hands. In a few seconds, she was sure to be trampled.

There wasn't enough time for Carolyn to climb over the fence and drag Maggie to safety. Needing to get as close as possible, she jumped to second rail and leaned forward. "Stay down and cover up," she shouted to Maggie with her hands cupped to her mouth. Meanwhile, Dixie stood over Maggie with a confused look. The sharp tug on the lead rope had alerted her to danger, but she was unaware it was coming from behind. Maggie had headed for the fence before she could spot Bojangles. Carolyn's only chance was to have Dixie turn around and face Bojangles.

Lifting her fingers to her lips, she blasted a long and loud whistle. Dixie lifted her head and pricked her ears. "Run Dixie! Run hard, girl" Carolyn yelled as she raised her right arm and threw it forward like a baseball pitcher. Sensing immediate danger, Dixie responded instantly. Twisting violently, she spun around and bolted straight for Bojangles. Her natural instinct to flee was suppressed by a greater urge. In the distant corner of her mind, she heard the ancient call to protect her foal. She had to stop the raging stallion at all costs, even if she paid with her life.

Both horses charged towards each with flared nostrils, flattened ears, and raised tails. Dixie had the heart of a thoroughbred, but she was outsized and out-muscled by the massive stallion. There was no way she would survive the crash.

Carolyn and Paddy, who had just arrived on the scene, watched in horror as the horses continued to charge at full speed on a collision course. Pounding hooves thundered to a deadly drumbeat as Dixie and Bojangles kicked up clumps of grass. The two horses drew closer and closer until they were only a few feet apart. "Dixie, no!" Carolyn screamed in terror. Paddy reached over and squeezed her arm. In a blink of an eye, it was over. At the last second, the horses sideswiped each other and veered away, turning in a tight circle. The hard, glancing blows didn't faze either horse.

"Now's your chance! Get up and run!" Carolyn yelled to Maggie. Maggie lifted her head with a pained look. She twisted and turned, but the leg brace had pinned her good leg to the ground. With a loud grunt, she reached around and tried to lift the brace.

"It's no use. I'm stuck, I can't untangle my legs," she cried out in frustration as she pounded the ground with her fist. There was no way she could even crawl to the fence.

"Stay down and be still," Carolyn ordered calmly. "You'll be okay, buckaroo. Trust me on this one." Once again, Maggie buried her face in the grass and covered her head with her hands. Cocking her head to the side, she overhead Carolyn and Paddy hastily making a rescue plan. Little did she know that all they could do was wait with her. At the moment, everything depended on Dixie.

After the horses turned, they charged again, this time skidding to a stop about ten feet directly in front of each other. They shook their heads wildly and snorted excited breaths. The challenge had been issued. It was time to fight or flee. Both horses raised their heads and repeatedly sniffed the air, hoping to smell fear in their opponent. It was a weakness that would be quickly exploited. After a brief exchange of snorts and angry whinnies, both horses fell quiet and stared hard at each other. Their rippled muscles quivered with excitement, waiting to see who would make the next move. Neither horse was backing down. A menacing bluff or one violent blow could decide the battle.

"I think we're getting the situation under control," Paddy said tensely to Carolyn. "Be ready to go in when I give the word. No sudden noise or movement. And don't take any chances." He spoke loud enough for Maggie to hear, hoping his voice would calm her fear.

"Gotcha covered," Carolyn replied in a hushed tone with her hand over her mouth.

Bojangles made the next move. He snorted madly and pounded the ground with his front hoof. With a furious squeal, he reared up and flailed the air with his forelegs. A quick lunge would crush Dixie's skull. As he hovered high above Dixie, his black eyes rolled back in his head, revealing two blood-shot white orbs that glowed like hot coals. Dropping to the ground, he clawed at the dirt and bellowed an evil, high-pitched whinny that sounded

141

from the depths of hell. Steam rose from his body as if his heart was on fire.

Dixie was equal to the challenge. Rearing up, she flailed the air with lightening-quick jabs like an angry boxer. Her high-pitched scream was a frightening battle cry that sent chills down Carolyn's spine. Though undersized, Dixie matched the stallion squeal for squeal and snort for snort. After touching down, she violently kicked up her hind legs to show Bojangles that she also could deliver a killing blow. Both horses stood their ground and glared angrily at each other, their heaving bodies dripping a thick, heavy sweat. Neither horse was ready to turn and run.

"Now is our chance. You take Dixie, and I'll take the devil," Paddy whispered cautiously. Carolyn quietly climbed over the fence and moved toward her pony, praying the battle was over. If the horses started to jab at each other, their hooves could inflict deadly blows, cutting deep into muscle and tendon.

"Down Dixie. Easy now, girl. It's over," Carolyn cooed in Dixie's ear as she grabbed the lead rope. Dixie flicked her ears and blew softly through her nose. She sensed the fight was over. "That goes for you too," Carolyn said, glancing down at Maggie. "Stay put until I tell you to get up."

"I read you loud and clear," came the muffled reply. Maggie breathed easier now that Carolyn was in the pasture. Remaining flat on the ground, she turned her head and peeked around her arms to watch Paddy disarm Bojangles.

Once Carolyn had control of Dixie, Paddy slowly entered the pasture and stepped towards Bojangles. The situation was still extremely dangerous. He was now the intruder. If Bojangles viewed him as a bigger threat than Dixie, the horse could suddenly attack. One blow from a razor-sharp hoof could easily kill him. His heart raced with fear. To steady his trembling hands, he squeezed the lasso with a death grip.

Despite being smaller than his foe, Paddy had a large advantage. He had horse knowledge; he knew exactly what Bojangles was thinking. For the last few minutes, Bojangles had forgotten his years of training as the hot blood of a wild stallion surged through his veins. After years of being trapped in stalls, paddocks, and starting gates, he was finally free. Today, he was the leader of the herd. It was a power that would not be surrendered easily.

Paddy stopped a few feet from Bojangles and stood slightly off center while maintaining constant eye contact. When the horse's breathing slowed, he raised the lasso to his chest and stretched it out in front of his body. Bojangles jerked his head and rocked back on his hind legs. Recognizing the challenge, he lifted his head high and pricked his ears forward. That was the signal Paddy wanted. Now it was time for him to impose his will. He gradually lowered his arms and tossed the rope on the ground. Bojangles lowered his head and sniffed it. Quickly rising, he breathed deeply and exhaled a long and shallow breath. The anger in his eyes disappeared. A look of calm masked his face.

Paddy shifted his body and tilted his head in a series of movements that were virtually undetectable. He was speaking a silent language, and Bojangles was listening to every word. Paddy was declaring that he was the now leader of the herd. Bojangles had no reason to fear for his safety. After slowly raising his right hand to his chest, he sharply threw it forward and held it parallel to the ground. Bojangles remained motionless, waiting patiently for the next command. When Paddy dropped his arm, he turned and galloped to the far corner of the pasture. The order had been obeyed.

"I'll be glad when that one's gone home in another two weeks," Paddy sighed with relief as he wiped the sweat from his brow with the back of his hand. "Miss Roberts can have the devil all to herself."

Carolyn extended a hand and lifted Maggie to her feet. "Are you okay?" she asked as Maggie brushed the grass from her clothes and hair.

"Not a scratch on me," Maggie replied nervously, her hands still shaking from the ordeal. "Guess I really screwed up."

"Horsefeathers! You did a great job today. You didn't panic. You should be proud of the way you handled the situation," Carolyn said, trying to comfort her friend. Maggie's body wasn't bruised, but her ego was black and blue. "When you're

144

around horses, things like that happen. Why if it wasn't for you falling down, you and Dixie would have made it out of there."

"Yeah, if only I didn't fall down," Maggie said glumly. "If only I didn't have to wear this stupid brace."

"Carolyn's right, you know," Paddy interjected. "Everybody falls down in life, and everybody wears a brace of their own design. Sometimes you see them and sometimes you don't. And most of the time, the biggest ones are the hardest to see."

Carolyn and Maggie looked at each and shrugged their shoulders. Paddy was again talking in circles like the night of the trail ride. They weren't exactly sure what Paddy was talking about, but it sounded like good horse sense.

"Here you go, cowgirl. I think this belongs to you." Carolyn said, handing Maggie her hat. Miraculously, her most cherished possession had escaped without a mark.

"Hummmph," Maggie grunted. "I'm not much of a cowgirl. I'm more like Maggie Banana instead of Maggie Montana. Heck, I can't even take a horse to pasture."

"But that was some crazy dance you did out there," Carolyn joked. "It looks like you were inventing a new dance with all that twisting and turning. Next time, find a better dance partner."

"Guess I am a better dancer than a cowgirl," Maggie replied dejectedly. "And don't worry about a new partner. I have someone in mind."

"Just remember, it's all part of the cowgirl code. When you fall off of the saddle, you climb right back on," Carolyn politely reminded her.

"You're absolutely right," Maggie readily agreed. "Come to think of it, I owe you guys big time for saving my life, and a real cowgirl always repays her debts. I don't how, when or where, but someday I'll make good on my word. I swear on the cowgirl code."

Carolyn smiled and put a hand on Maggie's shoulder. "Now that's my saddle pal," she said cheerfully. "Oh, and by the way, no swearin' allowed. It's against the cowgirl code."

Maggie smiled weakly at the joke. "And Paddy, you were simply amazing," she gushed. "You might not be a leprechaun, but you're a magician with horses."

"Just something you learn with time, and I spent a lot of time around horses," Paddy replied humbly, somewhat embarrassed by the praise. "I learned to speak their language years ago. One day you'll be able to do it. I see it in you. You've got a lot of horse blood running through your veins." He wasn't being kind in his comments just to boost Maggie's confidence. He felt it deep in his old Irish bones. It was the same feeling when he first saw Carolyn on a horse. At that very moment, he knew that she was born to ride.

Carolyn and Maggie had the ability to communicate with a horse on an emotional level. Some horseman called it "horse whispering," but

Paddy called it "horse listening." It wasn't ancient Indian magic but a skill in the art of "talking" with a horse through body language. If pressed for an explanation, Paddy would simply say it was a gift from God and leave it at that. He could teach people to talk to a horse, but he couldn't teach them to listen. In his heart, he knew that both girls could talk and listen. They just needed more experience with the language.

"Hey, what about me?" Carolyn joked, trying to lighten the mood. "Ain't I one of the good guys in a white hat?"

"Ah, shucks, pardner," Maggie replied in her Texas drawl. "You're Carolyn Clark, Queen of the Cowgirls. That says it all."

"Well said, buckaroo. But the Queen of the Cowgirls also says that you'd better check your makeup," Carolyn replied, dabbing her cheek with her finger.

Maggie reached up and rubbed her cheeks. Tears had mixed with the dirt to coat her face with a thin layer of caked mud. "Must be the sweatin' from all of that hard work. 'Cause everybody knows that cowgirls only cry over horses, cowboys, and spilled milk," she chuckled.

"And speaking about horses, what about Dixie? She's the real hero!" Carolyn proudly proclaimed.

"You're right, again, pardner," Maggie shouted with glee. "Let's here it for Dixie!"

"Hooray for Dixie!" the trio shouted in unison. At the sound of her name, Dixie shook back her head and neighed softly. "Ah, shucks, gang. It was nothing. Just doing what a horse has to do," she seemed to say.

"If I didn't know any better, I'd swear that pony understands what we're saying," Paddy chirped. He grabbed Dixie's halter and handed it to Maggie. "Ma'am, I believe you deserve the honor of escorting our hero home."

Maggie took off her hat and placed it gently on Dixie's head. On TV westerns, the good guys always wore a white hat. Today it wouldn't be any different just because the hero was a horse. As Maggie led the way back to the stable, Carolyn and Paddy followed a few feet behind, discussing how Bojangles would be handled for the next two weeks. Maggie leaned close to Dixie and whispered in her ear. "About that promise to repay my debt. Well, that goes double for you, girl. I don't know how I going to do, but I am." Maggie knew that no matter what happened in her life, this was one promise she would keep.

Chapter 8 – Ponytails to Pigskins

On Monday morning, Maggie was back on the job with her cowgirl hat tilted back on her head. Only today, she was busy leaning instead of cleaning. There wasn't a lot of elbow grease being applied to her shovel. She'd work for a few minutes and then break for a minute. The usual happy-go-lucky smile was etched across her face, but something was amiss. She was strangely silent. Any other day, she would babble endlessly at the sound of her name.

Every few minutes, Carolyn glanced at Maggie to make sure that her friend was still in the stable.

Each time, Maggie was staring off into space. Carolyn had a pretty good idea what was bothering her. Over the weekend, she tried hard not to think about the incident in the pasture, but it was impossible. What if she had done this or that, she kept asking herself. Second-guessing offered a lot of possibilities but no easy answers. To end the mental torture, Carolyn finally decided that what happened in the pasture was fate, and no one could have changed the events. It was time to move on with life and accept the facts as they were. Maggie was a courageous tenderfoot with the potential to be an excellent horsewoman. Paddy was an amazing horse magician with a dark secret. Carolyn was a modern day Annie Oakley who feared becoming a teenager. Dixie was simply the greatest horse in the world even if she couldn't jump over a crack in the pavement, and Bojangles was a devil of a horse.

Carolyn studied the expression on Maggie's face. Maggie wasn't spooked, but she had that faraway look in her eye. It was hard to tell what she was thinking or feeling. Carolyn knew that a lot of people became "horse shy" after a bad experience in the saddle. Usually, they'd let it fester like a bad saddle sore and then quit instead of finding a cure. If Maggie was suffering from the affliction, she had to get right back in the saddle and headed down the trail. If she wanted too long, there was a good chance that she would join the Tuttle boys as riding academy dropouts.

Just before the lunch break, Carolyn decided to break the silence. After all she was working in a stable, not a library. "That was a heck of a way to break in a hat. Next time you might want to just roll it in your hand instead of rolling it across the prairie," Carolyn joked, hoping not to sound like a smart aleck.

"Think nothing off it, pardner. Next time you get a new hat, I'll do the same for you," Maggie giggled.

Carolyn was glad to see that Maggie hadn't lost her sense of cowgirl humor. "I was thinking you need to get back right back in the saddle," Carolyn suggested.

"I was thinking that I'd better get back to work before I was fired," Maggie said in a serious tone. "What did you mother say about the incident?"

"She was upset with me and Paddy more than anything else. She said we know better and should have paid more attention to what's going on," Carolyn replied. "And she wasn't at all surprised about Dixie. She was just doing what a girl has to do."

"Then it's time to get back in the saddle, the sooner the better," Maggie shot back eagerly.

Carolyn was somewhat surprised at the answer, sure that Maggie would hem and haw and put it off for another day. The tenderfoot had a lot of grit.

"Then, we'll saddle up this afternoon and ride the fences this afternoon," Carolyn announced. She knew the healing power of the fence, whether you were sitting on top of it or riding alongside it.

When a cowgirl has the blues and needs to leave her worries behind, she rides the fences. There might be a plank to be hammered or a wire to be spliced, but fixing the fence was not the sole purpose of riding the fence. Sometimes a cowgirl just needed to be alone with her thoughts and her horse. In the open spaces, she had ample time to ponder the mysteries of the universe that plotted to make her life miserable.

After lunch the girls saddled up Dixie and Cherokee and headed to the farthest corner of the farm. Today's ride was about mending the invisible fences that protect a friendship. Riding was always guaranteed to loosen tongues, and it never took too long to loosen Maggie's once she was in the saddle. Carolyn knew exactly what she had to say.

"After an incident, some people get a little horse shy and start thinking too much about what they're doing and why they're doing it," Carolyn said thoughtfully. "And to a cowgirl, thinking can be like stinking. You do it a lot and not too many people want to be near you."

Maggie laughed at the joke, knowing exactly what Carolyn was talking about. She appreciated Carolyn's concern. "After Friday I never wanted to ride again, but then I remembered how hard I worked to get here and how much I love it. It was a no-brainer," Maggie replied earnestly. "And then I thought about what you said the other night. The cowgirl code got me in the saddle, and it's going to keep me there. I just didn't know it at the time."

"Well, that's mighty good news. For a minute there, I thought you might spook and hightail it out of here," Carolyn replied.

"But what I really thought about was the farm. When school starts in a couple of weeks, I'll be out of a job. That's what really had me down. I hate to see it all end," Maggie said somberly.

"I know how you feel. I'll be losing my only student," Carolyn said, her voice tailing off. The thought had been in the back of her mind since Maggie's first lesson. Not only was she losing a student, but she was losing Maggie's deal.

Over the weekend, Carolyn had a lot of time to think about becoming a teenager. One question led to another which led to a state of perpetual pre-teen confusion. It was like trying to count clouds. As soon as one had been counted, it broke apart into two or three more. Completely confused and utterly overwhelmed, she went to the "fence" for some answers. As always, the fence on a sunny day was best remedy for a cloudy mind.

Sitting on rail, Carolyn assessed her pending teenage situation. She was comfortable with the physical changes in her body. That was happening to all of her girlfriends. It was the mental changes that had her worried. Would she start thinking differently about the things that she loved? Would she start acting differently now that she was becoming an adult? She knew she had to grow old

153

but did she have to grow up? The last question was the scariest. In the dark corners of her mind, a thousand questions were lurking. Many of the answers would take years to find. All of her friends had the same questions, and as they went their own ways, they would find different answers.

Surviving the teenage years was going to be like riding a carousel. Carolyn knew that she had to keep changing horses until she came full circle. That certainly didn't mean discarding Dixie. It meant that she had to expand her horizons as her mother liked to say. Someday and somehow, she was certain that it would all lead back to the Jolly Jockey. But now she had to make the first move. It was time to step on the spinning wheel, climb aboard a painted pony, and reach for the brass ring. It just so happened that Maggie was selling tickets for the ride. It was time to ask the ticket-taker one of those thousand teenage questions.

"You know that deal about teaching me to become a teenager. When can we start?" Carolyn stammered.

Maggie leaned out of the saddle as if the words had struck her broadside. She bit her lower lip and tilted her head to the sky, trying to hide the silly grin on her face. "How about if we saddle up this afternoon?"

"Saddle up. We're already saddled up," Carolyn replied with a puzzled look.

154

"Nah, I mean saddle up as in get going. We need to find a place to relax and watch a little television," Maggie explained.

"A good western, I hope," Carolyn sighed.

"Not close, pardner. It's the Buddy Deane Show. Live from Television Hill on Channel 13," she announced, holding her a fist up to mouth for a microphone.

"Enough already! What's it about?" Carolyn begged impatiently, wishing she had kept her mouth shut. She could ride the teenage carousel another day.

"It's about teenagers. How else can you learn to be a teenager? Seeing is learning, and learning is doing. Something like that," Maggie pronounced with glee. She couldn't wait to settle her deal with Carolyn. Maybe she didn't know that much about horses, but nobody in the city of Baltimore knew more about the Buddy Deane Show. She probably knew more about the show than Buddy. After all, she had inside information from a real teenager.

Returning to the farmhouse, the girls kicked off their boots and plopped down on the couch in the family room. Carolyn turned on the television and flicked the channel knob to channel 13. Fuzzy black and white images appeared on the screen. As the picture tube warmed up, a dance floor filled with teenagers slowly crystallized. The Buddy Deane Show was in progress, and every teenager in Baltimore who wasn't in the studio was watching at home or a friend's house. Maggie immediately began teaching Buddy's introductory course, spouting off the names of every dance and dancer.

"Could you turn up the volume a little? It's not only about dancing; it's about music," Maggie pleaded. As soon as the volume jumped, so did Maggie. In a flash, she was on her feet, clapping her hands and swaying to the music. Carolyn paid little attention to her animated instructor. She fell back on the couch with her eyes glued to the television, drawn to the light like a moth. Inch by inch, the dancing images pulled her closer until she was kneeling directly in front of the screen. Any second, she would be sucked into the picture tube. Then, if Maggie looked hard enough, she might see Carolyn tucked away in the far corner of the dance floor. She'd be easy to recognize, the only dancer wearing a cowgirl hat and riding boots.

The Buddy Deane Show was a popular, televised record hop that aired six days a week for two hours a day. In 1959 Baltimore's coolest teenagers strutted their stuff in front of the TV cameras for their fellow teens. The boys wore sport coats and ties, pegged legs pants, and pointed toed shoes with tapered heels. The hair was slicked up and slicked back in pompadours like Elvis Presley. The girls wore cardigan sweaters and blouses, straight skirts that rested just above the knee, and cha-cha heels or saddles shoes. Their hairdos were teased, layered, lacquered, and piled high in a beehive. A select group of teens known as "The Committee" stalked the dance floor to ensure the rules of conduct were being followed. No t-shirts, high-heels, gum chewing, soda drinking or public displays of affection were allowed. Maggie danced and Carolyn watched until Walter leaned on the horn.

"Well, what did you think?" Maggie asked as she gathered her stuff.

"If that's all it takes to be a teenager, then I think it will be a hayride," Carolyn said confidently, hoping to hide her doubt. In her heart, she knew that it would be a challenging process. The minister called it spiritual. The biology teacher called it physical. The guidance counselor called it emotional. Parents, who seemed to have forgotten that they were teenagers not too long ago, called it eternal because it made days seem like years. Even Mrs. Clark was the first too admit it wasn't always a smooth transition. Some of Carolyn's family members like Uncle Frank were still going through the process thirty years later. Of course, Uncle Frank didn't mind growing old; he just didn't want to grow up.

"Nothing's ever that easy, but I think it's a start in the right direction," Maggie replied. "Over the weekend I'll get some records from my baby sitter and teach you to dance next week."

"You're going to teach me to dance?" Carolyn laughed in disbelief.

Maggie shrugged off the comment. She heard it a thousand times before. "If you think I'm good on a horse, wait until you see more on the dance floor,"

157

she boasted, heading for the door. "Make sure you have your record player ready to go. You do have a record player, don't you?"

"Of course, I have a record player. How else would I listen to the Sons of the Pioneers?" Carolyn replied with mock sarcasm.

"You've got to hear the word to be part of the herd. It's time to make the scene with Buddy Deane," Maggie replied, imitating a late night disk jockey.

After Maggie left, Carolyn watched the rest of the show. Maggie's comment about the herd stuck in her mind. She may have been joking, but it was the truth. Being a teenager was being part of the herd. The dances, the music, the fashion, and the language were part of the herd mentality. The teenagers on the show were Carolyn's herd, and somewhere deep in her soul there was a longing to join. She'd have a better chance of being accepted if there was a similar show in the west. Maybe Wyoming had a Buffalo Buddy Deane Show or Texas had a Buckskin Buddy Deane show.

She pictured teenagers in the latest western garb, kicking up their heels to the latest country and western tunes. That would be an awesome show. She wouldn't need a fashion makeover or have to learn new dances. She just had to be herself. But on second thought that wouldn't work. The Buddy Deane Show belonged to Baltimore. The kids on the show were friends and family. She belonged to this herd like wild mustangs belonged out west. If she was to survive as a teenager, she would have to learn the ways of the Baltimore herd. "I've got the word from the herd. I want to be a dancing machine with the Buddy Deane," she joked as she tried to mimic Maggie's DJ voice. All that was missing for the herd was a brand. Carolyn chuckled at the crazy thought of teenagers being wrestled to the ground and branded on the buttocks with a "BD." Then at the end of the show, the corral would be opened and newly-branded members would roam the teenage landscape as official "Deaners."

While Carolyn couldn't picture herself dressed like the girls on television, she had no trouble picturing herself at a record hop. She liked to dance, even if she didn't know all the latest teenage dances. Flipping back the throw rug in front of the television, she created a small dance floor. With her eyes glued to the dancers, she mimicked their every move as her stocking feet slid smoothly across the hardwood floor. Shaking her body and gently tossing her head, she quietly clapped her hands to the beat as the music flowed through her body. Unofficially, Carolyn Clark had just joined the teenage herd. She wasn't quite ready to give up the Sons of the Pioneers, but rock and roll was here to stay. It was time to start warming up the branding iron.

Monday's dance session sizzled from the moment that Carolyn turned on the television. After a warm-up dance, the camera panned to the star of the show who was breaking into a wide grin.

159

"What time is it?" Buddy asked with delight. "It's Madison time," he shouted before anyone could answer.

"Goodness, gracious, great balls of fire," Maggie shouted, jumping to her feet. . "That's our song. It's Baltimore's own dance," she squealed hysterically. At that moment, Carolyn knew that Maggie was destined to advance from TV tour guide to teenage tribal leader. The Madison was a rock and roll line dance with calls from one of Baltimore's top disc jockeys. The series of chorus steps featured references to popular TV shows, Hollywood celebrities, and sport stars. With a strong backbeat and a jazzy rhythm, the song had feet moving and hands clapping in a hurry. Even the so-called "wallflowers," those on the show who didn't dance a lot, found a place within camera range.

When the song ended, Maggie turned down the volume on the television and pulled back the rug. Racing to the phonograph, she gently placed a record on the spindle and waited for it to drop to the spinning turntable. "It's our turn to do The Madison. Just follow me. It's like a barn dance except there's no barn," Maggie said enthusiastically.

Carolyn watched closely as Maggie shuffled and stepped to the music with the ease of a professional dancer. There was no doubt that she danced better than she walked. When the song was over, Maggie played it again with Carolyn as her dance partner. On the third take, Carolyn had a solo.

"When I say hit it, I want you to go two up and two back with a big strong turn and back to the Madison," Maggie called out with the DJ on the song. "You're lookin' good. Hands up. Relax the legs. Just like riding a horse." Carolyn smiled as her own words from the riding ring came back to haunt her. The pupil was now the teacher. And as always, the teacher was right. Dancing was like riding a horse.

After Carolyn finished, it was back to the show where a selected group of dancers were demonstrating the latest fad dance, the Bob-a-Loop, named after the popular toy.

Maggie and Carolyn were quickly on their feet when Mrs. Clark abruptly ended the session.

"Carolyn, there's a phone call for you. You can take it in the kitchen," Mrs. Clark shouted over the music.

"Freeze and hold it," Carolyn joked as Maggie was in mid-step. "It's probably one of the pony club members." A few minutes later, she returned to the living room with a tight grin on her face.

"What's up? You look like a cat that just swallowed a canary," Maggie asked.

"You're not going to believe this, but I just got a job offer," Carolyn said, shaking her head from side to side.

161

"But you already have a job here. Who in Baltimore would want to hire a sweaty and stinky cowgirl?" Maggie joked.

"A herd of horses, the Baltimore Colts, who else?" Carolyn blurted out.

"Why that's a football team. What do you have that a football team doesn't?" Maggie asked in disbelief.

"A pony, what else!' Carolyn shouted with a belly laugh. "They want a mascot, a horse and rider to circle the field every time the home team scores."

Maggie immediately pressed Carolyn for details about the conversation. Carolyn explained that Mr. Bob Tuttle, the public relations director for the team, was so impressed with her pony that she had first crack at the job. All she had to do was go for an interview and sign a few papers. Simple as that, the job was hers. The team was even going to supply a uniform and pay her twenty dollars a game.

"Wow! That is so cool. When are you going to interview?" Maggie asked excitedly.

"I have to think about it," Carolyn replied hesitantly.

"What's there to think about? This is the chance of a lifetime," Maggie clamored. The sound of Walter beeping his horn ended the conversation and the dance lesson. "Keep me posted, pardner," Maggie requested as she ran out the door.

For the rest of the day, Carolyn thought about the job offer. Mr. Tuttle had already spoken with

Mrs. Clark. It was okay with her as long as it didn't interfere with school, but the decision was Carolyn's. At first, it seemed like a "no brainer." Carolyn would simply take the job. It offered good pay and a chance to meet new people. If things didn't work out, the Baltimore Colts could always find another mascot. There were plenty of girls in Maryland with white ponies. But Carolyn didn't want this for herself; she wanted this for Dixie.

The job was possibly the last chance for Dixie to start another career. There was no guarantee the riding academy would have any students next summer, even with the new flyer. The idea about a riding academy for handicapped kids was still on the drawing board. As things stood, if Maggie stopped taking lessons, Dixie would be unemployed.

After dinner, Carolyn went to the fence to think. In the distance, she watched Dixie grazing with the other horses. Her pony looked as fit as any horse in the pasture, but looks were deceiving. Dixie could stop on a dime and turn on a dollar, but she couldn't jump. Last year's tendon injury not only ended her jumping career but almost ended her life. Paddy's "horse doctoring" healed the leg, but Dixie would never jump again in competition. And that's what she loved to do because she was an athlete like Bojangles. If nothing was found to fill the void, she would spend the rest of her life in the pasture. That wasn't a bad thing for a horse, but Dixie deserved a better fate.

Since the injury, Dixie earned her keep as a companion pony. Mrs. Clark used her to escort skittish horses to the track and befriend new horses in the stable. Dixie was just like Mrs. Clark, a gracious lady who knew how to care for her clients. But since the injury, she lost some of that twinkle in her eye and bounce in her step. At times, she was moody which was unlike her. Even though her leg had healed, she limped on occasion. She was hurting on the inside, and Carolyn felt her pain.

Carolyn hated to admit it, but she felt a guilty when thinking about Dixie. Their great times might be only memories in the near future whether or not Dixie found a new career. Horse and rider were going through life changes. Dixie was growing old, and she was growing up. Somehow she had to accommodate both events. Being a teenager was becoming harder with each passing day, and she wasn't even thirteen yet.

Looking at the clouds, Carolyn thought about her future. She was growing out of her pony like she was growing out of her clothes. If she wanted to be a competitive jumper like Miss Roberts, she'd have to have a new horse. What would a real cowgirl like Dale Evans say to her, she wondered as she imagined a heart to heart talk with one of her heroes. The answer was easy. Friends weren't thrown away because they changed. A friendship was about giving, not about taking. For a cowgirl, it was that plain and simple. She would care for friend forever. To take care of Dixie, she would take the job.

Carolyn meandered back to the house with her thumbs jammed in her pockets, her hands dangling at her side. Every few feet, she stopped to watch the sun sinking behind the ridge. A warm glow radiated throughout her body. She felt good about her decision. If the job didn't work out, she had no regrets. She was standing by a friend. How could she go wrong? The Baltimore Colts were like family to most of the people in the city. On Christmas mornings in Baltimore, almost every boy and a lot of girls hoped to find a royal blue jersey with two white rings around the shoulder and the number 19 on the front and back. For the rest of the holiday season, Johnny Unitas, Baltimore's most famous Colt, could be seen quarterbacking a team in every schoolyard and playground. He came in all shapes, sizes, ages, and colors. And this fall, Carolyn and Dixie would be joining Johnny and the Baltimore Colts at Memorial Stadium.

Carolyn wanted to sign the contract as soon as possible in case she had second thoughts about the job. It was now time to put this decision behind her and start worrying about other things, such as how she and Dixie would perform in front of thousands of people. Since the beginning of summer, worrying had become a full-time occupation. If it wasn't the riding academy, it was Dixie, Maggie, teenagers, or Buddy Deane. The list was endless. "Worry, worry, have to hurry. Hurry, hurry, have to

165

worry," she lamented as she got out her clothes for tomorrow's interview. Worrying was like riding a rocking horse. It moved back and forth, but it didn't get you where you wanted to go. Carolyn knew that she had to starting moving forward. The interview was a step in the right direction.

After arriving at Memorial Stadium, Mrs. Clark escorted Carolyn to the second floor offices of the Baltimore Colts. In the foyer, Carolyn stopped for a last minute check in front of a mirror. She straightened her blouse and tugged at her skirt. Somehow, she couldn't convince her mother that she should wear a western outfit so the Baltimore Colts could see what a real cowgirl looked like. Mrs. Clark paid no attention. Her daughter was going to dress like a professional businesswoman even if it meant wearing her Sunday best. Sometimes, cowgirls and horsewomen didn't see eye to eye on things.

"I'll wait out here," Mrs. Clark said calmly. "Just remember, do what you want to do. Be polite and be honest. If you change you mind, Mr. Tuttle will understand."

Carolyn took a deep breath, pulled opened the door and headed for the receptionist's desk. "Carolyn Clark to see Mr. Tuttle," she said nervously.

"He's waiting for you in his office. Third door on the left," the receptionist replied with a polite smile.

Carolyn walked slowly down the hall. Except for a few team photographs on the walls, the place looked like any other business office. Carolyn had seen more football pictures in her dentist's office. For a team named after horses, there wasn't anything too horsy about the headquarters of the world champions.

Three doors down, Carolyn stopped and peered into the office. Mr. Tuttle was talking to his secretary with an obvious eye on the door. "Miss Clark, please come in. I've been looking forward to meeting you. I heard so much about you from my sons," he announced cheerfully. After the introductions, he led Carolyn to his inner office. "Have a seat and we can talk about your future as a Baltimore Colt."

As Mr. Tuttle thumbed through some documents on his desk, Carolyn took a seat in one of the oversized leather chairs and glanced around the room. It was a football museum, exactly what she expected from a football team. Autographed pictures of past and present players filled the walls. One wall was filled with framed blue and white jerseys. On the corner of the desk was a team helmet, white with a blue stripe down the center and a blue horseshoe on each side. The built-in bookcase behind the desk was filled with footballs, framed pictures, and a pair of bronzed high-top football cleats. Next to the shoes were pictures of the Tuttle family.

Carolyn instantly recognized the Tuttle Gang. The boys were wearing their Viking Mountain t-shirts and holding a football. She abruptly shifted her eyes to the object next to the picture and stared in disbelief. It was a deflated chunk of cracked and battered leather. Carolyn squirmed in her seat and fumed. She had been tricked. The mascot job was a hoax. The Baltimore Colts wanted Dixie to kick footballs. Somehow the Tuttle boys had convinced their father that Dixie could sell tickets to the games. Fans would pack the stands to see the Dixie the Football Pony blast another ball through the goalposts. When the time came, she was going to politely inform Mr. Tuttle that she was not interested in the job, no matter how much it paid. Dixie was not a circus act for hire.

Carolyn listened intently as Mr. Tuttle explained the job, but her eyes kept shifting to the Tuttle ball. After finishing his sales pitch, Tuttle stood up, grabbed an autographed football from the shelf and held it up to his face.

"Carolyn, sportswriters called last year's championship the greatest game ever played," he said proudly. "This ball represents a great moment in Baltimore's football history." He paused and set the ball on his desk. Turning around, he grabbed the Tuttle ball and held it above his head, careful not to hold it near his face. "This ball represents many great moments in the future," he said, his voice rising in crescendo like a storefront preacher. "And the future of football belongs to the fans. We

168

need someone to reach out to fans of all ages, and that someone is you. The Baltimore Colts want you and your pony to join our team."

Mr. Tuttle stopped and studied the blank look on Carolyn' face. He was afraid that his passionate plea had fallen on deaf ears. Carolyn sat perfectly still and stared at the Tuttle ball. His speech had been spellbinding. She was ready to jump out of the chair and shout "Alleluia, brother Tuttle!"

"What do you say, Carolyn? Are you ready to join the team?" Tuttle asked, flashing a broad smile.

"Will Dixie have to kick footballs or race players around the field?" Carolyn asked warily, still sensing that Tuttle was not being completely honest.

"Nothing like that at all. You'll only ride around the field after the Colts score," he replied. Sensing Carolyn's reluctance, he knew it was time to seal the deal. He walked over to the wall and removed two pictures. "Here are your coworkers," he said, handing her a picture of the Colts band and cheerleaders in their western costumes. "And here's your workplace," he said, handing her an aerial view of the stadium.

Carolyn studied the pictures carefully. Her new teammates belonged in Buffalo Bill's Wild West Show, and her new workplace was shaped like a horseshoe. This was easier than expected, she thought. "Well, then, Mr. Tuttle, you have yourself a deal," Carolyn said gladly, extending her hand.

"I'm afraid I'll need more than a handshake to close the deal," Mr. Tuttle joked as he picked up a contract from his desk. Mrs. Clark was called into the office to read the fine print and sign as Carolyn's witness and guardian. After the contract was signed in triplicate, Mr. Tuttle handed Carolyn her copy. "Welcome to the Baltimore Colts. Good luck on your career. I'll see you opening day," he said with a firm handshake.

Walking out of the lobby, Carolyn passed a painting of Johnny Unitas, standing on the sideline in his uniform. Who knows, she thought. One day there might be a picture of her and Dixie hanging next to Johnny.

Back at the Jolly Jockey, Maggie waited impatiently for Carolyn to return. When she heard the sound of tires crunching gravel, she hurried from the stable. By the time she hobbled into the parking lot, Carolyn was standing next to the car with her arm raised over her head. Dangling from her fingers was the contract. From the broad smile on Carolyn's face, Maggie knew immediately that she had taken the job. Reaching up, she plucked the piece of paper from Carolyn's hand and began to speed read.

"You're going to be on television," Maggie squealed deliriously. "Everybody in Maryland watches the football games on TV. You'll be as famous as Buddy Deane."

"I'm, I'm going to do, to do what," Carolyn stuttered in shock. She snatched the contract from

170

Maggie and began to read the small print near the bottom of the page. There it was in black and white. "I also agree to allow the Baltimore Colts exclusive rights to use my image for television broadcasting purposes, to include live and taped events as authorized by management officials."

"Today the National Football League, tomorrow the Buddy Deane Show," Maggie cheered, thinking Carolyn could be her ticket to the teen show. "Once, you have star power, Buddy will be begging you to appear on the show. Better yet, you'll have your own television show. I can see the Hollywood headlines now. Carolyn and Dixie replace Dale and Roy as the stars of TV westerns."

Carolyn lowered her head and huffed. All of this talk about becoming a TV star was unnerving. The limelight might be good for Dixie but not for her. She was content to be Carolyn Clark, cowgirl of the Jolly Jockey. Mr. Tuttle said there would be some changes in her life, but Carolyn didn't thing they would come this quick. The ink was barely dry on the contract, and Maggie already had her billed as the next Dale Evans.

That evening, Carolyn visited Dixie in her stall to talk about the new job. "Girl, I have some great news. I got you a new job. You're going to be on the field with the most famous football team in the world. It's going to be a lot of fun, but first we have some work to do." The enthusiasm in Carolyn's voice was contagious. Dixie lifted her head and pricked her ears forward as if she understood every word. When Carolyn was finished talking, Dixie nickered quietly. The two girls had a deal.

Maggie's wry comments about becoming a star had sounded an alarm. The clock was ticking, and Carolyn was running out of time. School was starting in another week and that meant Maggie would only be at the farm on Saturdays. Opening day for the Baltimore Colts was three weeks away and that meant she didn't leave much time to prepare Dixie for her debut. The first thing on Carolyn's "do" list was to speak with Paddy about teaching an old pony some new tricks. She had a few ideas about how to make Dixie the star of the show but needed some technical advice. But more than anything else, she looked forward to spending time with Dixie. The daily practice sessions in the ring would renew the bond between two old friends. To Carolyn, the contract was already paying more than twenty dollars a game.

Chapter 9 – Cowgirl Up

Dawn was still an hour away, but on this lazy Sunday morning, the Jolly Jockey Farm was already bustling with activity. Dixie paced in her stall while Inky Dink stalked the stable for something or someone to chase. Carolyn's parents and Paddy sat on the front porch and sipped coffee, waiting for daybreak and the Sunday newspaper. Only one resident had not started the workday.

Carolyn slowly opened her eyes and peered through the early morning darkness. The shapes that filled her bedroom remained cloaked in shadows. Reaching behind her head, she fluffed up her pillow with a few quick jabs and pulled her blanket snugly under her chin. The clock on her dresser read 5:59 a.m. There was still time to catch some sleep, but a queasy feeling in the pit of her stomach made that impossible. The butterflies had returned with a vengeance. Closing her eyes, she tried to relax.

In the dark void underneath her eyelids, a carousel magically appeared. It was the one with the antique wood horses and blinking lights that Carolyn had seen at Ocean City, Maryland's oceanfront resort town. Calliope music blared in the background as the carousel slowly began to turn and gain speed with each revolution. Within seconds, the carousel was a blur. Sensing danger, the horses came to life and jumped from the platform. With panicked faces and high-pitched whinnies, they raced from the building with their riders desperately clinging to their necks. Spectators screamed in horror and followed the horses in a stampede down the boardwalk. Only one horse remained on the carousel, desperate and determined to finish the ride. Its rider leaned forward in the saddle and tightly clenched the reins.

The carousel became a whirl of colors, lights, and strange noises. White smoke swirled in a funnel cloud as the motor overheated. Showers of red and orange sparks sprayed from beneath the platform. The carousel's machinery rumbled louder and louder as the acrid smell of burning rubber filled the air. A high-pitched, ear-shattering whine

174

signaled the beginning of the end. With a thunderous, metallic explosion, the gearbox shattered into a thousand pieces. Anchor bolts snapped like twigs. With nothing to hold it secure, the carousel rocked violently from side to side, flipped on its side, and then rolled out the building. Picking up speed, the giant wheel rolled across the beach and splashed into the ocean where it bubbled and gurgled before sinking to the bottom of the Atlantic. A white cloud of steam hovered over the watery grave. Carolyn sprang open her eyes, unable to look at the horrible sight. The carousel vanished in the darkness of her room. Beads of sweat dotted her forehead as her heart pounded furiously. She had finally recognized the last rider. It was none other than Carolyn Clark.

"If today was Monday, then it would be all over," Carolyn sighed as she rolled over, hoping to fall back to sleep. Monday would be an ordinary, boring school day with no worries unless there was a big test. But today would be anything but ordinary and boring. Today's test was tomorrow's front-page news. Today was her debut with the Baltimore Colts. She dreaded the thought. How could a seasoned horsewoman who performed before hundreds of spectators be as fidgety as a newborn colt? Hoping her new job was a dream like the Pony Express, Carolyn closed her eyes again. This time the dark void slowly filled with vapors of light. When she finally opened her eyes, she was still in her room, and it was still Sunday

175

morning. "At least, there wasn't a carousel," she mumbled. She blamed the whole episode on Maggie's wild and wacky tales about carousels. That's all Maggie talked about when mucking out stalls. From now on, Carolyn vowed to start yodeling when Maggie started talking about carousels.

With darkness gradually fading from the room, a bed, a desk, and a bookcase began to take shape. Pictures hanging on the wall slowly became portraits of shadows. Suddenly, a weak beam of daylight streaked through the window. Carolyn lifted her head and followed the path of the light across the room. It landed directly on the closet where she hung her clothes. She gasped softy, blinking her eyes in disbelief. Her blue and white Colts uniform pulsated with an eerie glow as if it had come to life. With each passing second, the tiny spotlight grew brighter until the uniform glowed in a brilliant white light.

"The light of the world," Carolyn whispered softly as she remembered her pastor's favorite quote from scripture. "Prayer, that's the answer to my problem," she giggled excitedly. She immediately threw off the covers and jumped out of bed to get ready for church.

At the Sunday morning service, the Reverend Theodore Goodwin proved to be a creature of habit. With dramatic flair, he slowly climbed the pulpit steps and then paused before proclaiming his immortal words. "Lord, give us strength this

Sunday and every Sunday of the season to accept victory and defeat with equal grace. Lest we never forget; there is a time to pray and a time to play." About the same time every year, he recited the sermon by heart with a fervor that promised a journey of redemption to a heavenly paradise. Carolyn always thought the good reverend was just preaching scripture. But now, it finally dawned on her that he was really talking about football. Every football fan in church knew it. It was the time of the season for the Baltimore Colts, and the heavenly paradise was another championship.

Carolyn bowed her head with a small prayer for herself and Dixie. "O Lord, I know there are a billion prayers headed your way this morning," she whispered silently. "I know they are more important than a football game, but I'm just asking for a small favor. It would be greatly appreciated if you could give Dixie and me a little extra courage today. Amen."

Knowing God was extremely busy on Sunday mornings and couldn't personally answer all of his calls, Carolyn searched for a sign that her prayer had been received if not answered. First, she looked at Reverend Goodwin who was busy dramatizing his opening day sermon. Then, she gazed at her fellow worshippers who were busy watching the reverend and probably thinking about the football game. Finally, she looked up towards the rafters and smiled. She found her sign. A brilliant beam of light filtered through the stained glass window and bathed the pulpit in a rainbow of colors. Prayer was light, and light was prayer. If light from the heavens could pass through the pulpit to the congregation, then prayers from the congregation could pass through the pulpit to the heavens. "Lord, thank you kindly," she whispered and bowed her head.

The spiritual discovery wasn't a miracle, just science. It would be there next Sunday at a slightly different angle. But deep in her heart, Carolyn hoped the ray of sunlight was a pipeline of faith that could carry her prayer to the heavens above. With light traveling at 186,282 miles per second, she calculated that her prayer would reach its destination before the reverend's final Amen. That was plenty of time to have it answered before the start of the game.

By the time Carolyn changed her Sunday dress for work clothes and ran out to the stable, the hard work had been done. Paddy had finished feeding the horses and mucking out the stalls. Carolyn now had more time to prepare Dixie, and today she needed every minute. She made a mental note to repay Paddy for another favor but knew that would never happen. All she could do was add it to the list. Paddy was just like her, another kindred horse soul. He was glad to help because he loved to be around horses.

"Top of the mornin' to you, Miss Carolyn," Paddy hailed cheerfully in his thick Irish brogue from the far end of building. "It's a beautiful day to be about God's business."

"God's business is not what I'm worried about today. It's the football business that has me scared to death," Carolyn replied somberly, hoping for a few words of encouragement. In the distance, Paddy's whistling faded away to silence. A door slammed shut. Obviously, Paddy hadn't heard her reply. She thought about chasing after him for a pep talk, but there wasn't time. Dixie needed to be prepped.

"Hey there, Dixie girl! It's time to suit up for the big game," Carolyn sang out as she headed towards Dixie's stall. Usually, the sound of her voice produced a soft nicker or a loud snort depending on Dixie's mood. But today, there was only silence. Carolyn cautiously poked her head in the stall. To her surprise, Dixie was gone, but the stall wasn't empty. Leaning against the far wall was Paddy with his arms folded and his cap pulled down over his brow. He raised his head, looked Carolyn straight in the eye, and then winked.

"Yer lookin' at this all wrong, lass," he said with a mischievous grin. "Ya got to remember that God's work is serious business and football is serious play. Work hard and play hard, but always remember to have fun." He snapped the cap from his head and slapped it against his leg. "Work and have fun. Work and have fun!" he cackled with devilish delight. "Now get to your pony, there's work to be done."

179

With hands on hips, Paddy kicked up his heels and clicked down his toes. Bits of straw flew in the air as he twisted one leg in front of the other in his version of an Irish jig. Spinning out of the stall, he grabbed Carolyn by the hand and danced down the aisle to the staging area where Dixie was waiting. Clutching his cap to his chest, he bowed and pointed to Dixie with an exaggerated sweep of his arm. "Madame Clark, the princess from the royal House of Welsh requests your company this day. Her bath and breakfast have been completed."

"Why, thank you so much, Squire O'Brien. As always, your services as the royal coachman are greatly appreciated. There will be a commendation for today's performance, I do believe. " Carolyn giggled in her best Irish accent that wasn't too Irish.

"And may I inquire as to the situation of Miss Inky Dink?" Paddy asked.

"Mom said that with all of the commotion at the stadium, it's best if she stays home today," Carolyn replied, dropping her accent. "If everything goes smoothly, maybe we can bring her next time. But I'll be with Dixie every minute of the day, so the princess shouldn't be lacking for friends."

"As you wish, madam. I will see to it that Miss Inky Dink finds suitable activities to fill her day."

"And Paddy, thanks for cheering me up. I really needed it,' Carolyn said sincerely.

"Always a pleasure to serve anyway I can," he drawled dryly. He bowed again and disappeared around the corner. His whistling was now accompanied by a barking dog.

Carolyn was still smiling when she turned her attention to Dixie. Paddy knew exactly what he was doing. From the far end of the stable, he had read her face like an open book. The bard of the Jolly Jockey had struck again, always popping up at the most unlikely moments. Perhaps, he was a leprechaun as Maggie believed. How else could someone be so humorous yet so mischievous?

"Good morning, girl! It's time to get ready for our big day," Carolyn announced as Dixie's ears pricked forward in anticipation. She nickered softly when Carolyn nuzzled her check and stroked her neck.

Carolyn glanced at her watch and immediately grabbed a brush and comb. There wasn't a second to spare. After a few minutes of feverish stroking, Dixie's coat glistened like new fallen snow. Now that her arm muscles were warmed up, Carolyn was ready for her version of a Wild West shoot-out. Setting aside the grooming basket, she grabbed the box of blue and white pom-poms and placed them on a stool at arm's length. Lifting her arms to her shoulders, she curled and stretched her fingers. There may have been faster hands among the famous gunslingers of the Old West, but none faster than Carolyn at her stock-in-trade. "Carolyn Clark's my name and braiding is my game," she snarled. Taking a deep breath, she blew a stream of hot air into her fists and reached for the box. After loading up her hands with pom-poms, she slowly dropped them to her hips.

"Whenever you're ready. Go ahead and make your move," she sneered. Dixie snorted and flinched. That was the signal to draw. Carolyn drew her hands like six-shooters and fired a volley of pompons with deadly accuracy. With blazing quickness, she twisted, turned, knotted and tied the pom-pom in one motion, pausing only to reload with more pom-poms. Minutes later, she lifted her hands to her face and blew on her fingertips to cool them off. The fastest hands east of the Mississippi had struck again. Blue and white pom-poms sprouted from Dixie's braided mane like a bouquet of spring flowers. To finish up the task, Carolyn delicately twisted Dixie's tail into a fancy braid. "Carolyn Clark's my name and braiding is my claim to fame," she said proudly.

"Oh, Dixie, what a lady you are today, my dear. You look simply magnificent," Carolyn exclaimed with delight as she stepped back to admire her handiwork. She walked Dixie to the full-length mirror outside the tack room. Dixie stared hard at the reflection. She had seen herself in the mirror many times but never with blue and white pompons. After rolling her head for a few seconds, she flapped her lips and turned to face Carolyn with smiling eyes. She liked her new look. The makeover was success.

"Aye, a lovely lady, indeed. There's none lovelier except for you. Now I think it's time that you powder your own nose," Paddy said admiringly. He had snuck up on Carolyn and watched her put the finishing touches on Dixie. "Run along. I'll load Miss Dixie in the trailer."

"Oh, my gosh! It's almost the stroke of twelve," Carolyn shrieked after looking at her watch. She gave Paddy a big hug and a kiss on the cheek before sprinting to the house and up the stairs to her bedroom.

After braiding her hair into a ponytail, Carolyn sat on the edge of her bed and stared out the window with a blank look. She was having serious doubts about her makeover. At times like this, Carolyn envied her mother. Mrs. Clark had the business of people and ponies down to a science and practiced it as an art. She made friends easily and seemed to know just what to say and when to say it. A minute after meeting her, you felt as if you had known her for years. People called it business savvy, but most of it was nothing more than horse sense delivered with a smile. Today Carolyn hoped that a little bit of that business savvy would rub off on her. All she had to do was follow Dixie's lead and Maggie's advice. "Just watch Dixie and do what she does," Maggie said. "Remember, she's a people pony and you're a pony people." The grammar wasn't correct, but the message was clear. It was time to focus on people instead of ponies. For Carolyn, that was a very difficult task. She was more comfortable in a stable full of ponies than a room full of people. To Maggie and Mrs. Clark, it was a dreadful situation for a pre-teen, and they weren't shy in reminding her. But Carolyn took their advice to heart without any hard feelings.

Next to the stable, Paddy was hitching the horse trailer to the pick-up truck. In a few minutes, he would be walking up to the house and handing the truck keys to Mr. Clark. Time was running out, yet Carolyn suddenly felt content to sit on the bed for the rest of the day. Maybe she should switch with Paddy and let him ride while she finished the chores, she thought. The old leprechaun would be a real crowd pleaser as a mascot. At halftime, he could grab a microphone and entertain the crowd with his stories. Eventually, he would have his own football show before the game. After that, it would only be a matter of time until the team was renamed the Baltimore Shamrocks at Paddy's prompting.

Carolyn's mind continued to wander. Nervousness was racing into a full-blown case of stage fright, and a lack of confidence was not the cure. Now she was certain that she would crack under the pressure like a rookie jockey coming down the backstretch with a lead in the Kentucky Derby. Something drastic was bound to go wrong today as it did with Maggie's first lesson. Dixie would fall or she would fall. Dixie would spook or she would spook. Straps would break or clothing would tear. In broad daylight, Carolyn's dream job would turn into a nightmare. Fans would laugh or boo. She could take the abuse, but she wasn't sure how Dixie would respond. Would the fans break

Dixie's heart? If they did, would she be the same loveable pony?

Walking across the room, Carolyn stopped briefly at her desk and stared at the pile of textbooks. Too bad she couldn't spend the day doing homework, she mused. Twenty dollars a game, which seemed like a fortune yesterday, now looked like fool's gold.

Carolyn removed the uniform from the closet door and laid it on the bed. Reaching down, she lightly ran her fingers along the front of the jacket. The wool blend was surprisingly soft to the touch, not itchy or scratchy. Although the jacket no longer glowed, it was still warm as if the sun had breathed life into the fabric. She lifted up the hangar and held it at arm's length. It was the same outfit worn by the Colts marching band, blue pants with white fringes along the legs, a white jacket with blue pocket flaps and blue fringes on the sleeves, and a blue ascot. It was a snazzy outfit straight out of an Old West movie. The uniform was instant cowgirl. Just add a horse, and Carolyn already had one of those.

Carolyn cautiously changed into the uniform, taking extreme care with the buttons. For some unknown reason, a button always fell off her jacket whenever she dressed for a competition. Today she didn't want to ride in front of fifty-five thousand strangers with a safety pin fastened to her jacket or pants. There were too many other things waiting to go wrong. After pulling on her white boots, she stood in front of the mirror and posed. Staring hard at her reflection, she slowly cocked her head from side to side and then leaned forward until her nose was inches from the glass. Everything looked fine, but something was missing.

Leaning back, she reached behind and plucked the blue felt hat from the chair, gently placing it on her head. Every true-blue cowpoke knew the hat was the most important part of an outfit. It spoke volumes about the person underneath it. With a low crown and a flat brim, the style was more rancher than cowpuncher, but it was a genuine cowgirl hat. Carolyn squinted until her eyes were narrow slits. With the tip of her index finger, she began nudging the hat into position. That's how it was done on the TV westerns.

After tipping the hat slightly to the front and tilting it slightly to the right, Carolyn stepped back for a full view and posed with hands on hips. She couldn't believe her eyes. Standing in front of the mirror was a full-fledged, genuine cowgirl from the top of her blue hat to the bottoms of her white boots. "If that ain't a kick in the britches," she hooted as she smoothed the brim of the hat with her thumb and index finger. "Carolyn Clark, a rootin' and tootin' real live cowgirl. Why Annie Oakley, eat your heart out!"

Carolyn tugged on her sleeves and spun around like a ballerina. From every angle, the view was perfect. "When you're going to work, dress your best. When going to rodeo, dress your very best," she proclaimed, remembering the line from a cowgirl book. Today was the biggest horse show in Maryland, and she was dressed for the occasion.

"Carolyn, we're ready to go," Mrs. Clark called up the stairs impatiently.

"I'm almost ready. Just another minute," Carolyn shot back. There was one more thing to do. She had to be sure the picture in the mirror wasn't a lie. Dashing to her desk, she grabbed the framed picture of Gail Davis, the star of the TV show "Annie Oakley." It was always within view for extra motivation during homework. While Carolyn didn't look anything like the real Annie Oakley, she bore an uncanny resemblance to the TV Annie Oakley. That alone was more than enough reason to become a big fan of Miss Davis. Two years ago, she had written a fan letter to Miss Davis and received an autographed picture with a cheerful thank-you note. From that moment, she was a fan for life.

Racing back to the mirror, Carolyn held the picture on top of her shoulder. To her amazement, Gail was dressed in a blue and white-fringed cowgirl outfit that closely resembled her costume. Both cowgirls even had the same style of hat. "Why Annie, I mean Miss Davis, we could be sisters. Ain't no brag, just a natural fact as they say," she stated proudly. If the producers of the television show ever needed a young Annie Oakley, the part belonged to Carolyn. She could even bring her own wardrobe.

187

Three quick beeps from the truck horn sounded the alarm. Carolyn bounded down the stairs and out the door, jumping into the front seat with a smile on her face as wide as the brim on her hat. Miss Davis and Annie Oakley had come to the rescue of a lonesome cowgirl.

It was a few minutes after high noon when Mr. Clark put the truck in gear and pulled away in a cloud of dust. Still smiling, Carolyn gazed out the side window, hoping for a quick trip to the stadium and a quicker return. She wanted to be out of Baltimore town by sundown.

Chapter 10 - Instant Replay

As usual, Mr. Clark played tour guide during the trip. Carolyn had no doubt that if her father wasn't a jockey, he'd be working at a museum or monument. Although Mr. Clark didn't read a lot of books around the house, his knowledge of local trivia rivaled any history teacher. He was a walking and talking trivia book. His delivery was casual, but there was always passion in his voice. Behind the wheel of a car, he became a real-life Gabby Hayes, the bearded, tobacco chewing, old codger who was Roy Rogers' sidekick. Gabby had something to say about everything, and Mr. Clark had something to say about everything in Baltimore. He spit out facts and figures like a ticker tape machine. His favorite topics were old people and old buildings because they had a lot of hard luck stories to tell, and hard luck was once good luck. Every time he drove into the city, it was a chance to speak on their behalf.

As Carolyn listened, she looked out the window and fumed. She had no idea that a football created so much traffic. On any normal Sunday, the main artery to the city was an open country road, but today it was clogged with parked buses of all shapes and sizes as football fans boarded for the ride to the stadium. If the fans spilling into the streets weren't enough congestion, every traffic light seemed stuck on was red. At this rate, Carolyn calculated arriving just as the game ended.

"Ladies and gentlemen! To your right is the latest tribute to that most famous of horses, the Baltimore Colt. Destined to be remembered in the hearts of the young and old," Mr. Clark exclaimed with the fervor of a circus ringmaster. The announcement jolted Carolyn from her traffic temper tantrum. How could she have missed such a famous landmark during her previous trips, she wondered. She heard the same stories every time she went to the racetrack with her father. With eyes wide open, she looked out the window at an empty asphalt parking lot littered with hamburger wrappers and paper cups.

"I don't see anything," Carolyn moaned impatiently.

"Quick! Look up before the light changes," Mr. Clark instructed.

"Up where?" Carolyn replied as she rolled down the window for a better look.

"Up there!" said Mrs. Clark, pointing to the sky.

Carolyn stuck her head out the window and gawked. Perched halfway up a candy-striped pole was a gigantic, plastic statue of a boyish football player with bulging eyes and a broad smile, wearing number 35. High-stepping off the top of the sign, he carried at his chest a giant hamburger named the "Powerhouse." With two patties of freshly ground beef, melted cheese and shredded lettuce on a double-deck seed roll with pickle and a secret sauce; the "banquet on the bun" was nearly half the size of the statue. It was a meal that no mortal could eat much less carry. No wonder the poor boy's eyes were bulging out of their sockets.

The statue was the logo for Alan "The Horse" Ameche, the fullback who scored the winning touchdown in last year's championship game. When he decided to open a restaurant, his instant football fame became a fast food fortune. Word about the new drive-in "burger joint" spread like wildfire. A few weeks after the grand opening, his place became the popular weekend hangout, a gathering place for teenagers, cars and Colts fans. "Meetcha at Ameche's" was the phrase on every teenager's lips.   Maggie talked about the place whenever it was time to eat.   According to Mr. Clark, it was the most popular hangout for teenagers next to the Buddy Deane Show.

As the truck pulled away, Carolyn chuckled at a silly thought. If she and Dixie became famous, they could have their own plastic statues atop a pole. The place could be named "Dixie's." With a catchy slogan, Dixie soon could be challenging Alan Ameche for hearts and souls of Baltimore's teenagers.

While Carolyn and her mom were discussing a lunch date at Ameche's and whether it would be a chocolate or vanilla shake with their burger and fries, Mr. Clark shifted his talk from a football player to a football game. No one in Baltimore could mention Alan "The Horse" Ameche without talking about the greatest game ever played, the 1958 championship game between the Baltimore Colts and the New York Giants. As always, Mr. Clark replayed the first sudden death championship game as if standing on the sideline with the team which he wasn't. While he launched into his play by play commentary, Carolyn remembered her own version of the game.

What a game it was! What a day it was! Uncle Frank, one of Mrs. Clark's brothers, had invited every family member within driving distance to watch the game at his house. He promised the sporting experience of a lifetime. "It's better than a ticket to the game. You'll be on the standing on the sidelines," he proudly boasted. Very few turned down the offer. When Mr. Clark pulled up to the house, people were already parking on the front lawn. Uncle Frank personally greeted every guest at the door of his brick rancher and led them to the family room where the momentous event would take place. In this inner sanctum, "man" and "machine" would be united in harmony to celebrate the game of football.

The "man" was none other than Uncle Frank, a true Baltimore blue blood. He was blue collar, blue crab, and Colts blue in every fiber of his being. Even his house was trimmed in blue and white lights at Christmas time. As tall as he was wide, he was a walking brown-eyed refrigerator with a crew cut. He was as tough as the steel he poured from the blast furnaces at Sparrows Point, yet as gentle as a summer breeze blowing off the Chesapeake Bay. Small tattoos adorned both massive forearms, a mermaid on one and crossed anchors on the other with the motto "Semper Paratus," which was Latin for "Always Ready." Friends jokingly said he would give you the shirt off his back as long as it wasn't a Colts jersey, and that was probably the truth. Say anything about Uncle Frank without fear, but never utter a foul word about his beloved Baltimore Colts. They were revered as family. One unkind word about the team and the wrath of Uncle Frank rained down like molten lava, a blistering heat that was hotter than his homemade crab seasoning.

Colts and crabs summed up Uncle Frank's life. Until football training camp opened, his life's pursuit was to find the best, which usually meant the cheapest, crabs in the city. If a Baltimore Colt player ever opened a crab house, he would crawl there gladly on his hands and knees at least once a week for a carryout order. But in the third week of July, Colts replaced crabs. Instead of driving around the city looking for crabs, he drove out to the small, rural college where his team practiced. He knew the players on a first name basis and was always greeted with a hearty handshake and a slap on the back. He sent cards and cakes to them for birthdays and anniversaries. If a rookie needed a place to stay or a home-cooked meal, his home and kitchen were open twenty-four hours a day, seven days a week. Uncle Frank was married to the two loves of his life, his wife and his football team, for better or worse, richer or poorer, and in victory or defeat until death do they part.

Uncle Frank's paneled family room was a personalized football museum dedicated to the Baltimore Colts. In the bookcase next to the television was an autographed football from the 1957 team, guarded by a family portrait and an autographed picture of Johnny U. Team souvenirs, to include pennants, programs, pictures, drinking glasses, and coffee mugs, filled the space normally reserved for books. The motif was blue and white; the theme was horses.

A season ticket holder since the team relocated in 1953, Uncle Frank religiously attended every home game and some of the away games within driving distance. When he couldn't find a ticket to Yankee Stadium in New York for the championship game, he found the best seat money could buy. He would watch the game in front of his brand new Admiral television set. The "machine," as he called it, was a giant 17-inch television with a high-intensity, instamatic screen, a stereo record player, and an AM-FM radio, all tastefully mounted into a handcrafted walnut cabinet. In every appliance store, this marvel of technology was the flagship of the television fleet. Uncle Frank brushed aside any questions about the price with a wave of his hand. No expense would be spared in witnessing the game of the century. Even the food and beverages were on the house. But there was a price to pay for all of this hospitality. All guests had to abide by Uncle Frank's golden rule and root for the Colts on every play. You could criticize the other team or the referees, but never the Baltimore Colts. The players were his boys in battle, engaging in football warfare for the honor of their city and state. Their will to win would never be questioned. Any infraction would result in banishment to the kitchen where the game was on the radio.

The room was packed wall to wall with people. Men, women, children jostled each other for the best view of the television that was centered against the far wall. Most of the assembled faithful had followed Uncle Frank's suggestion and wore something blue and white as a sign of unity. With the kick-off only minutes away, all eyes were trained on the Admiral. As grand marshal, Uncle Frank had the honor of turning on the set. Almost instantly, crystal clear images appeared in various shades of black and white.

As the Baltimore Colts ran on the field, the room erupted with a deafening roar. And then the cheering suddenly stopped. The room fell deadly quiet. Necks craned as eyes strained to see what happened. Total darkness had descended upon the field. Not a player was in sight. Everyone immediately grumbled the same opinion. Those dastardly television executives in New York pulled the plug so the fans in Baltimore couldn't watch the game. Hoping the blackout was simple a technical glitch, Uncle Frank's faithful prayed for deliverance.

"Torpedoed! The television has taken a direct hit," Uncle Frank yelled in horror when the television remained dark. Uncle Frank, who rose to the rank of chief petty officer in the United States Coast Guard during World War II, quickly recovered from the initial shock and swung into action. Quick as a cat he sprang from his recliner. With a flick of the wrist, he turned on the small television atop the Admiral. Seconds later, the Colts emerged from the darkness and ran onto a smaller field.

"Semper Paratus!" Uncle Frank bellowed with a sigh of relief, falling back into his seat. Wiping his brow, he called for his favorite drink, a bottle of National Bohemian beer, the one proudly advertised as being brewed on the shores of the Chesapeake Bay when, in fact, it was brewed on the banks of Baltimore's harbor. His quick action under fire had saved the day. The old television was a life preserver. Uncle Frank's guests were not going to abandon ship and watch the game somewhere else. Such an idea was unfathomable to an old mariner. To Uncle Frank, the Coast Guard motto of "Always Ready" was a way of life. If the team ever took a sea cruise, Uncle Frank was the man they wanted at the helm.

At halftime, Uncle Frank did a damage control check. The problem wasn't in New York; it was in his living room. The picture tube had unexplainably died. The Admiral was a casualty right out the box, despite a lifetime warranty on parts and labor. "Never did know an admiral worth a damn. They should have named the darned thing The Chief. That would have been a television to depend on," Uncle Frank grumbled to the delight of the guests. He may have lost his Admiral but not his sense of humor. The old chief even joked about painting the old television orange in case of another emergency.

Carolyn really didn't pay much attention to the game. It was too confusing with too many players and too many rules. She could tell the difference between real colts, but all of the football Colts looked the same in uniform. Every player had a different number and a different position, and, of course, every position had a different title, such as quarterback, halfback, fullback, end, guard, and tackle. Offensive players tried to move the ball down the field while defensive players tried to stop them. Every play looked like a stampede of wild horses with two herds moving in opposite directions. Often the action seemed comical as players ran around the field, tripping and falling over themselves.

To Carolyn, the real action was in the living room, not on the field. It was more fun to watch her relatives than the players. They were the game within the game. Following Uncle Frank's cue, they cheered the Colts and booed the Giants. He grumbled; they grumbled. He mumbled; they mumbled. He spoke; they listened, especially when he talked about Johnny Unitas. All Carolyn needed to know about football and the Baltimore Colts was one name and one number. The fate of Colts rested on the arm of their quarterback, number 19, John Unitas or Johnny U, as he was affectionately nicknamed by fans.

He swaggered on the field with bowed legs as if he had spent years in the saddle. He stood on the sideline with hands on hips, ready to draw at a moment's notice. He was a sheriff without a badge, just the number 19 on his jersey. He called all the plays and answered to no one. He didn't have a white cowboy hat, just a white helmet with a blue stripe down the middle and blue horseshoes on the sides. He didn't have cowboy boots, just his trademark high top, black leather cleats. He didn't even have a shootin' iron, just a golden arm that fired passes downfield with deadly accuracy. Without ever looking in his eyes or shaking his hand, Carolyn knew the fabric of his character. Johnny U was cut from cowboy cloth. If he wasn't a football player, he'd be a bull ridin' and bronco bustin' cowpoke.

Calm, cool and collected under fire, Johnny U drove his Colts down the field for a field goal that tied the game in the final seconds. Minutes later in the overtime period, he once again drove his Colts down the field with some daring plays. He passed when he should have run; he ran when he should have passed. When he handed the ball to Alan Ameche who plunged into the end zone with the winning touchdown, an earthquake hit Baltimore. The family room shook to its foundations as people jumped up and down with a thunderous, foot-stomping cheer. Family members who had not spoken in years hugged one another and toasted drinks like it was New Year's Eve. Everyone celebrated madly but Uncle Frank. He sat quietly in his chair and stared at the screen with a tight smile. His body was in Baltimore, but his spirit had taken flight to New York. He was running with the fans who stormed the field to celebrate with the players. Clenching his teeth, he wiped a small tear from the corner of his eye and then leaned forward to gently pat the old television for a job well done. In victory, the marriage of "man" and the "other machine" was a blissful if not perfect event.

Carolyn's slowly scanned the room, trying to capture the faces frozen in time. Years from now, she wanted to affectionately remember the game for the Clark family archives. It was destined to be a comedy classic. If only she had a movie camera, she thought. Her film would be titled appropriately "Faith, Family, Football and Uncle Frank."

The victory celebration stopped suddenly when a news bulletin interrupted the post-game show. All eyes and ears turned to the television for an update. Team doctors reported that Gino "The Giant" Marchetti, the star defensive end who broke his leg making a crucial tackle late in the fourth quarter, was expected to make a full recovery. Bloodied but not bowed, the fallen warrior watched the final climatic moments from a stretcher on the sideline. "Those Italian guys are as tough as nails. You know Gino fought at the Battle of the Bulge," Uncle Frank commented proudly as if he had just been elected to the Sons of Italy. Carolyn knew that next year there would be an autographed picture of Gino on the bookshelf.

A broken leg, a busted television and a bruised ego were the costs of the day's battle. It was a small price to pay for victory. "A calm sea doth not a good mariner make," Uncle Frank joked as guests filed out the front door underneath the blue and white Christmas lights that shined like a lighthouse beacon in the early evening. His Christmas gift had arrived three days late, but it was worth the wait. By the following morning, he was ready for the 1959 season and another championship.

Chapter 11 - Wild West Show in Baltimore

Carolyn and Mr. Clark finished their replays at nearly the same time. The rest of the ride passed in silence until the tour guide made his last announcement of the day.

"Ladies and gentlemen, to your right is the home of the most famous of Maryland horses, the Baltimore Colts," Mr. Clark declared. Memorial Stadium loomed straight ahead.

Carolyn twisted her head out the window for a better view as her father circled the parking lot. The gigantic bowl looked more massive than it did a month ago for her interview. Due to her nervousness, she didn't remember the imposing facade at the main entrance. On the soaring concrete wall bordered with red brick, ten-foot stainless steel letters in a modern art style spelled out a tribute to Maryland's war veterans who sacrificed their lives for freedom. "Time Will Not Dim the Glory of Their Deeds," Carolyn whispered repeatedly. The words had special meaning in her family. Her uncles always had a war story about a friend who never made it home from one of those distant battlefields.

High above the stadium's rim, pennants fluttered in the breeze. Triangular flags in team colors signaled this year's contestants in the National Football League. With colts, lions, rams, eagles, and cardinals, the league sounded like a collection of zoo animals instead of football teams. Next to the Colts, Carolyn's favorite teams were the San Francisco 49'ers and the Washington Redskins because they reminded her of the Old West. She knew about New York Giants from last year's championship game but had no idea about the Green Bay Packers. They sounded like a moving company from Wisconsin. She wondered when a team would be named the cowboys. That would instantly become her second favorite team. With colts and cowboys, she might become a real football fan after all.

The area around the stadium resembled an open-air market in a National Geographic magazine. Vendors crowded the sidewalks with tables and carts. Their voices filled the air with song-like ditties, selling hot dogs, pretzels, caramel popcorn, team souvenirs, and game-day programs. The longest lines were for the peanut vendors; further proof to Carolyn that Colts fans were simply nuts for their football team.

Not to be outdone by the vendors, Baltimore's "men in blue" added their own musical contribution. On every street corner, traffic cops tooted their whistles and waved their hands to keep foot and vehicle traffic moving at a steady pace. Long and short, high and low, the shrill bursts were a common language to the people in the streets who moved in rhythmic response.

At the main crosswalks in front of the stadium, mounted police stood guard as cars and pedestrians played a continuous game of chicken. To Carolyn, a chance to see the city's horse patrol unit was always worth the trip. She saw them every year when her pony club rode through the streets of downtown Baltimore in the annual Thanksgiving Day parade. Their dark blue uniforms with sharp creases and black spit-shined riding boots were well-known trademarks. Their horses were big and beautiful animals, always well-groomed for public appearances. Carolyn easily pictured herself sitting in one of those shiny black saddles, marshalin' a football game with a large silver badge pinned on her chest.

Mr. Clark flashed his VIP pass at the parking lot checkpoint. The security guard didn't question a horse trailer at a football game and pointed to a tunnel entrance at the far end of the stadium. A second after Mr. Clark turned off the ignition, Carolyn jumped out and stretched her arms over her head with a yawn, ready to turn around for home.

The cavernous room under the grandstand was a perfect staging area. It was close to the field yet quiet enough to give Dixie a break during the game. Carolyn glanced at her watch and headed for the back of the trailer. The game was an hour away, but there wasn't a second to waste. Mr. Clark spread a blanket of straw on the concrete floor, stacked a few bales of hay, and then unloaded Dixie. While Dixie snacked, Carolyn and Mrs. Clark brushed her white coat to high sheen that glowed in the dull light of the tunnel.

"Are you ready, girl?" Carolyn asked as she reached up and adjusted a few of the pom-poms. Dixie snorted and bobbed her head.

"Well, there's no doubt Dixie's ready for the show. How about her rider?" Mrs. Clark asked enthusiastically.

Carolyn hesitated. "I think so. How do I look?" she asked nervously.

Mrs. Clark stepped forward and pulled down the sides of Carolyn's jacket. She slowly ran her fingertips over the front of the jacket to smooth the wrinkles. Reaching up, she straightened the hat that was tilted far to the side. Carolyn frowned in jest because she knew it was coming. Her Wild West look was out of fashion for today. Mom was a horsewoman, not a cowgirl.

205

"Without a doubt, I'm standing in front of Baltimore's own Annie Oakley," her mother proudly exclaimed as she stepped back. Carolyn grinned. The comparison to Annie Oakley was a wagonload of confidence. "But there is one thing missing," her mother drawled.

Carolyn panicked. "Oh no, what did I forget?" she asked, her face turning pale white. Her wagon of confidence just took a wrong turn and plunged off the cliff.

"That smile! Where is the Annie Oakley smile?" her mother asked. "If you're smiling, then Dixie and the rest of the fans are smiling with you. Show the fans you're having fun. Today is just one big Wild West show. It's not a competition."

Carolyn cracked a wide smile as Paddy's words about fun echoed in her head. Mom was right as usual. The fans had come to see the Baltimore Colts, not Carolyn and Dixie. "Then it's time to ride the magic carousel," Carolyn declared jubilantly, repeating Maggie's mantra from the riding ring.

"As they say in football, it's time to take the field,' Mrs. Clark added. "Just remember to relax. Everybody out there is nervous, players, fans, and mascots. It's a natural thing."

"Thanks for the Annie Oakley comment. It really helped," Carolyn replied as she gave her mother a hug. Grabbing hold of the reins, she led Dixie toward the light at the end of the tunnel and disappeared into the bright sunshine.

"Mom's right, girl," Carolyn cooed in Dixie's ear as she slipped her a treat. "Now let's go make Annie proud of us."

Carolyn stepped onto the field and stopped dead in her tracks. The view of the stadium from ground level was stunning. It was nothing like the picture on Uncle Frank's black and white television. A rainbow of freshly painted colors, bright enough for sunglasses, replaced the shades of television gray.

But color wasn't the only thing missing from Uncle Frank's television. While the lens of the television camera captured detail, it didn't accurately capture size. The stands rose at a steep angle like mountain bluffs while the playing field stretched like a grasslands prairie, wide enough and long enough for a stampeding herd of buffalo. Taking a picture of a football stadium with a TV camera was like taking a picture of the Grand Canyon with a pocket camera.

Carolyn knelt and rubbed the grass with her fingers. The blades were soft and thick as a shag carpet. As she looked up, Dixie looked down, their eyes meeting along the way with the same thought. Dixie was in horse heaven. As green as an Irish spring, the field was a giant salad bowl. Carolyn's toughest job of the day might be keeping Dixie from eating on the job.

Following her mother's advice, Carolyn walked Dixie around the cinder track, stopping every few steps to look and listen. Even though Dixie was a seasoned performer, she needed to get comfortable with her new home. At midfield, Carolyn stopped behind the Colts' bench to watch the action. Both teams were scattered across the field in warm-up drills. Footballs filled the air as quarterbacks hurled spiraling passes downfield. Galloping receivers snared the balls in mid-flight and sprinted to the end zone. Massive linemen collided with one another in bone-jarring blocking drills. Grunting and snorting, they kicked up dust like raging bulls.

When the players jogged to the locker room, Carolyn watched the fans navigate to their seats. Everyone was smiling and waving; their voices drifting down to the field like the whispers of autumn leaves. Carolyn wasn't sure if they were smiling and waving at her, but she was positive they were looking in her direction. So far, the stadium was a home on the range where seldom was heard a discouraging word, and Carolyn hoped that it stayed that way until the end of the game. In the back of her mind were the stories about rowdy fans throwing trash on the field and screaming insults at the top of their lungs. That made her nervous because she wasn't sure how Dixie would react. Today was not the day for horse or rider to be spooked.

Moving away from the bench area, Carolyn crossed her fingers and prayed that she could finish the walk without being noticed. She knew the odds were stacked against her. How many people wouldn't notice a cowgirl and her pony at a football game? The answer came three steps later. Carolyn froze in her tracks as the sound of her name was hurled from the stands. Terror filled her heart. The wrath of an angry fan was upon her. Those stories about unruly fans were true. "Carolyn, up here! Up here!" a deep voice boomed. Carolyn turned with a stiff wave and a weak smile, her eyes rapidly scanning the crowd. She couldn't imagine how someone could have singled her out so quickly. She strained her eyes to find the voice, but there were too many faces. It was scary to think that a fan already knew her name.

Just as Carolyn turned back to the track, she saw movement in the corner of her eye. From an upper aisle, a crazed fan was running towards her, shouting her name wildly. Carolyn chuckled at the sight of Uncle Frank charging down the steps. "I've been looking for you since I got here," he said huffing and puffing. After catching his breath, he leaned over the rail with his request. "I need two favors from you if you don't mind. First, I need you to autograph my program, and then I need a picture of you, me and Dixie."

"Oh, I don't know Uncle Frank. Can I do these things?" Carolyn asked hesitantly.

"Can you do these things? Of course, you can do these things. You're part of the team. You're a Baltimore Colt!" trumpeted Uncle Frank. Grabbing the rolled up program from his pants pocket, he thumbed through the first couple of pages, his big meaty hands nearly ripping the pages in half. Sweat dripped from his face as if his head had been steamed in a crab pot. "Look, right there on page five. That's you next to the band and cheerleaders," he exclaimed, pointing to the picture in the corner of the page.

"Look Dixie!" Carolyn shouted excitedly, recognizing the photograph. About a month ago, the team photographer had visited the farm to take some promotional pictures. "But I feel kind of funny doing this kind of stuff since I'm not one of the players," Carolyn added bashfully.

"Nonsense," Uncle Frank insisted, handing her the program and a pen. "You're the prettiest colt... I mean filly. I mean you and Dixie are the prettiest fillies. Ah, shucks, Carolyn, you know what I mean."

Carolyn knew exactly what Uncle Frank meant. He had the same look on his face when the Colts won the championship last year. She couldn't say no to Uncle Frank even if it was against the rules. Nervously fumbling with the pen, she signed her name next to the picture. Uncle Frank then removed the camera from around his neck and coaxed a nearby fan to take pictures of the trio. The man eagerly obliged in return for his own autograph and picture. He wanted his own mascot souvenirs for his young daughter at home.

"This is the greatest day of my life, Carolyn. Who would have thought that a family member would be a Baltimore Colt! I'm going to put that picture on my bookshelf, right next to Johnny U," he boldly declared, hanging the camera around his neck. "Got to run along. Have a great day, kiddo. Just remember, Semper Paratus!"

"Yeah, I know, Uncle Frank, always ready," Carolyn replied nonchalantly. With a silly grin on his face, Uncle Frank lumbered up the steps and disappeared into the crowd. Carolyn shook her head in amazement. Her first encounter with a fan was a breeze, even if it was Uncle Frank. Too bad, Maggie wasn't around to witness this fine display of public relations skills. Carolyn was convinced the rest of her encounters would be just as easy. All she had to do was nod and let the fans do the talking.

Turning around to face the field, Carolyn bumped into a solid blue curtain. Startled by the collision, she stepped back to see what was blocking her path. She slowly began inspecting the stranger from the tips of his shoes to the top of his head. "Oh, my goodness," she gasped in disbelief. The black high-top shoes with white shoelaces and the crew cut were dead giveaways. There was only one Colt in the herd with those markings. It was Johnny U, and he was standing right in front of her. "Semper Paratus!" she groaned. She was prepared for anything but a meeting with "Mr. Colt."

"Welcome to the Baltimore Colts," Johnny said cheerfully as he extended his right hand. "I couldn't help but hear you and your Uncle Frank. I think I would have figured out who you were sooner or later. The pony was a sure clue. You don't see too many colts out here without helmets and cleats."

Carolyn grasped Johnny's hand firmly, making sure her grip wasn't too loose or too tight. That was a trick she learned from watching TV westerns. Roy Rogers always said the strength of man's handshake reflected the strength of his character. From the feel of it, Johnny had plenty of character. His handshake was firm but not forceful, and strong but not strangling.

"It's a pleasure to meet you, Mr. Unitas. My name is Carolyn and this is my pony Dixie," Carolyn said nervously, the words stumbling out of her mouth. Suddenly, her face was hot, and her feet were cold. She opened her mouth to speak, but the words were stuck in her throat. Hopefully, the cinder track would turn to quicksand, and she would vanish from sigh without further embarrassment.

Seeing that Carolyn was a damsel in distress, Johnny came to rescue. "I couldn't help but overhear you and your uncle. Sounds like he's your biggest fan," he said casually.

"Uncle Frank is the biggest Colts fan ever. He even has a picture of you on his bookcase," Carolyn replied quickly.

"You mean it's still on the middle shelf next to that old football," Johnny chuckled. "I have to admit that I know Uncle Frank. He's quite a character, a Baltimore original."

Carolyn slouched with relief. She could talk all day about Uncle Frank and the Baltimore Colts. As she told her story about the championship game, Johnny nodded his head and laughed.

"I'll be riding around the track every time the Colts score today. Do you think I'll be riding a lot?" Carolyn asked at the end of her story.

"That's a hard to say. It depends on how well we play. I wish I could tell you, but I can't," Johnny replied modestly.

Carolyn grimaced. If Johnny U didn't have an answer, she might as well saddle up and ride home. Seeing the look of disappointment on Carolyn's face, Johnny quickly recovered the fumbled conversation. "I guarantee that we'll score at least once, just for you and Dixie. That way you and Dixie can meet all the fans," he responded with a chuckle.

Carolyn laughed along. That's exactly what she wanted to hear. Yes, siree, talkin' to good ole Johnny U. was like shootin' the breeze with some of the cowpokes back at the bunkhouse, she thought. Johnny's prediction got her tongue waggin' once again. And then it happened, an unexpected, serious breech of cowgirl etiquette from out of the blue.

"Sir, I think you'd make a great horseman," Carolyn blurted out. All she could do was keep talking and hope her comments weren't taken the wrong way.

"And how so?" responded a bewildered Johnny.

"It's your hands, sir. They're big and strong, yet gentle to the touch. Just the kind of hands to talk to a horse."

"Talking hands?" Johnny pondered as he held his hands to his face.

"They let you communicate with your horse so he knows exactly what you want done. It's like a stagecoach driver with his team," Carolyn explained frantically, searching for the right words.

"I never thought of it that way before, but you're absolutely right. I'm a driver with a team of ten colts. I like that idea a lot. Sportswriters write a lot of things about me, but nobody has ever mentioned my talkin' hands. Maybe you should be a sportswriter. That way you could talk about my fast hands and not my slow feet," Johnny said jokingly, his tight grin now stretching into a broad smile.

"Today I'll just try to be a good horsewoman. If good riders make good writers, I'll give it a try," Carolyn replied with a joke of her own, relieved to see that Johnny was still smiling. When kids at school teased her about her horse hands, she took it as a compliment. Thank goodness Johnny U had a sense of humor as large as his hands.

From the bench, someone yelled to Johnny and pointed to the end of the field as the players headed to the locker room. Johnny held up a finger. He needed another minute with the new Colt. "Well, time for me to saddle up my horses," he joked, placing his right hand on Carolyn's shoulder. "But just remember, one thing. Win or lose, football is just a game, and games are supposed to be fun.

You and Dixie are part of the team so have fun today."

"That sounds like a touchdown to me," Carolyn replied as Johnny jogged toward the tunnel. "Wow! We really are Baltimore Colts. Now let's do as the man said and have some have some fun," she said to Dixie. Win or lose, she had two things in common with Johnny U, big hands and big hearts.

After finishing her walk around the track, Carolyn met with the band director for any last minute instructions. Nothing in the plans had changed. Other than smiling, waving and having fun, she was to circle the field every time the Colts scored a point. "Don't race your horse wildly and watch out for people standing on the track," the band director instructed hurriedly. He then quickly reviewed the rules for riding on the field and ended with a short pep talk. "And one more thing, be ready for anything, especially at the introductions," he added with a sly grin.

Carolyn met with her parents at the open end of the stadium without a second thought about the band director's last comments. Pre-game activities were only minutes away. It was time to be a spectator for a few minutes.

Three short whistle blasts from the drum major signaled the start of the show. To the beat of a muffled drum cadence, the world famous Baltimore Colts Marching Band marched underneath the goalpost. At midfield, the band halted and stood at attention. Fans stood and inhaled a deep breath.

Like the calm before a mighty storm, an eerie silence settled over the stadium. All eyes were riveted on the band. On a quick count from the drum major, the brass players snapped their horns to their lips. A split second later, he did an about face and twirled his baton in a series of spins before bringing it to rest at his side. The crowd remained still and quiet. The flags of the color guard flapped gently in the breeze.

Now it was up to the band to make the first move in this pre-game showdown with fans. On cue, the drum major thrust his baton high over his head, pumped his arm twice, and high-stepped forward. Following his lead, the band strutted down the center of the field, playing the sweetest music this side of the Chesapeake Bay. As the first notes of the Baltimore Colts Fight Song reached the stands, the crowd finally exhaled with a mighty wind. "Let's go, you Baltimore Colts, and put that ball across the line," they sang in a rousing plea for victory. Horse fever raged, spreading from one fan to another like a wildfire. Carolyn listened hard for rest of the words to the song.

"That's your cue," Mrs. Clark said as the band played another chorus. Carolyn grabbed the reins and lifted herself into the saddle. She trotted Dixie down the track to meet the band at the other end of the stadium. With all eyes on the field, no one seemed to notice a girl and her pony. So far her luck was holding up.

As expected, the introduction of the Detroit Lions met with a frightening round of boos. The band followed hard on the heels of the last player and formed two parallel lines extending from the goalpost to mid-field. Dixie stood at attention next to the drum major. It was time for the fans to cheer for their heroes. Memorial Stadium was a giant powder keg filled with fifty-five thousand sticks of dynamite.

"Ladies and gentlemen, please welcome your world champion Baltimore Colts," the announcer crooned in a silky baritone. The fuse had been lit. One by one, he introduced the starting players by position, college, jersey number, and name. Running underneath the goalpost and through the band line, the blue jerseys were greeted with a wave of deafening cheers. The fuse on the powder keg sizzled and sparked as the line of players near the tunnel dwindled. Finally, one lone player stood in the shadows with hands on hips and shoulders hunched forward.

"At quarterback," the announcer continued before pausing. Ka-boom! The crowd exploded in thunderous applause as Johnny U snapped the chinstrap on his helmet and ran onto the field. Goosebumps rose on Carolyn's arms and legs, and the hair on her neck stood on end. Not even Uncle Frank's television could capture the emotion of the moment.

After the introductions, the band was to close ranks and march down the field to their seats in the end zone. That was Carolyn's cue to finish her lap around the track. But the band remained frozen in position. Carolyn glanced at the drum major, but he was staring straight ahead. She then remembered that sometimes the governor, the mayor, or some other dignitary would be introduced at the end. Could it be the President of the United States, she wondered. Sometimes the president threw out the first pitch for a baseball season opener. For a football game, he could flip the coin for the referees. Perhaps, he could start a new tradition, the ceremonial first kick-off. The president could tee up the ball up and kick it downfield to one of the Colts. It could be like the first pitch in baseball.

The crowd grew restless, buzzing like a swarm of angry bees. Since last December, they had been waiting for the new season to begin. They couldn't wait any longer.

A high-high-pitched whine crackled over the public address system. Static electricity charged the air as all eyes shifted to the tunnel. A second later, the announcer's voice silenced the din of the crowd. Only this time Carolyn finally recognized the voice. It was the same soothing baritone that echoed throughout the stable during the summer months when Paddy listened to baseball games on the radio. Every horse in the stable, even Dixie, knew the voice of Chuck Thompson, the play-by-play announcer for the Baltimore Orioles. No wonder Dixie had remained so calm during the introductions. Carolyn patted her on the neck to let her know that something big was going to happen.

"Get ready, girl! Here we go!" she called to Dixie, expecting the name of President Dwight Eisenhower to be announced.

"Ladies, gentlemen, and fans of all ages, please give a warm welcome to the newest members of the Baltimore Colts..." the announcer paused. The crow inhaled and went silent once again. Waiting turned to wondering. Did the Colts trade for new players? The microphone crackled again. "Please welcome," the announcer continued gleefully, "Miss Carolyn Clark and her pony Dixie."

The crowd exhaled. Polite applause feathered in the air. But instead of fading out, the cheers gradually increased in volume until they reached a deafening crescendo. Horse fever had flared up once again. Highly contagious among Colt fans, it raged out of control quicker than you could say Johnny U. A Baltimore Colt was a Baltimore Colt. It didn't matter if it had two legs or four legs. The newest Colts would be treated like the rest of the team. That's what made Baltimore a special place for football.

Carolyn stiffened at the sound of her name. She couldn't believe her ears. Surely, there must be another Carolyn Clark and Dixie! Sweat beaded on her forehead as her face turned crimson. Her head started swimming. The fever had spread to the field. "A sip of sweet water," she mumbled incoherently. A cool drink from a clear mountain stream would douse the fire. Everything was getting hot. Even the saddle felt like it was on fire. Any second now, she expected her uniform to burst into flames.

"Someone please help me," she begged silently as she squeezed the reins, afraid the she would fall out of the saddle. What a sight for the crowd, she thought as she pictured herself being dragged across the field by her pony. The fans would cheer even louder, thinking it was part of the act.

Carolyn's worst nightmare was coming true. Surely, this had to be a dream like Bitter Creek. She blinked but nothing happened. She blinked hard two more times, still nothing. Suddenly, a voice in the confusion called her name. "Carolyn! Take the field!" the drum major shouted with a wide grin. Carolyn turned her head and leaned to the side. The sound of her name snapped her back to reality. What had seemed like hours in the saddle had only been a few seconds.

"But I'm not suppose to be on the field," she shouted back, remembering her instructions from the band director.

"Until we march off the field, it's our field. Hurry, up! Everyone's waiting," the drum major urged, this time waving his hand forward. "We've got a football game to play."

Carolyn took a deep breath and exhaled, regaining her composure. Her ears stopped ringing, and her head stopped spinning. She knew exactly what to do next. She would give the paying customers their money's worth. That's what Annie Oakley would do. The fans wanted a Wild West show, then that's what they were going to get. By the time, she was done with these greenhorns, the names of Carolyn Clark and Dixie would be on the marquee right under Johnny Unitas.

"Okay, girl! Ride the magic carousel," Carolyn commanded as she snapped the reins. Dixie galloped underneath the goalpost as if leading a cavalry charge and skidded to a stop at midfield. Carolyn lifted her hat high over her head and waved it at the crowd. "Dix-ee! Dix-ee!" chanted the fans in unison. Carolyn scanned the crowd who were on their feet and clapping. A mere tip of the hat was not going to be enough to satisfy them. It was time for an encore. Carolyn pulled back on the reins and leaned forward. "Up, girl," she barked, gently brushing her cheek against Dixie's neck. As Dixie reared high in the air and flailed her legs, the crowd cheered louder. Landing with a kick of her hind legs, she spun in a tight before charging to the far end zone. Applause roared down the stands like an avalanche. Any second Buffalo Bill Cody would be running onto the field with a pen in one hand and a contract in the other. A new star had been born, and Dixie was her name.

Back in her corner of the field, Carolyn slid off the saddle and nuzzled Dixie. "You were just fantastic out there. Maybe we should name you Cinderella. You are certainly the princess of this ball," she cooed, slipping her another treat. Dixie nodded and gave a loud high-pitched whinny that startled the nearby fans. They didn't know what she was saying, but they cheered again. It was love at first sight.

Once the game started, Carolyn stood next to her parents and waited for the Colts to score. Ground level wasn't the best seat in the stadium, and being a little shorter than the average jockey didn't help either. Sitting on Dixie improved the view but blocked the view of the fans behind her. When the teams moved to the far end of the stadium, it was impossible to see the action. To solve the problem, Mr. Clark brought along his Japanese transistor radio. To listen to the game, he plugged in the earpiece and stuck the radio in his shirt pocket. The radio announcer, high above the field in the press box, saw every play unfolding. If a player was running down the field, he knew it would be a touchdown seconds before the player crossed the goal line. If a kick was in the air, he knew if it was headed between the goalposts.

Wanting to ride at a moment's notice, Carolyn and her father worked out a series of hand signals to communicate over the crowd noise. A thumb's up was saddle up because the Colts were threatening to score. A thumb's down was dismount because the Colts weren't threatening to score anymore. Two thumb's up was the signal to ride like the wind because the Colts have scored.

A few minutes into the game, Carolyn got the first thumb's up of the season as the Colts drove to the goal line. Electricity surged through her body as she vaulted into the saddle and watched her father fumble with his hands in a nervous fit. When the crowd started to cheer madly, Mr. Clark slowly raised both hands in clenched fists. Carolyn tensed in the saddle. Suddenly, the crowed groaned, and Mr. Clark turned his thumbs down. The Colts had fumbled the ball to the Lions. Carolyn climbed out of the saddle to continue waiting. The scene was repeated twice in the first quarter and once in the second quarter. Instead of riding a carousel, Carolyn was riding an elevator. "Up and down and all around, and one, two, three, Colts kick," she mumbled to herself every time she had to dismount. The routine sounded more like the latest teenage dance craze than a football game.

At halftime the Colts had no points, and Dixie had no laps around the track. When the players headed for the locker room, the crowd clapped politely. A few fickle fans booed. Everybody in the stadium was frustrated. By now they had expected at least one touchdown. Even Johnny U seemed to be frowning. The hot-handed and cool-headed quarterback was having a bad day throwing the football. He threw high when he should have thrown low and threw low when he should have thrown high. When he did finally throw a perfect pass, the receiver dropped the ball. Johnny's passes clunked around the field as if he was throwing horseshoes instead of footballs. His talking hands

223

were stone silent, and his team of ten Colts was not pulling together.

The halftime show featured the marching band, and Carolyn watched with special interest. The band director had suggested using her and Dixie in some of the musical numbers. With every note, the high-stepping band proved why they were one of the finest bands in the country. They were a high-octane blend of music and movement as they strutted up and down the field in those great looking western outfits. Every fan would admit that the band was worth the price of a ticket even if the Colts lost the game. Too bad the band wasn't around at the turn of the century, Carolyn thought. They could have been the opening act in Buffalo Bill's Wild West Show. As the band finished their performance, Carolyn clapped and then glanced at the gigantic scoreboard behind the end zone seats. There was nothing to see but zeroes.

"Mom, do you think we'll score any points in the second half?" she asked nervously.

"I really don't know. It's all part of the game. Sometimes, they'll score no points, and sometimes they'll score them in bunches. That's what makes it fun. You don't know what's going to happen," Mrs. Clark replied, sounding a little bit like Johnny U.

"Just have patience," Mr. Clark added. "Sometimes, it takes a while to get comfortable on the field. It's like a horse at a new track. Once, he feels at home, it's off to the races. You'll see."

224

Since Carolyn didn't know a lot about football, she could only hope that her father's knowledge about horses applied to Baltimore Colts. Turning to Dixie, she voiced her own opinion on the game. "I hate to say it, but I'll go down in football history as the girl who jinxed the great Johnny U. I knew all that talk about horse hands would be bad luck. Next time I'll give him a rabbit's foot instead of advice." Dixie seemed to agree. She stared straight ahead without a sound.

When the Colts took the field for the second half, the crowd was back on its feet. But once again, they cheered in vain. The Colts offense stalled, unable to move the ball across mid-field. On this summer-like day, Johnny U. had icicles hanging from the ends of his fingers. But midway through the quarter, his hands started to thaw. Passes spiraled with deadly accuracy into the hands of receivers. Yard by yard, the Colts moved downfield within the shadow of the goalpost. Seconds later, Alan "The Horse" Ameche plunged over from the one yard line for a touchdown as he did in the championship game. The referee raised both arms in the air to signal a touchdown, and the crowd erupted in celebration. Carolyn looked at her father who was holding both thumbs above his head, but this time she didn't need a signal.

"Giddy-up, girl," she shouted wildly as she flicked the reins and pressed her heels. Dixie bolted down the track for their first official ride as a Baltimore Colt.

Dixie went quickly to a full gallop. Her stride was smooth and measured; her breathing strong and steady. As the crowd cheered, she responded with a surge of power. While her legs pumped like giant pistons, her steps remained soft as if floating above the track. Any second Carolyn expected her pony to sprout wings and soar high above the stadium to join the small planes pulling advertisement banners.

Carolyn leaned forward as Dixie charged fearlessly towards the closed end of the stadium. The air was cool and dank in the foreboding shadows of the triple-tiered stands. The howling cheers swirled like a trapped cyclone, growing louder with Dixie's every step. Carolyn's plan was to ride though the danger zone as quickly as possible.

Just as the noise reached an ear-splitting pitch, the stadium went silent. Carolyn was suddenly riding in a dream. There was no sound only movement, movement that slowed with each passing second. The faster Dixie charged, the slower she ran. Instead of floating off the ground, she was sinking in a quagmire of cinder. Carolyn pressed her heels hard and snapped the reins. Dixie stretched her legs as far as they would go. White plumes of cold breath streamed from her nostrils, but she ran even slower. Another bout of horse fever, Carolyn thought. Pulling hard with her left hand, she steered Dixie through the sharp turn at the end of the oval and headed down the straightaway on the other side of the field. Blinding sunlight was

226

drawing nearer. A few steps later, Dixie crossed the divide between darkness and light. Once again, she was running hard and moving fast. With the noise of the crowd flooding her ears, Carolyn reached up and touched the brim of her hat. She smiled as a warm breeze splashed her face. The fever had been broken. The scoring drought was officially over.

Johnny U proved better than his word. The Colts scored a total of three touchdowns within twelve minutes. After each score, Mr. Clark gave the thumbs-up, and Carolyn was off to the races. On the next two rides, there were no evil forces lurking at the closed end of the stadium. It was still dark and cold, but the warmth of the fans made it seem like a sunny day in the park. Along the way, Carolyn slowed Dixie to a trot and stood in the saddle, waving to the crowd. They responded by blowing kisses.

After the third touchdown lap, Dixie was panting and starting to sweat. Her pristine coat was spotted with flecks of cinder from the track, giving her the appearance of an Appaloosa. Carolyn knew it was time to slow the carousel. Even she was beginning to feel the effects of the heat. With the temperature in the middle 80's, the wool blend uniform was not as cool as it looked. She wondered how cowboys out west survived without shorts and t-shirts.

To the delight of the fans who thought it was part of the act, Carolyn trotted Dixie off the field with a tip of the hat. Underneath the stands, Mr.

Clark was waiting with buckets of water for a quick sponge bath and a long drink. Back on the field, Carolyn hoped for a quick end to the game. To her delight, Johnny U heard her silent plea. There was no more scoring. The Colts had tamed the Lions 21 to 9.

When the gun sounded to end the game, Dixie took her victory lap. Even though her gallop had slowed, there was still a bounce to her step. Seeing Dixie on the move, fans gathered along the rail next to the field. They stretched their arms to touch their new hero, but Carolyn kept a safe distance. Dixie didn't bite or kick, but she was tiring. Carolyn didn't want a well-meaning fan to startle her. Along the route, Carolyn leaned over to shake a few hands, but mostly just tipped her hat and smiled. That was the proper way for a cowgirl to thank the audience at the end of a show.

Around the backstretch, Carolyn brought Dixie to a walk. On the field, players from both teams huddled in small groups. Fans lingered along the front row of seats for an autograph, a picture, or a quick chat. For the most part, the stadium emptied as quickly as it filled it. But across the field, Carolyn noticed a crowd gathering where the horse trailer was parked.

Carolyn halted Dixie behind the goalpost, content to wait until the last doggies headed out to pasture. Hunching forward in the saddle, she breathed a sigh of relief and wiped her brow with her good luck bandana that had been stuffed in her pants pocket. It had been a hard day's ride, exhausting but deeply satisfying. There were no accidents, and Dixie had her day in the spotlight. In a few minutes, Mr. Clark would load the trailer, and then it was homeward bound. This time Carolyn looked forward to the ride. She couldn't wait to hear the tour guide replay today's game. With new material, she was certain her father would be most entertaining.

The herd at the tunnel entrance was thinning when a doggie bolted across the field towards Carolyn. She immediately recognized the breed. "There's a policeman who needs to see you right away," Mrs. Clark shouted, waving her arms for Carolyn to hurry up.

"Did we do something wrong?" Carolyn asked with a worried frown.

"Just go see for yourself," her mother replied calmly.

Carolyn jumped out of the saddle and briskly walked Dixie towards the tunnel. What could possibly ruin such a perfect day, she wondered. As she drew closer, a man forced his way through the crowd and approached her. The words "Baltimore Police" were embroidered across the front of his cap, and a large silver badge was pinned to the chest of his windbreaker. Carolyn was worried. Any time the marshal called, it was bad news. It was either be out of town by sundown or spend the night in the calaboose.

"Miss Clark," the man inquired politely. "My name is Officer John, and I'm with the Police Boys Club. Every Sunday I bring to the boys to the game and…"

"If it's about riding on the field, it won't happen again. I promise," Carolyn interrupted, hoping to plead her case before the evidence could be presented.

Officer John blinked and straightened his neck, clueless about Carolyn's comment. "As I was saying," he continued politely. "You and your pony were all they talked about. I was hoping you could take a few minutes to meet the boys and sign a few autographs."

"Oh, yes, meet the boys. It would be a pleasure," Carolyn said hesitantly, forcing a weak smile. She had already met fifty-five thousand strangers. Now she had to meet the boys. They were probably like the boys in school who teased her about horses. But maybe this group would be different since they had the law on their side. Even if they weren't, it was part of the job so it had to be done. The words of the team's public relations director echoed in her ear. "Carolyn, a good time for the fans is good business, and good business is our business." True to the cowgirl code, Carolyn put a smile on her face and prepared to meet her guests.

Under the watchful eye of Officer John and his assistant Officer Jim, the boys lined up in an orderly fashion. Young and old, they all looked the same in

230

their white t-shirts with a huge blue police badge in the center and the words "Baltimore Police Boys Club." Some wanted autographs, but most wanted to touch either Dixie or Carolyn, just like the fans at the rail. Carolyn didn't mind the tugging on her uniform, but she was worried that a yank or a slap might spook Dixie. Arms reached out and waved in the air. Carolyn tried to shoo them away, but there was just too many. Dixie, the true southern belle, stood politely and accepted each hand without a flinch. "Boys, be careful when you touch her and don't give her any snacks," Carolyn cautioned. The brown paper bags with leftover popcorn and peanuts were quickly closed.

One by one, the boys stepped forward with questions. At times, they came in rapid-fire succession. How long have you been riding? Where did you buy your pony? How did you train your pony? And the question on everyone's lips, can I ride your pony?

Carolyn did her best to answer each question in three words or less. Finally, after about fifteen minutes, the line was gone except for one young boy. Slowly, he shuffled forward to within a few inches of Carolyn, tilted his head back, and stared into her blue eyes. From the mean look on this cowpoke's face, Carolyn knew he had some serious business to attend.

"Are you a real cowgirl?" the boy asked bluntly.

Carolyn paused and thought for a second. She had been asking herself that question for the last year. Only she never had an answer until today. "I got a horse, a saddle, a Stetson, and a paying job, so as of today, I'm officially a cowgirl," she replied cheerfully. The boy seemed satisfied with the answer, standing silent as if gathering his thoughts. In fact, he was gathering courage. "Do you have a boyfriend?" he asked shyly, still looking up at Carolyn.

"No, but I bet a handsome fella like you has a girlfriend," Carolyn kidded.

"Not until I met you," the boy replied with a sheepish grin.

Carolyn had a sneaky suspicion that answer was coming. "Well, I ain't ready to settle down with any cowpoke just yet. I still got a lot of ridin' to do before I tie the knot. No, hard feelings now," Carolyn replied in her Texas twang, trying to make light of the moment.

"I understand. No hard feelings," the boy said with a frown.

"Why, don't worry. Someday you'll find yourself some pretty little cowgirl to twirl around the dance floor. I just know it," Carolyn said warmly.

"I don't dance very well," the boy replied sadly.

"You're in luck 'cause neither do I. Sometimes I think I got two left feet stuffed in these boots," Carolyn said extending her hand. The young cowpoke shook hands and laughed along with Carolyn. Someone whistled, and the boy ran to catch up with his friends. The Carolyn Clark Fan Club had another life-long member.

Officer John thanked Carolyn for her time and invited her to visit the club as an honorary member. As the boys mingled in the parking lot, Carolyn could hear them asking Officer John to buy a horse for the club. When the bus pulled away, she tipped her hat and waved. "Happy trails to you until we meet again," she sang softly. She had to admit they were a well-behaved group of young men.

Wearily, Carolyn trudged to the trailer alongside Dixie, still chuckling at the last conversation. "Dixie, as cowboys like to say, we've been rode hard and put up wet. Time for us to head for the bunkhouse," she lamented. A long soak in a tub of hot water with a bar of perfumed soap would be the perfect ending to the perfect day for both girls. Thank goodness, Paddy had promised to bathe Dixie.

Back at the farmhouse, the phone was ringing off the hook when Carolyn walked through the front door. Her biggest fan was waiting impatiently to speak with Baltimore's newest sports star.

"You and Dixie were just fantastic," Maggie gushed.

"But how would you know?" Carolyn asked, wondering how news could spread so fast.

"My father was at the game. He has tickets for the whole season. I told him to watch for you and

233

let me know everything that happens," Maggie blabbered. "I even listened to the game on the radio. When you were introduced, I jumped from the sofa and started cheering like I was at the game. Of course, mom told me to be careful so that I didn't get hurt."

"Well, Dixie did all the work," Carolyn responded modestly

"But you and Dixie are a team. You both did all the work," Maggie replied. "And you know, I've been thinking about today's game. I have a business offer for you. We can talk about it on Saturday."

"A what? Not another business..." Carolyn shrieked as the sentence ended in a dial tone. "Can't wait 'til Saturday," she muttered under her breath with a smirk. The last time she heard those words she ended up with a hired hand. "Paaard-neeers, forever," she drawled, echoing Maggie's words to close the deal.

After a late supper, Carolyn dragged herself up the stairs to her bedroom. Her bunk had never looked more inviting, but there was one more chore to finish. No chore was more important than homework. The "homework clause" was an official part of the mascot contract. If the grades slipped, the Colts had to find a new mascot. Carolyn and Dixie would be out of a job, no questions and no second chances. It was a fair deal to Carolyn, but tonight homework was going to be an uphill climb on a very steep and rocky trail. The thought of reading a chapter about man and machine during the Industrial Revolution produced an extended yawn. Where was the chapter on cowboys and cowgirls of the American West, she wondered as she opened her history book. To stay awake, she needed to read about real horses instead of iron horses. Minutes later, her head bobbed and her eyes fluttered. The bed was now calling out her name. After a few scribbled notes, the assignment was complete.

Carolyn slipped between the fresh sheets, pulled the blanket up to her chin and closed her eyes. But sleep would not come easy. One minute she was falling asleep at her desk in a hard, uncomfortable chair, and the next minute she was lying wide-awake in a feather bed. Replaying the day's events only made her more energized. Maybe counting fans would make her drowsy. The trick always worked with sheep in cartoons. Carolyn squeezed her eyelids. Instantly, thousands of fans rushed at her with pens and paper in hand, screaming for autographs. The line stretched from her bedroom door to the parking lot of the stadium.

Carolyn bolted upright and shuddered. Counting fans was definitely not the answer. Rubbing her eyes, she gazed around the room. A streak of pale moonlight beamed across the room. Carolyn followed the light from the window to the closet door. "Bulls-eye," she said sleepily. Her uniform once again glowed with a ghostly presence. "Ride the magic carousel," she whispered repeatedly until her voice faded. As she stared at the dull light, her eyes slammed shut. She fell back on the pillow with a vision of her and Dixie riding on a dream.

Chapter 12 – Some Phony Pony Baloney

The sports section from Monday morning's newspaper was waiting for Carolyn on the kitchen table. The front-page headline boldly declared yesterday's victory. On the inside page, a much smaller headline proclaimed: "New Colts Score Big with Fans." A short article about the new mascots included a picture of Carolyn and Dixie racing around the oval. Carolyn gagged on her spoonful of cereal. Her secret life had been exposed to the public. But on second thought, there was no reason to worry. Not too many middle school students read the sports page. Carolyn didn't give the article another thought until her homeroom classmates gave her a standing ovation. After the applause faded, the principal took to the airwaves and noted the achievement of Miss Clark and her pet pony during morning announcements. Someone had even cut out the article and posted it on the school bulletin board.

Carolyn smiled and thanked everyone for the kind remarks. She patiently answered everyone's questions, remembering the words of the Colts public relations director. Much to her relief, the hysteria died down quickly. On Monday, everybody in school wanted an autographed picture. By Wednesday, only her classmates had any questions about the mascot job. On Friday, only a few friends stopped by her desk to chat about homework and the weekend.

On Saturday morning, Carolyn was glad to be back in the ring with Dixie and Maggie. She enjoyed being a hometown hero for a day, but preferred to be a hometown horsewoman. After all, Dixie was the real star of the show. The attention would have been much nicer if her classmates wanted to be her friend because she was Carolyn Clark, horsewoman, not Carolyn Clark, Baltimore Colt.

Since the start of school, the summer week at the Jolly Jockey had been condensed into a Saturday. Maggie had her riding lesson in the mid-morning and then hung around the farm for the rest of the day. The only difference was that now she wasn't getting paid for any work, but that didn't

238

matter. The Jolly Jockey was still her summer dream, and she was determined to ride that dream for as long as she could. There was nothing else an urban cowgirl could want.

"Quit and cross your stirrups," Carolyn barked to Maggie. Maggie pulled the stirrups across the saddle and then swung her legs in a series of exercises to develop balance and strengthen muscles. To advance as a rider, Maggie would have to learn to use her legs to communicate with her horse. Strong legs delivered a loud and clear message, and Maggie was getting stronger every week.

After the lesson, Maggie retrieved her knapsack from the tack room. By the time she entered the family room, Carolyn had the TV warmed up. The Buddy Deane show was minutes away. Maggie plopped down on the couch without a word, her knapsack at her side. Throughout the morning, Maggie was unusually quiet which meant that she was busy thinking about her latest scheme. Carolyn had learned from previous deals with Maggie not to ask. She hoped that Maggie had forgotten about their conversation after opening day, but that was wishful thinking. The knapsack was the clue. The only things Maggie carried around the farm were a violin case, a canvass music bag, and a cardboard record box. Carolyn wondered about the contents of the knapsack, she didn't want to ruin the suspense by asking. It would out come out in due time.

"Ready to get down to business," Carolyn gushed as Buddy announced the first song.

"Exactly what I had in mind, the business of business," Maggie replied eagerly as she unzipped her knapsack and pulled out a scrapbook and a note pad. Carolyn winced at the sight. The moment was at hand. "You're the biggest thing to hit my school since saddle shoes," Maggie said. "All week everybody was talking about Carolyn and Dixie. Of course, I had to cash in on your celebrity status and tell that you were a good friend of mine. And of course, nobody believed me. They couldn't see any reason why a celebrity like you would hang around a cripple like me. But that's another story."

Opening the scrapbook, Maggie removed Monday's sports article. "Miss Clark, this is just the beginning of great things for you and your pony," she said enthusiastically as she held the newspaper clipping in front of her face. "What you need to promote your career is a business manager, and I believe I'm the right person for the job."

Carolyn raised her eyebrows and rolled her eyes in mock surprise. She had to admit that it really wasn't a bad idea. "Dixie's the star of the show. Go talk to her. Maybe she needs an agent," she joked as she sat down on the couch.

Maggie wasn't laughing. She pressed her lips together and stared hard at Carolyn. "This is your future here. This is serious business. I need to talk and talk now," Maggie responded sternly. The tone of her voice got Carolyn's attention. Maggie was sounding just like her mother.

"Okay, you win. You've got two minutes," Carolyn declared. "Then it's back to the show. I was hoping to get some dance time today."

Maggie smiled cutely and flipped opened her notebook. "I was thinking that if you and Dixie become full-fledged celebrities, we could schedule personal appearances to raise money for the riding academy. If things really get rolling, we can sell souvenirs and put the money back into our non-profit company."

"Now that's an idea that I like," Carolyn said eagerly. "Who could say no to such a worthy cause?"

"Of course, we'll need a business plan. First, I could be your business manager, and then, maybe, your business partner," Maggie blurted.

"Congratulations on your promotion," Carolyn roared with laughter. "In two minutes, you went from manager to partner."

Maggie was unfazed by the comment and immediately began reading from her notepad. Carolyn listened intently as Maggie spoke about budgets, expenses, fundraising, special equipment, and another pony. An academy for handicapped children was Carolyn's dream, but she never saw herself as a businesswoman. She needed Maggie's business savvy to run a successful riding academy.

"Let's see how the next couple of games go. If I'm still a member of the Colts by then, I'll make a decision about a business manger," Carolyn replied. Fame was a fickle. In a week, she could go from heroic to hapless, and their business plans would be back on the drawing board. "But either way," Carolyn added. "We're definitely doing the academy, somehow and some way."

"Sounds good to me, pardner," Maggie said with a handshake and a smile. "Now, let's get to the show." Maggie grabbed Carolyn's hand and lifted her from the couch. They lined up and faced each other, their steps mimicking the dancers on the screen. The Deaners were doing The Stroll, the latest of the teenage line dances. In the background, the do-wop vocal group, The Diamonds, was exhorting teenagers to grab a partner and stroll down the center aisle. When Maggie strolled into the kitchen to get a snack, Carolyn peeked at the scrapbook. The pages were blank except for the last one. Taped to the top of the page was a hand-written note with horse doodles that said "Reserved."

"Have a picture for your last page?" Carolyn asked when Maggie returned.

"Not yet. It's a special place for a special picture. It's out there somewhere. I just have to find it," Maggie replied with a mischievous grin as she pointed to the window.

"You're sounding more like Paddy everyday," Carolyn said with a shrug. There was no telling what Maggie had in mind, and Carolyn didn't want to risk asking about it. It might be another business deal.

On Sunday, the Colts lost to the Chicago Bears by a score of 26 to 21. In many ways, the game was a repeat of the previous Sunday except for the outcome. Despite the heroic efforts of Johnny U, the Colts could not pull out a last minute victory. They scored three touchdowns which resulted in three trips around the oval. Each time the fans greeted Carolyn and Dixie with thunderous applause. Win or lose, the fans always stayed loyal to their team. If they couldn't cheer for the players, then they would cheer for the mascots. After the game, Carolyn overheard Johnny U talking to reporters. "The Bears played a tremendous football game today," he said in congratulating the winners. "But I could have done a better job of driving my team of Colts. I threw some of those passes as if I had hooves instead of hands." The reporters laughed, and Johnny cracked a quick smile. That was typical Johnny U, a humble winner and a gracious loser. Carolyn chuckled at Johnny's choice of words. The conversation with the press had a familiar ring to it. Maybe after the season, she would offer Johnny free riding lessons. It would be good publicity for the Colts and the riding academy.

As Carolyn walked Dixie to the tunnel, fans were already lined and waiting to meet the newest Colts. The line looked much longer and younger than it did last week. Today Mr. Tuttle was mingling with the crowd which was odd. Usually, he was in the locker room arranging interviews with players and reporters.

"Great game, Carolyn, even though we lost," Tuttle said with a pat on the back. "But out here everybody is a winner. You're the hottest sports story in town."

"And I thought it was just my wool uniform," Carolyn replied sarcastically, knowing that Tuttle would never miss an opportunity for free publicity.

"Parents and their kids have been lining up since halftime to meet you and Dixie," Tuttle replied, ignoring Carolyn's comment.

"Then I guess I'd better strike while the iron is hot," Carolyn stated smartly as she went to greet her fans.

"Now that's the attitude to have," Tuttle declared merrily. "Today's autograph is tomorrow's ticket."

"Colts Lose But Mascots Win Again" was the inside headline to Monday's sports section. It was no wonder that parents who weren't football fans were driving to the stadium to meet the mascots. In the article, the writer compared Carolyn and Dixie to Dale Evans and Buttermilk with pictures of the duos next to each other. Carolyn was flattered by the comparison, even though she suspected that Tuttle was behind it. She cut it out and stuck it on her bulletin board. No doubt, it would pop up in Maggie's scrapbook.

For the rest of the week, Carolyn weighed Maggie's offer. Mr. Clark had an agent who was paid to find rides for his clients, but her situation was quite different. What could a business manager or agent do for her? She was an entertainer, not really an athlete. Twenty dollars a game was plenty. She didn't need someone to walk into Tuttle's office and ask for a pay raise or more playing time. If anyone needed an agent it was Dixie. She was the athlete in the act. On any Sunday, she ran for more yards than all of the running backs in the league combined. But Dixie didn't need an agent, she had Carolyn to look out for her best interests. And no one was more qualified for the job.

With the team on the road for the next two games in Detroit and Chicago, Carolyn was sure the publicity would fade away. On Saturday, she was going to tell Maggie that she didn't need a manger, agent, or partner. But Maggie was more than welcome to join the mascot team and come to the games. Those plans changed drastically with a surprise visit from Mr. Tuttle on late Friday afternoon. Carolyn had been looking forward to a quiet weekend of TV westerns, Buddy Deane, and homework.

"The Pony Express has arrived. Just wanted to drop off some things before I meet the team at the airport," Tuttle declared as he squeezed through the front door with a large box and mailbag in his arms. Rushing to the kitchen, he dropped the box and dumped the bag on the table. Letters addressed to Carolyn and Dixie spilled out in a pile over a foot

245

high. Since the debut of Carolyn and Dixie, the team's business office had been flooded with requests for autographs from the new mascots. In two weeks, Carolyn and Dixie had received more fan mail than some players received in a year.

"I knew the pony idea was a winner," Tuttle said proudly. "We just needed the right horse and the right rider, and we got both."

Carolyn opened a few of the letters that were stacked on top. All were requests for an autographed picture. Some even had questions for either Carolyn or Dixie. From the writing, Carolyn could tell that most of the letters were from younger fans. There weren't too many grownups fans who signed their names in crayon. Carolyn thumbed through the pile and randomly inspected the envelopes. The return addresses were as far away as Illinois and Michigan, places where the Colts had already played.

"You mean all of this is my mail?" Carolyn asked in disbelief.

"Not all of it. Some of it is addressed to Dixie," Tuttle replied with a chuckle. "Like I said, I found the right rider. I just hope she's the right writer."

"You mean I've got to answer all of these letters?" Carolyn asked somberly. She worried about what would happen when the Colts played the teams from Los Angeles and San Francisco. There could thousands of letters in a pile that reached the ceiling.

246

Tuttle saw the worried look on Carolyn's face. "Just answer them at your own pace. There's no deadline," he said reassuringly. "This is the fun part of the job. It's a chance for you to connect with your fans. You're a star."

Carolyn remembered the time that she wrote a fan letter to Gail Davis, the TV Annie Oakley. Everyday she raced home from school to check the mail, looking for a postmark from Hollywood, California. When the letter finally arrived, she carefully opened it and gently lifted the autographed picture. Rubbing her fingers along the edge of the photo, she read the inscription over and over until she was reading between the lines. It was exciting to think that her favorite starlet had touched the same picture. It was even more fun to wonder if Ms. Davis had thought about the person who requested the autograph. Surely, a letter from The Jolly Jockey Farm in Maryland must have made her curious about the writer. This time Tuttle was right. Connecting with your favorite star was a thrill for fans of all ages. The only problem was that Carolyn didn't see herself as a star. Dixie was the star of the show. But since Dixie couldn't write, the job belonged to Carolyn.

"But what will I send them?" she asked.

"Since you're on a football team, you send them a football card," Tuttle replied with glee as he opened the box tucked under his arm. The box was filled with pre-stamped postcards that featured a black and white picture of Carolyn and Dixie at

Memorial Stadium taken by the team photographer on opening day. "Just sign the card, fill out the address, and drop it in the mail. When you run out of cards, I'll get you some more. The next batch will be in color."

After Tuttle left, she counted the letters. There were already a hundred and fifty-two members in the Carolyn and Dixie fan club. Back and forth, she looked at the pile of letters and then the box of postcards. There was only one solution to the problem.

On Saturday afternoon, Carolyn waited anxiously for her new business manager to enter the family room. "Well, buckaroo, I thought about your business proposal, and it's a deal," Carolyn said excitedly, not immediately telling Maggie about the sudden change of heart.

"Super! When do we get started?" Maggie asked eagerly, placing her scrapbook on the coffee table.

"Right now," Carolyn replied as she led Maggie to the kitchen. "As of today, you are officially president of the Carolyn and Dixie fan club."

"Wow!" proclaimed Maggie as she stared at the mound of letters. "I knew that you and Dixie were going to be stars. You'll be number one on the charts before the season is over," she added, referring to how rock and roll songs were rated for play on the radio.

With the Buddy Deane Show in the background, the girls went to work, digging into the pile and sorting the letters. In addition to requests for autographs, there were requests for pony rides and school visits. There was even a request for one of Dixie's horseshoes. While Maggie answered questions on the back of the cards, Carolyn did the signatures. Every member of her fan club was getting a genuine autograph for a souvenir.

On Sunday morning, Maggie returned to finish the job. By late afternoon, the last card was signed and addressed. With Mr. Clark home for the day, Maggie eagerly accepted the invitation to stay for dinner. To her delight, the only difference between lunch and dinner was the room. Lunch was in the kitchen, but dinner was always in the dining room. To horse people, Sunday dinner was a formal occasion, a chance to polish up the antique silverware and dust-off great grandma's fine china.

The Sunday meal was always the same, a pioneer feast of fried chicken, mashed potatoes with plenty of thick gravy, fresh string beans, applesauce and corn bread. But for Carolyn, this feast was a famine. Her hand ached so bad from signing autographs that she could barely lift her fork. The price of fame was already taking its toll, but she decided to bear her pain in silence. Meanwhile, Maggie couldn't wait to sit down with Mr. Clark and discuss her new job as business manager. In between bites of food, she chattered endlessly about her ideas to promote Carolyn and Dixie.

This time around Mr. Clark was a captive audience. He just nodded as he slowly chewed the small portions of food on his plate. As a jockey, he had to constantly watch his weight at the expense of a home-cooked meal. While not doing a lot of serious eating, he was doing some serious listening and thinking. When Maggie dove into a plate of cherry pie and vanilla ice cream, Mr. Clark saw his chance. "What you need is a pony-mobile to ride to the games," he suggested in a dead serious tone. "Take the back seat out of that big, four-door sedan, and you'll have enough room for Dixie. Going to the games would be like driving in a parade. People could stand along the streets and wave."

"A brilliant idea, Mr. Clark," Maggie shouted with glee. "But why be like a parade when we can be a parade!" With that comment, Maggie and Mr. Clark were off to the races in an exchange of ridiculous ideas.

Carolyn just nodded her head and rolled her eyes. None of it made any sense to her. The fun was becoming annoying. She couldn't be sure that her father and Maggie were joking, knowing their personalities. Why would Dixie need a vehicle to carry her in a parade, she wondered. Horses were made to carry people. Sedans were not made to carry horses.

Carolyn was ready to open her mouth and put an end to the silliness, but decided not to spoil the fun. As she finished a second helping of desert, Maggie and her father were now engaged in a can-you-top this contest. At Christmas, Dixie would appear in the Christmas parade as the newest member of Santa's sleigh team, and Carolyn would be a jolly elf. For the Saint Patrick's Day parade, Dixie would wear a green blanket, green pompoms, and a green top hat; and Carolyn would be a leprechaun. The annual Easter and the Fourth of July parades had Carolyn and Dixie in costume. Of course, Dixie would arrive in the pony-mobile for all events.

By the time Walter beeped his horn, Carolyn's career had been planned for the coming year. When Maggie headed for the door, Carolyn expected to receive an appointment book and a business card from her new manager.

After dinner Carolyn walked outside for some fresh air and headed straight for her fence. Climbing to the top rail, she took her usual seat to enjoy the last few hours of daylight. "Home, home on the range where seldom is heard a discouraging word," she whispered wistfully. Today the fence was a wooden chain that connected her to the family, the farm, and her future. And yet today, she came to the fence to be disconnected from the family, the farm, and her future.

Staring into the distant horizon was always good therapy. Blue skies and green forests were always a soothing sight. The warm breeze on a cool evening was like a gentle hug from Mother Nature. In the great outdoors, problems seemed to fade into the twilight. Was the sky a bluish pink or a pinkish blue, Carolyn wondered. Was an Indian Summer really Indian or really summer? Those were the questions that required some serious thought on a lazy Sunday afternoon, not what parade she would be attending. So much had happened so quickly over the last month, Carolyn wasn't sure what to think. Somehow every thought circled back to the Baltimore Colts, and right now, she wasn't sure if she really wanted to be a Baltimore Colt.

"Got room for another rail bird," a familiar voice sounded behind Carolyn.

"Ah, mom, there's always room for you. Pull up a seat," Carolyn responded warmly. Mrs. Clark climbed to the top of the rail and balanced herself next to Carolyn.

"With all the commotion at dinner, you didn't have too much to say about your publicity campaign. Thought you might want to talk about your future with someone who would listen," Mrs. Clark said sincerely.

"It's all of this stuff about being a Baltimore Colt that's bothering me," Carolyn said glumly. "It seems that everybody wants to be my friend because I'm some kind of celebrity, not because I'm Carolyn Clark. I now have a business manager and an unofficial fan club. Even Dad's getting into the act with this pony-mobile nonsense. It's becoming a bit too much. Everybody sees me, but I'm invisible to my friends and family."

Mrs. Clark listened intently and then put her arm around Carolyn's shoulder. "The easy answer is that it's part of life. The hard answer is trying to explain what part," Mrs. Clark said softly. "This is just one moment of your life. There are thousands of moments ahead of you. You should just try to enjoy being a mascot as much as you can. Fame and fortune are fleeting. Today's heroes are tomorrow's has-beens. Just look at your favorite TV shows. They're on the air for a season or two then replaced by new shows. Actors and actresses move on with their careers, but they always have fond memories of what they did."

"I never really looked at it that way. It is kind of fun to see everybody getting involved, but I want to be remembered as Carolyn Clark, horsewoman, not Carolyn Clark, football hero," Carolyn said dolefully.

"Well, I guarantee you'll be remembered for more than being a mascot," Mrs. Clark stated bluntly. "This mascot craze is just a fad. It won't last forever. You have your whole life ahead of you. One day, you'll be telling your grandchildren about the legend of Carolyn Clark and Dixie because no one will have remembered. It will be something you'll always be proud of. Now enjoy the sunset. I'll see you back in the bunkhouse, and we'll treat ourselves to another bowl of ice cream."

Carolyn watched the sun sink below the ridgeline. For a brief moment, the hilltop was ablaze with a blinding orange light. And then as if a switch had been flipped, darkness covered the valley. Carolyn clapped politely as the curtain

253

came down. She jumped from the fence and slowly headed for home, whistling "Happy Trails." The sunset never looked more beautiful and the light in the kitchen never more inviting. Light into darkness and darkness into light was the way of the world, she mused. Mothers of all types have a way of making things better, whether it was with words or the weather.

The Colts won their two road games and returned home with high expectations from the fans. The city was being whipped into championship frenzy, but the season was still young. The next home game was a 38 to 21 win over the Green Bay Packers. Carolyn and Dixie had a busy day with six laps around the field as the Colts scored five touchdowns and a field goal. Johnny U and the Colts were red hot. Their record stood at 4 wins and 1 loss. After the game, fans near the tunnel were already talking about a second championship.

Heeding the advice of her mother, Carolyn cheerfully greeted her legion of young fans with a wave of her hat and a broad smile. From now on, she was only going to worry about making herself happy. Everyone else would have to fend for themselves. She liked horses more than football, and that's what she was going to give her fans. They came to see Dixie, not the Baltimore Colts. "Pony power to the people," she whispered under her breath as she grabbed a pen. To Carolyn's surprise, the words came right out of the blue. She liked them so much that for the rest of the day she signed autographs with "Pony Power Rules, Carolyn and Dixie."

Today's game also marked Maggie's debut as unofficial usherette. Dressed in a blue and white western shirt with a royal blue skirt, she handed out picture cards and answered questions about the mascots. With her cowgirl hat scrunched squarely on top of her head, she was easy to spot in a crowd. Annie Oakley had Buffalo Bill Cody as a pitchman; Carolyn had Maggie. Even Mr. Clark got into the family act. The jolly jockey leaned against the trailer and regaled older fans with his hair-raising tales of famous horse races.

On the ride home, Carolyn made a few mental notes about her job. First, the Clark family, to include Paddy and Maggie, would officially be known as the Pony Power Team. Second, she had to ask Mr. Tuttle for more picture cards. She expected a sack of mail from Wisconsin, home state of the Packers, to arrive at the end of the week. Third, and most important, she had a wonderful time by simply being herself.

As usual, Monday started a normal week at the farm. The first two days of the week were schoolwork and farm chores, a pleasant repetition that formed Carolyn's week. But on Wednesday morning, a bombshell landed on the doorstep of the farmhouse that shattered the daily routine. The day would be known forever in Jolly Jockey history as "Black Wednesday."

Mrs. Clark wasn't surprised to see the police car pull up to the house. Recently, there had been a rash of burglaries in the area. An out-of-state gang was targeting farm equipment, to include equine items. An unlocked tack room was an open invitation for thieves. Saddles and bridles worth thousands of dollars could be easily sold on the black market. Expecting a courtesy visit, she casually strolled out to meet the officer.

Sheriff Sims quickly introduced himself and proceeded to official business. "Ma'am, I have a search and seizure order for stolen property on the premises of the Jolly Jockey Farm," he stated in an official voice. "Is this the address for the business operating under the name of the Jolly Jockey, owned by Mr. and Mrs. William Clark of the same address?

"Yes, this is the home of the Jolly Jockey, and, yes, I am Dorothy Clark, one of the owners," Mrs. Clark responded with mild surprise. "Perhaps, you can tell me what this is all about?"

"Ma'am, I'm looking for a white Welsh Pony, known as Dixie. The animal is to be seized and secured by the court until the hearing to determine ownership."

"The pony is in her stall, but I can assure you this is a mistake. We have owned the pony for over five years," Mrs. Clark said nervously.

"Ma'am, the pony was reported stolen from a horse farm in New York. It seems that the recent publicity about the pony attracted the attention of someone claiming to be the real owner."

"Well, I going to have to speak to our lawyer about this," Mrs. Clark protested, becoming quickly annoyed with the sheriff's official attitude.

"That's your right, ma'am, but I'm here to serve legal papers and take custody of the horse until the hearing," Sims said as he handed the court documents to Mrs. Clark.

Mrs. Clark hurriedly read the documents. "You can't take Dixie away. That pony belongs to my daughter," Mrs. Clark shouted angrily, gesturing wildly with her hands.

Paddy who had heard the commotion came running from the stable. He grabbed the papers from Dot's hand while she continued to argue with the sheriff. "What kind of shenanigans are you trying to pull here?" he rudely interjected, his squeaky voice piercing the air. As the sheriff explained the situation, a horse trailer rumbled up the driveway.

"If you take Dixie, then you have to take me," Mrs. Clark said defiantly.

"Ma'am, if that's what you want then I'll have to place you under arrest," the sheriff said bluntly, clearly irritated with Mrs. Clark's bickering. Before either person could say another word, Paddy interrupted the showdown.

"Dot, it won't do any good to spend the night in the hoosegow," he said, grabbing her by the arm. "You don't have a choice here. The law's the law.

257

You go into the house and call Willie and Mr. Tuttle, and I'll assist the officer."

"But what will I tell Carolyn. She'll be crushed." Mrs. Clark pleaded

"You just tell her the truth. That's all you can do." Paddy replied solemnly.

While Mrs. Clark made her phone calls, Paddy had an off-the-record conversation, but Sims was tight-lipped. He wouldn't even tell Paddy where Dixie was being stabled.

Paddy took his time in loading Dixie, hoping that Sims would change his mind, but Sims hurried him along with a stern look and a wave of the hand. Paddy was allowed to give the hostlers a list of Dixie's dietary needs and a bucket filled with her grooming gear. "Boys, she's a gentle horse," Paddy said. "Just give her some kind words and a smile, and she'll do anything you want." A minute later, Dixie was headed down the road in a strange trailer surrounded by strangers. That would panic a lot of horses, but Paddy wasn't worried. On Sundays Dixie performed for thousands of strangers. She would be fine. It was Carolyn that had him worried.

Back in the kitchen, Mrs. Clark was sitting at the table, nursing a cup of coffee. After Paddy poured a cup for himself, Dot gave him an update. Tuttle offered the services of the team's lawyer, and she accepted. Until the hearing, they had to wait for justice to be served.

"I smell a rat here," Paddy fumed. "They're calling us horse thieves, and I don't like that one bit."

Mrs. Clark crossed her arms and leaned back in the chair. "Paddy, I hate to admit it, but Dixie could have been stolen," she said with a frown. "She was given to us by Doc Higgins. He said the horse was given to him as payment for a medical bill. As luck would have it, the breeder went out of business right after that. It will be impossible to track him down."

"I have connections in the horse world. I'll get to the bottom of this if it's the last thing I do," Paddy declared, banging his fist on the table and spilling coffee down the sides of the cups. "I may be a lot of things, but I'm not a horse thief."

"Well, I'd better get ready to give Carolyn the bad news," Mrs. Clark sighed. "She'll be home in a few minutes."

As usual, Carolyn jumped off the school bus and dashed up the driveway, lumbering under the weight of her knapsack. Coming home to the farm was the highlight of her day. She couldn't wait to greet Dixie and the other horses. As she headed for the stable, Paddy cut her off in the parking lot.

"Woe-ah, slow down there, lassie," he shouted. "Before you do anything else, you need to speak to your mother. She's waiting for you inside the house."

"Just let me see Dixie first and I'll be on my way," Carolyn gushed.

"It's best you go inside first. I think it's more important." Paddy replied solemnly.

Carolyn saw the worried look on Paddy's face. "Is Dad alright?" she asked nervously. Her father's safety was always on her mind. Racing horses at thirty miles an hour around a tight oval was a dangerous occupation. Spills and injuries were common. To the jockeys, it was part of the job. To the families, it was a serious injury waiting to happen.

"No, your father is fine, but you need to speak with your mother," Paddy answered in a halting voice. Carolyn turned and sprinted to the house.

Mrs. Clark heard the screen door squeak open and immediately recognized Carolyn's footsteps. "Sit down next to me," Mrs. Clark said, patting the sofa. "We need to talk horsewoman to horsewoman." The court papers were setting on the coffee table.

Carolyn took a seat with a rather confused look. If it wasn't her father, then who could be in trouble, she wondered. From her mother's grim look, she was sure that there had been a death in the family. She just hoped it wasn't Grandma Clark who had been ill.

"Who or what are we talking about?" Carolyn asked hesitantly.

"It's about Dixie," Mrs. Clark stated as calmly as she could.

Carolyn's faced turned pale white; her pulse quickened. "Dixie's been hurt," she cried out.

"No, that's not the case," Mrs. Clark replied. "Dixie is just fine, but there is a problem." Mrs. Clark explained the visit from the sheriff and showed her the court documents. She told Carolyn that lawyers from the Colts would handle the case. "I'm sure it's just a case of mistaken identity. Dixie will be home in a few days," she added reassuringly.

Carolyn didn't hear her mother's words of encouragement. She heard only that Dixie was gone. "I don't believe it. It can't be true," she wailed. "How could they take Dixie?"

"These things happen in the horse business," Mrs. Clark replied as she gently placed her hand on Carolyn's thigh. "You just have to be…"

Carolyn pushed away her mother's hand before her mother could finish her sentence. She bolted from the sofa and raced towards the stable. She had to see for herself. Paddy was standing just inside the stable entrance, knowing that Carolyn would be heading his way in a frenzied state. He let her pass without a word.

With a look of terror, Carolyn poked her head inside the Dixie's stall. "It's true. They took Dixie away. Oh, how could they?" she bawled as tears streamed down her face. She leaned against the side of the stall and slumped to the floor where she sobbed bitterly.

Paddy stood at a distance and watched with sadness, his own eyes growing moist. With his arms folded, he lowered his head and waited. When he was sure that Carolyn's tears were starting to run dry, he walked over to the stall. "Lassie, I know exactly how you feel," he whispered gently as he sat down next to Carolyn. "Sometimes friends are apart for reasons that we don't understand, but deep in your heart you're never far from each other. You got to believe that. It's one of those mysteries of life." He placed his hand on Carolyn's forearm and squeezed gently.

"Is it always this hard?" Carolyn asked, wiping away the tears.

"I hate to say it, but it is, especially with the ones you love," Paddy replied softly. "It never gets easier, no matter how many times you do it. But it's important to know that Dixie is safe and sound. The hearing is scheduled for Friday morning. By noon, she'll be back in her stall where she belongs. You'll see."

"But I don't know if I can wait that long. I feel like my heart has been broken in two," Carolyn sniffed repeatedly.

"Well, I can mend broken horses. Let me see what I can do with broken hearts," Paddy said tenderly. He stood up and lifted Carolyn to her feet. After dusting the loose straw from her clothes, he pulled out of a handkerchief and dried her tears. With his arm around her shoulder, he pressed her to his side. Together, they walked back to the house. There was already a chill in the late afternoon air. Deep down in his Irish bones, Paddy felt an evil wind blowing from the north. From somewhere in

New York, he figured. That's where most gangsters and gamblers could be found.

Carolyn sat down at the dinner table and stared at her plate. Usually, she said grace, but tonight Mrs. Clark gave thanks for the meal. How could she be thankful when her pony had been rustled in broad daylight, Carolyn thought. In her heart, she didn't feel thankful; she felt abandoned. Not even meatloaf and mashed potatoes drenched in gravy, one of her favorite meals, could cheer her up. She took a few bites and quickly excused herself, racing up the stairs. She needed to be alone. If she couldn't be at the fence, then her bedroom was the next best place. Sitting at her desk, she opened her history book and tried to read, hoping that it would take on my off Dixie. But her mind was blank. She stared at the pages like she stared at dinner. Small teardrops splashed the pages, leaving circular stains. No matter how hard she tired, she couldn't stop thinking about Dixie.

Carolyn needed to get outside before the walls closed in, but it was already nightfall. Instead she would have to be content with the view from her bedroom. Turning off the desk lamp, she dragged her chair over to the open window and sat down. Propping her elbows on the sill, she gazed into the evening darkness and inhaled the cool night air. Somewhere out there on a distant farm, Dixie was alone and lonely, poking her head out of the stall and searching for Carolyn. Hopefully, the stable boys were taking good care of her. Paddy had given them one of Dixie's blankets, but Dixie needed more than the creature comforts of home. On a night like this, Dixie needed a friend. It would have been nice if the sheriff had let Inky Dink tag along.

Lost in her thoughts, Carolyn didn't hear the gentle tap on the door. "Mind if I come in and sit a spell?" Mrs. Clark asked as the door squeaked open.

"Mom, there's always room for another cowgirl, especially you," Carolyn replied.

"Seems like we're becoming a pair of old saddle pals. All we do is sit and talk," Mrs. Clark replied with an easy laugh, trying to ease Carolyn's pain. She pulled up a chair and stared out the window with Carolyn. For the next few minutes, the two horsewomen sat in silence. Mrs. Clark knew exactly how Carolyn felt. She remembered as a little girl when her first pony died from old age. She was heartbroken for months. "I just got off the phone with the sheriff's office," Mrs. Clark piped up. "They've taken Dixie to Tyler Taylor's farm. Nobody takes better care of horses than Tyler except you and me."

"Can we go see her?" Carolyn asked hopefully.

"Not yet, we have to get the court's permission to do that. They have an officer on guard around the clock to see that Dixie is safe. Tyler said he would call in the morning. He's personally looking after Dixie."

"I guess if there's any good news today, that's it," Carolyn said glumly, disappointed that she couldn't visit Dixie. Dixie was being held prisoner for a crime that she didn't commit. The law was supposed to protect the innocent; instead it was punishing the innocent. Why couldn't the court let Dixie stay at the farm until the case was decided? Why couldn't the court take her as a prisoner in place of Dixie? After a minute of biting her tongue in silence, she turned to her mother. "Mom, why did this have to happen?"

Mrs. Clark wasn't surprised at the question. She knew that sooner or later it would be asked. She had been searching for an answer since the sheriff left with Dixie. "I think what you're asking is why bad things happen to good people," she replied. "That's a tough one to answer. Some people say things just happen as part of life. Others say it's a test from God."

"But what do you think?" Carolyn asked solemnly.

Mrs. Clark paused to collect her thoughts. "I think I'm somewhere in between. Good and bad things happen in every life. I guess that's where faith comes into the picture. You have to believe that God has a plan for each person. Just like you have to believe that God has a plan for you and Dixie."

"Mom, you sound like Pastor Goodwin, but I believe what you're saying," Carolyn chuckled softly. "At this point, all I can do is pray that everything will turn out right."

265

Mrs. Clark reached over and hugged Carolyn, kissing her gently on the forehead. "Now, cowgirl, what do you say you hit the hay. You just have to get through one more day."

Carolyn put on her favorite flannel pajamas, the ones with galloping horses. Before climbing into bed, she knelt beside her bed and folded her eyes in prayer. "Dear Lord, even though it's not Sunday, I know there are a lot prayers coming your way tonight," she whispered piously. "But I just have one request. Could you please bring Dixie home?"

Carolyn snuggled under the blanket but seconds later started tossing and turning. The bed was like a ship upon a stormy sea as she rolled from one edge to the other. No matter how hard she tried, she couldn't get comfortable. If she didn't stop moving, she was certain to get seasick, and she already had an upset stomach. Finally, she rolled her head to the side and stared out the window in despair. Thoughts of Dixie clouded her mind like a thick fog. All she could see was Dixie pacing around her stall with sad eyes. Closing her eyes, she thought about Dixie in happier times. She remembered the day when her father brought Dixie home. It was love at first sight for both horse and rider. One after another, the memories came in gentle waves and flooded her mind with soothing warmth. Gradually, she drifted off in a peaceful sleep with the sweet thought of her and Dixie riding into the sunset.

Chapter 13 - The Source of the Horse

Thursday was the longest day of Carolyn's life. Everything in the universe moved in slow motion. At school she stared at the wall clock and counted the seconds until the buses arrived for the ride home. Her sullen frown was the only clue that something was drastically wrong. When questioned by her classmates, she crossed her fingers behind her back and said she had a bad cold. A little white lie for the sake of others was never against the cowgirl creed. At morning announcements, she wanted to run into the principal's office and scream into the microphone that someone had stolen her pony. The student body would get a real-life civics lesson about justice. That would probably relieve her stress but get her into trouble with the law. The court had issued a "gag rule" that prevented any involved parties from talking about the case. It wasn't bad enough that someone was trying to steal her pony. Now Carolyn couldn't even talk about it. There was nothing just about justice.

Mrs. Clark was waiting in the kitchen when Carolyn returned home from school. Tyler had called twice during the day to report good news. Dixie was doing fine. She was eating well and making new pony friends in the pasture. Carolyn nodded and bit her lip. At least, her pony was doing well. All she had was an empty feeling in her stomach and an empty stall for her pony. To pass the time, she spent the rest of the afternoon in the stable with her painting set. There was a very important art project to be completed by Saturday.

That evening at dinner, Paddy had a news update on the great pony caper. True to his word, he made inquiries among his fellow horsemen. It didn't take long for the rumors to reach his ears, especially when it involved horses and gamblers. Shadowy characters in search of the "big score" inhabited the dark side of horse racing. If they weren't part of a scheme to make a quick dollar at the track, then they knew someone who was.

"Hudson Hills is a front for a bunch of New York gamblers who lost a ton of money on last year's championship game," Paddy stated confidently. "It seems these hooligans are friends of the owners. Their plan is to get ownership of Dixie and sell her to the highest bidder to recoup their losses."

"Then we should have no problem getting Dixie back?" Carolyn asked. "We can just tell the judge what you know."

"It's one thing to hear a rumor, but it's another thing to prove it in court," Mr. Clark interjected, not wanting Carolyn to get her hopes up to high. Like Paddy, he knew about the criminals in the horse business. Money was their master. For a few dollars, they would lie on a stack of Bibles and swear on their mother's grave.

"But I don't think this is about money. It's about revenge," Paddy declared with a look of disgust. "Revenge always fetches a high price. Maybe a price that no one in this room can afford. And I'm not just talking about money."

"We'll just have to wait and see what happens in court," Mrs. Clark said. "I'm sure the lawyers for the Colts are preparing an airtight case."

"Lawyers are rattlesnakes. They just slither around on the ground, waiting for their next victim," Paddy said snidely. "If I had my way, I'd go to Tyler's place, load up Dixie and head west."

"Maggie's relatives have a ranch in Colorado," Carolyn added with a quick clap of her hands, delighted that Paddy was willing to fight for the sake of law and order. She knew that he had a mysterious side, but she never pictured him as the

269

Lone Ranger, a man who struck fear in the hearts of the lawless. But Mrs. Clark had other thoughts about taking the law into your own hands.

"Just what I need, a Butch Cassidy and Sundance Kid," she sighed dramatically, referring to the Old West train robbers. To make her point, she held up her spoon for a microphone. "Horse thieves top tonight's news. Police catch the Hole in the Head Gang after their white pony was spotted galloping around a football field in downtown Denver. The gang's leader, Paddy O'Brien, also know as Butch, said they were just taking the horse for a ride when they took a wrong turn in Baltimore and got lost. His sidekick, Carolyn Clark, also known as the Kid, said that Paddy always had trouble reading a map. Police do not believe their story, and the pair will be charged as horse thieves."

Carolyn and Mr. Clark laughed so hard that they nearly choked on their food. Mrs. Clark dropped the spoon and leaned back in her chair triumphantly with her hands behind her head and a wide grin on her face. Paddy was stunned momentarily into silence. Mrs. Clark could be funny at times but never this funny. With a smirk on his face, Paddy turned to her and finished the news report.

"Ah, Dottie, but you forgot the most important detail," he said with a furrowed brow. "Police confirm that at the time of his arrest O'Brien was using a map of Ireland to flee from authorities." Paddy held up his coffee cup to toast Mrs. Clark.

270

He nodded and took a sip with his pinky finger extended. As everyone burst into a round of laughter, Paddy sat grim-faced like a seasoned vaudeville performer. The harder they laughed; the faster he sipped. When the liquid finally cascaded down his chin and into his lap, he broke into a wide smile and placed his cup gently on the table as if nothing had happened. Mrs. Clark and Paddy had proved that laughter was the best medicine for any ailment.

Carolyn's parents and Paddy talked about the case late into the night. When snippets of the conversation drifted upstairs, Carolyn opened her bedroom door and left it slightly ajar. They agreed that money was talking louder than words, and neither side wanted to pay for a lengthy trial. The National Football League was riding a wave of popularity due to last year's championship. The "sudden death" game was still the talk of the sports world. Tickets sales had soared during the off-season to record highs. Everybody, to include gamblers and gangsters, wanted a piece of the action that was professional football. If the accusation about Dixie being stolen was true, league executives didn't want the world to discover the current world champions were horse thieves. In this case, no publicity was the only good publicity. Any bad publicity would be swept under the rug. The owners of Hudson Hills, the horse farm claiming ownership of Dixie, would surely agree. Bad publicity would only lower the resale value of "their" pony.

Despite the negative talk, Carolyn went to bed with a smile on her face, even if it wasn't in her heart. Sleep came easy as some of her worries had lessened. Instead of tossing and turning, she continued with her fond memories of Dixie from last night. In a few minutes, she was sound asleep with a smile still etched across her face.

At 9 o'clock on Friday morning, court was called into session. Mr. and Mrs. Clark promptly took their spots at their lawyer's table. Behind them, Carolyn sat nervously next to Paddy and glanced around the courtroom as people shuffled into position. The last time Carolyn saw so many men in pin striped suites with slicked back hair was at a funeral. At that moment, she would have given anything in the world to be back in class and have Dixie back in her stall. A court drama could be exciting for a spectator but not for a potential witness.

A hush fell over the assembly when the burly bailiff announced the case. He stood next to the court reporter who was limbering up her fingers to officially record every word of the hearing. Lawyers for both sides, who had been huddling in quiet conversation, stood at attention behind their tables. "Your, honor, the first case on the docket is Hudson Hills versus the Jolly Jockey Farm to determine ownership of a disputed property, described herein as a white Welsh pony, approximately six years of age, and presently known as Dixie," he bellowed. Since this was a civil case and not a criminal case, both law teams agreed to waive a jury trial. Each side thought they could sway a country judge more easily than a jury of farmers. Judge Preston W. Cowherd's decision would be binding.

"Mr. Burns, you may proceed," the judge said dryly as he looked up from his papers. Mr. Wendell Burns, chief counsel for the law firm from New York City hired by Hudson Hills, stood erect and began to explain his case. By the way he walked and talked, Carolyn knew that he was a formidable foe. With his jet-black hair swept back on his head under a thick layer of hair cream, he was the slickest of city slickers. As he recited Dixie's life story, Carolyn folded her hands in prayer and leaned forward. She didn't want to miss a single word.

Burns was a smooth talker and a convincing actor. He paced in front of his table, pulling on the sleeves of his silk shirt to flash his diamond cufflinks and turning a diamond pinky ring on his finger. He was a man of wealth, wardrobe, and words and wanted everyone to know and remember it. Wasting no time, he quickly established a paper trail to prove that his clients were the true owners of Dixie. Every few seconds he held up a document and explained its meaning. Dixie's life unfolded in stack of veterinarian reports, business records, and affidavits from grooms and trainers. Much to

Carolyn's dismay, Judge Cowherd allowed each item to be introduced as evidence. Carolyn raised her hands to her chin. If she didn't know any better, she would swear that Dixie belonged to Hudson Hills. Burns was that convincing. She could only hope that her lawyer was an equal opponent.

Next up was Mr. Oliver Carson, an insurance fraud lawyer hired by the Colts to represent the Jolly Jockey. When called by the judge, he clumsily fingered through some papers and noisily slid back his chair. He slowly rose and slouched in place, looking down at his papers. With his black-rimmed glasses and rumpled suit, he looked more like a science teacher than a high-powered attorney. But looks were deceiving. He was sly and cunning in his own way, a perfect counterpoint to Burns. He rapidly introduced his own stack of records and statements to trace ownership of Dixie to the Jolly Jockey. Every time the judge accepted a document as evidence, Carolyn clapped silently and bowed her head. "A point for the good guys," she muttered under her breath.

With great oratory, Carson passionately portrayed the story of an orphaned pony from Maryland who was fortunately adopted by a loving family from Maryland. How could the pony not be a Maryland pony? The only time the pony stepped out of Maryland was to attend pony shows in nearby states. Carson saved his best for last. In closing, he stunned the court by requesting for dismissal of the case. "Your honor, since Hudson

Hills did not prove that Dixie was stolen, we beseech the court to declare her abandoned property. As such, the "finder's keepers" rule should apply, and Dixie should be rightfully awarded to the Jolly Jockey," he stated boldly.

Carolyn was ecstatic. Victory was at hand. Carson was simply brilliant. How could the judge not return Dixie to the Jolly Jockey? Cowherd took off his glasses, wiped them clean, and then replaced them on the tip of his nose. He was not impressed or amused with Carson's legal maneuver. He fervently believed that a case had to be proved beyond a reasonable doubt even if it resulted in unreasonable doubt. "Nice try, counselor, but simple solutions do not always solve simple problems, especially in a court of law," he replied dryly. Carolyn didn't know what he meant by that phrase, but she knew that victory had been snatched from the palm of her hand.

Cowherd proceeded to grill both lawyers in a gruff manner, seemingly irritated with the antics of both men. Although both sides presented convincing cases, neither was airtight. In some instances, it was impossible to tell fact from fiction, reality from fantasy, and coincidence from conspiracy. On one hand, Hudson Hills had proved ownership of a pony, but was it Dixie or some other pony? If the pony was Dixie, then why was the pony not reported missing or stolen for insurance purposes? On the other hand, the Jolly Jockey proved ownership of a pony named Dixie, but was it the pony that belonged to Hudson Hills? Where was the documentation to prove that Dixie was abandoned?

Judge Cowherd asked to see some of the evidence. Holding the documents at arm's length with one hand, he vigorously massaged the side of his face with the other. The decision was more difficult than he had anticipated. There were a least at a thousand white ponies stabled between Maryland and New York. Without any distinctive markings, it would be impossible to tell the difference among any of them. Hudson Hills had sufficiently documented initial ownership, but Cowherd had doubts about their paperwork. He was certain that some forms had been altered but had no way of proving it. After a few minutes of raising and lowering his glasses, he finally looked up and then slammed his gavel with a thunderous clap. "Court is recessed for fifteen minutes," he declared to a stunned courtroom. Everybody had been expecting a quick decision. Lawyers for both sides huddled together and whispered about strategies. At this point, no one was taking odds on a winner.

"What do you think about our chances?" Carolyn asked her mother, befuddled by all of the legal mumbo-jumbo that filled the air. Listening to Carson, it was obvious that Dixie was a native Marylander who should be listed as the official state horse.

"I don't know, honey," Mrs. Clark replied nervously. "I thought we made a strong case, but these things can go either way."

Carolyn was not encouraged by her mother's comments. "But what if we lose?" she asked hesitantly.

"If they win, we'll make an offer to buy Dixie," Mrs. Clark replied confidently. "If Paddy's right about the gamblers, we'll offer to buy her back and retire her from the Baltimore Colts. We'll do whatever it takes to get Dixie back home. And home is the Jolly Jockey."

Carolyn smiled weakly. That's what she wanted to hear, but she knew that was no promise. If only the judge would hear her side of the story, he might be swayed to decide in her favor. She just wanted to tell him how much Dixie meant to her and the Jolly Jockey.

"All rise! The court is now in session," the bailiff announced as the judge's chamber door swung open.

"All parties, please be seated," Cowherd proclaimed in a southern drawl. "I have reached a decision, and I will now explain that decision." Carolyn gulped hard and put her hand on Paddy's arm. They both leaned forward in their seats. An eerie quiet settled over the courtroom as all eyes turned toward the judge. Cowherd slowly scanned the courtroom to create an air of suspense for his momentous decision.

"As most of you know, I am a horseman, myself," the judge declared proudly. "To serve the best interests of Miss Dixie, the owner must be a capable horseman or horsewoman to the satisfaction of the court. Both sides will have the opportunity to prove they are best suited to be the owner. We will convene tomorrow noon at Mr. Taylor's farm."

Both legal teams looked at each with raised eyebrows. They were more befuddled than shocked. Cowherd was well-known for his odd decisions, but this one was the oddest. After conferring with the judge, Carson met with Mr. and Mrs. Clark. Each side would be allowed three character witnesses to demonstrate ownership. There would be more instructions tomorrow. Cowherd didn't want to reveal any more information for fear that one side might gain an advantage. Although Carson didn't say it, he viewed the judge's decision as a second chance for his clients. He was certain that Cowherd was ready to rule in favor of Hudson Hills. But for some reason, the judge had a soft spot in his heart for little girls and ponies.

Two names came right to mind for Carson's witness list, Carolyn and Paddy. Mr. and Mrs. Clark debated about which of them should be the third witness. Both had trained Dixie, but neither had a special bond with the pony. Mr. Clark plucked a quarter from his pocket for the coin toss. "Call it in the air Dot," he said to his wife.

"How about Maggie?" Carolyn blurted out as Mr. Clark was ready to flip the coin.

"That's an excellent choice. That girl and Dixie seem like sisters at times," Paddy quickly interjected. Heeding Paddy's advice, Mr. and Mrs. Clark nodded their heads in agreement. Carolyn felt a sense of relief. Now, she'd have a saddle pal by her side. When briefed about this mystery witness known as Maggie Farnsworth and her disability, Carson pursed his lips and straightened his tie.

"Sounds like she might be what I'm looking for," he said, staring out into space without further comment. In his head, the legal wheels were turning. Burns had a paper trail thicker than a city phone book. He fretted that he didn't opt for a jury trial and silently scolded himself for being so foolish. A jury of local people would never rule against a local girl and her pony, even if the pony didn't belong to her. Now he wondered if a local judge would rule against a local girl, her pony, and her crippled friend. Ever so slightly, his odds of winning had improved. If he couldn't win the case on motions, then he would win on emotions.

Back at the farm, Carolyn counted the minutes until Maggie arrived home from school. At 4 o'clock, Maggie would be dancing in front of the TV with a glass of Ovaltine in one hand and an Oreo cookie in the other. The Buddy Deane show would be blasting the latest Top Ten hits in the background until Mrs. Farnsworth yelled at her to turn down the noise.

"Maggie, it's for you," her mother called out. Maggie set down her drink and hobbled over to pick up the phone, hoping to get back to the show before the first song was over. Most likely, it was a classmate who needed a homework assignment.

"Maggie, I need your help. They stole Dixie," said the frantic voice on the other end of the line.

"Slow down, pardner," Maggie quickly responded, not immediately recognizing Carolyn's voice. "Is this some kind of trick or treat prank?" she asked, realizing that tomorrow was Halloween. Maggie was wise to such pranksters. Every Halloween, she was target of somebody's sick joke about her being The Hunchback or Frankenstein. But from the sound of desperation in the cracking voice, she knew that this was no trick. As Carolyn replayed the week's events, Maggie's heart dropped to her stomach with a sickly thud.

"It's time to circle the wagons, cowgirl, and you're in the middle with the rest of us pioneers," Carolyn said enthusiastically, hoping to convince her friend to testify.

"I don't understand what you mean," Maggie replied in confusion.

"I put you down as a witness in Dixie's behalf," Carolyn stated, explaining the court decision.

"Pardner, you know I'll do anything for you and Dixie," Maggie replied. "You can count on me."

After Carolyn hung up, Maggie plopped down on the couch and stared at the television. Images of Dixie galloped across the screen. Wiping away a tear, she went to tell her mother that's tomorrow's riding session was being replaced with a civics lesson.

"Why those wicked northern carpetbaggers," Mrs. Farnsworth growled. "These people come down here and think they can steal our horses. We are not suited to taking that kind of abuse. Never have and never will. Not only will you be there tomorrow, but I'll be there with you."

Maggie was speechless. Her mother rarely lost her composure about anything other than the women's society or the country club. It was a rare sight for a woman of her lineage to publicly rant, especially about a horse. Obviously, family history was the exception to social etiquette for the southern belles in Maryland. From the tone of Mrs. Farnsworth's voice, it sounded like a personal affront to her heritage. The Civil War was Maggie's first and foremost thought. Mom had numerous family members who had been sympathetic to the South during the war. It was rumored that Union soldiers had plundered the family estate. Maybe the Yankee raiders also stole their horses and torched the stable. It seemed farfetched, but no matter what the reason, Maggie was glad that her mother was in her corner.

Before climbing into bed, Maggie reached underneath her bed and slid out the box that housed her flying horse circus. From a jumbled pile of plastic arms and legs, she plucked the horse and rider that were to become Dixie and Carolyn. Even though the figures hadn't been painted, she easily pictured them as the real-life characters. After placing the pair on her nightstand, she turned out the light and fluffed up her pillow for a better view of her mounted guard. As the white plastic figures glowed dimly in the autumn moonlight, memories from the greatest summer of her life flashed though her mind. She vowed that no one was going to steal those memories without a fight.

"Dear Lord, it's Maggie Farnsworth again," she whispered softly, looking up at the ceiling. "You know how I always ask you to heal my leg. Well, tonight, I'm asking you to please bring Dixie home. If you can do that I promise never to bother you about the leg again." Maggie turned and faced the figures, hoping for a sign from beyond. She waited for the figures to vibrate and fall to the floor as they did in horror movies, but they remained still and silent. She then faced the window, hoping to hear a whispered voice proclaim "It's a deal, pardner." All she heard was the rustling of fallen leaves. That wasn't the response she wanted, but she didn't need a sign from heaven. She had faith, and her pastor always said that faith worked miracles. Faith had the power to change the minds of mothers, make summer dreams come true, and heal the crippled. If it could do all of that, it could easily bring home a pony.

Before closing her eyes, Maggie decided to sneak Carolyn and Dixie into tomorrow's court hearing. It never hurt to carry a good luck charm. She drifted off to sleep, silently reciting the promise that she made in the pasture after her dance with Bojangles.

Chapter 14 – Dixie Takes the Stand

Saturday dawned clear and crisp on the Taylor farm. Overnight, a cold front had swept down from Canada, coating the pumpkin fields in a white glaze. Today's court spectators were dressed in sweatshirts, sweaters, and blue jeans. They huddled in small groups and sipped coffee from steaming cups, talking mostly about the weather. Until the lawyers arrived, the scene looked more like a farm auction than a court hearing. Although their two-piece suits and wingtip shoes were ill fitted for the weather or the terrain, they reminded everyone that Taylor's corral was a court of law. The rules of the court were still in effect, and proper behavior, if not attire, was expected.

Judge Cowherd stepped from the front porch of Tyler's farmhouse into the brilliant sunshine. Dressed in a black robe, he strutted into the center of the corral with the ease of an emperor. Taking a position behind the portable podium, he pulled back his billowy sleeve and counted down the seconds with a look of grim determination. At exactly high noon, he drew the gavel from his side pocket and hammered the podium with a loud crack. Some spectators looked around to see if someone had fired a pistol. Judge Cowherd was obviously enjoying his time in the spotlight. He would have done well in the Old West, the Wild West or anyplace west of Maryland.

"As decreed yesterday," Cowherd boldly proclaimed. "The court's final decision will be based on the best interests of Miss Dixie, the current ward of the state. Each side will be allowed three witnesses and a total of fifteen minutes to demonstrate their custodial claim. In the event, Miss Dixie does not show a preference for either party, my decision will be based on the evidence that has been presented to the court."

Cowherd looked toward the stable with a smirk and rapidly rapped the gavel three times. On cue, a court officer walked Dixie to the corral. Carolyn's heart fluttered and skipped a beat at the sight. She wanted to run over and give Dixie the biggest hug in the world, but all she could do was stand on her toes and wrung her hands.

Paddy studied Dixie with a sharp eye as she was led from the stable. Since sunrise, he had been hanging around the stable with his fellow horsemen, waiting for a close look at his horse. After Dixie passed by, he walked briskly towards Mrs. Clark who was standing near Mr. Carson. Shaking his head from side to side, he motioned for Mrs. Clark to step aside. "Dot, the fix is in," he muttered angrily under his breath. "They drugged her, I tell you. I know it."

Mrs. Clark stepped toward the fence for a closer look. Dixie's ears were flat and her tail drooped but that could be from loneliness or boredom. Until she could she look into Dixie's eyes, she couldn't confirm Paddy's suspicion.

"She looks troubled, but that doesn't mean she's drugged," Mrs. Clark replied in a hushed tone as not to be overheard by the crowd. "Remember they had a 24-hour guard on her."

"Money talks louder than words. It'll buy you anything, even time by yourself to do your evil deed," Paddy snarled. He had seen this heinous trick too many times with racehorses. To fix a race, gangsters spiked the horse's feed or water. Depending on the medicine and the dose, the horse would either fall asleep in the starting gate or sprint around the track until his heart exploded. This was the same trick with a new twist. If Dixie didn't respond to anyone from the Jolly Jockey, then

Cowherd was bound by law to award Dixie to Hudson Hills even if the evidence was phony.

Paddy was frustrated. He knew that Dixie was drugged and the documents were forged but couldn't prove it. He thought about openly approaching Cowherd with his theory, but that would only get him escorted from the property for contempt of court. Somehow he had to outwit the "legal nitwits" as he fondly called them. "Think, laddie. You've got to think in a hurry," he whispered under this breath as he nervously chewed on the tip of his pipe.

Cowherd pointed to the legal team for Hudson Hills who were standing behind a small folding table crowded with leather briefcases. "Mr. Burns, you shall have first opportunity to address Miss Dixie."

"Your honor, we respectfully decline to exercise our option," Burns replied smugly. "We rest our case solely on the evidence presented to the court yesterday."

"As you wish," Cowherd responded with a tight grin as he silently applauded the decision. Placing the burden of proof on the Jolly Jockey was a brilliant legal move. For the moment, Burns had upstaged Carson's request for dismissal. Burns and Carson were squaring off in a high-stakes poker game, playing their cards close to the vest and not blinking an eye. Cowherd waited eagerly for the next card to be revealed.

Carolyn and Maggie held hands and listened intently. Their hopes soared when Burns declined the judge's request. They thought he had surrendered the case. When they realized that he was duping them, their hopes plummeted. They dropped hands; their bodies sagging from the latest legal blow to the stomach. They couldn't believe that Cowherd would let Burns kidnap the court. Now it was Carson's turn. Somehow he had to ride into the corral with his legal guns blazing to save the day. Hopefully, an Old West judge like Cowherd would appreciate such bravado.

"Mr. Carson, it's now your turn," Cowherd proclaimed. "Please have your first character witness address Miss Dixie. You have fifteen minutes and three witnesses. Any touching of the pony will be viewed as contempt of court, and the witness will be disqualified."

"Your honor, we'd like to call Miss Carolyn Clark to the podium," Carson announced as he waved for Carolyn. Carolyn suddenly felt light-headed as she nervously stepped forward. Shivers ran up and down her spine like a condemned criminal going to the gallows. Dixie's fate was now in her hands.

Carson quickly huddled with Carolyn and her parents. "It's simple," he said calmly, placing a hand on Carolyn's shoulder. "Get Dixie to follow you out the corral, and we win the case.

"I think I can do that," Carolyn replied, her knees knocking and her hands shaking. "We've been best friend for years. She listens to every word I say."

Carolyn glanced at her parents who nodded their encouragement. Looking back over her shoulder, she saw Maggie step from the crowd with two thumbs up, the same signal that Mr. Clark used when the Colts scored a touchdown. If Carolyn wanted to ride Dixie again, she needed to score a legal touchdown with Cowherd. She needed to be calm and cool under pressure. She needed Johnny U by her side to call the winning play.

Taking two deep breaths to calm her nerves, Carolyn entered the corral and gingerly approached Dixie, stopping two paces in front of her. Dixie appeared sleepy with sad eyes, but Carolyn wasn't alarmed. She always looked that way when Carolyn was gone for a few days. Upon hearing Carolyn's voice, she'd quickly respond with a soft whinny and start moving in Carolyn's direction. The officer, who was holding Dixie, dropped the lead line and stepped back.

"Dixie, it's me," Carolyn said cheerfully. "Come on, girl, it's time to go home." Dixie didn't flinch. Carolyn leaned forward until her face was inches away from Dixie's head. "Dixie, follow me, girl," she cooed softly. Once again, Dixie remained motionless. Carolyn's face was flush as beads of sweat dotted her forehead. Dixie was a total stranger. Had Dixie forgotten who she was in only three days or was she angry because she blamed Carolyn for being kidnapped, Carolyn wondered.

289

Carolyn stepped back to collect her thoughts for one last try. She had to shock Dixie from her trance. Raising her fingers to her mouth, she blew two shrill blasts that echoed over the pasture. "Run, Dixie! Run," she yelled at the top of her lungs as she threw her arm forward. Dixie stood like a statue. "Oh, Dixie, you've got to run," Carolyn pleaded as tears streamed down her face. She hung her head until her chin touched her chest and wept. All hope was lost. There was nothing else she could do.

"Eight minutes remaining," the bailiff called out as he kept a steady eye on his wristwatch.

Mr. Carson hurried over to Carolyn's side and held her hand. "Carolyn, it's going to be alright," he said, walking her back to his table. "She's not responding because she sees that you're nervous and thinks something is wrong. Let's give someone else a try."

Carson looked at Cowherd to find a sympathetic face, but Cowherd only glared back. "Those damn horse thieves," he muttered under his breath as he glanced at Burns and his cronies. He bit his tongue to bridle his rage. If he said anything out of line, Cowherd could rule against him. The judge had a reputation for being heavy-handed with mouthy lawyers who tried to upstage his court. Court observers called it frontier justice, but Carson didn't see any justice in allowing someone to steal a girl's pony.

"Your honor, we would like to call our next witness," Carson announced, pointing to Paddy. While preparing the case, horse people talked about Paddy's uncanny ability to communicate or "whisper" with horses. If anyone could talk to Dixie, it was Paddy. Carson needed an ace up his sleeve to win this hand, and Paddy was it. His strategy had been to save Paddy until the very end, but time was running out. He couldn't risk the remaining few minutes with Maggie.

"Any objections, Mr. Burns," Cowherd asked.

"None, your honor, as long as we adhere to your time limit," Burns replied impatiently.

"Proceed Mr. Carson, but be advised you have only seven minutes," Cowherd cautioned in a stern tone.

Paddy nodded as he walked by Carson. He didn't need a pep talk. He knew that he was the last hope for the Jolly Jockey. At the gate, he purposely fumbled with the latch, still trying to think of a plan. When the bailiff opened the gate for him, he realized that he could no longer delay the inevitable. It would take a miracle to lead Dixie from the corral, and today he was no miracle worker. If Carolyn couldn't get Dixie's attention, nobody in the world could. Dixie needed to see and hear clearly to respond to a voice command. As long as she was drugged, she might as well be asleep in her stall.

"Asleep in the stall," Paddy muttered under his breath as he swung open the corral gate. "That's it.

I got to stall for even more time." The effects of the drug could wear off any second. His plan was foolishly simple, part Paddy O'Brien and part leprechaun. To buy time, he would walk into the center of the corral and fake a heart attack. Clutching his chest, he would drop to his knees and fall face first in the grass. The court would have to recess while medics responded to the scene. That could be at least thirty minutes if he was a good actor.

Paddy almost laughed as he pictured Burns angrily objecting to the judge while he gasped a dying breath. There was no reason why he couldn't pull it off. After all, he came from a long line of vaudeville performers on the Irish stage. The theater was in his blood. Taking one last look at this watch, he flashed a mischievous grin to Mrs. Clark who was clueless. As he stepped into the corral, a squeaky voice suddenly piped up. The crowd craned their necks to find the source. As if parting a sea, Maggie stepped forward from a wall of spectators and hobbled towards Paddy.

"Paddy, please let me try," she begged. "You always said I had horse blood in me." After watching Carolyn's struggle, she remembered her promise to Dixie. She couldn't bear to lose Dixie and after losing Brownie. That loss was still a fresh scar on her heart.

Paddy didn't have to think twice. Maggie's idea was certainly better than faking a heart attack. He saw the emotional bond between her and Dixie because of their handicaps. It was the wink and a nod they gave each other whenever they were together. Maybe she could spark Dixie's memory. Glancing at Carson, Paddy pointed to Maggie and then to the podium. Carson shrugged his shoulders and nodded his approval. There was nothing else he could do. He had to rely on Paddy's intuition. Ponies were not his area of expertise. His legal ace would remain up his sleeve. Perhaps, Paddy had one of his own. But now the winning hand in this high-stakes game depended on Maggie Farnsworth, the Queen of Hearts.

"She knows you as a sister," Paddy whispered, not to be overhead by Mr. Burns. "Just be yourself. I think she might be waking up any second now. Take as much time as you need."

At the sight of petite, crippled girl, the lawyers standing with Burns snickered loudly. If this was their best witness, the case was over. It was time to pop the champagne and toast their victory. Their hearts of stone had no sympathy for the tragic play that was unfolding on the grassy stage, but they would watch with morbid curiosity. To them, the case was about winning or losing. It wasn't about what was best for Dixie. But Burns didn't like what he was seeing. He silenced his lawyers with a menacing stare. He knew this case was far from over.

Maggie stepped into the corral and patted the bulge in her jacket. Carolyn and Dixie were snugly tucked in her pocket. If she ever needed a good luck charm, it was now.   As Maggie wobbled towards Dixie, she remembered why she was a summer girl. The chilly weather had stiffened up her bad leg, making it extremely difficult to walk in a straight line. Her joints ached from the cold air, and the pain seeped through her body. Having to wear her leg brace over a thick pair of corduroy didn't make the walk any easier. With every step, she made a comical swishing sound.

Maggie approached Dixie from the side, dragging her leg along the ground. Dixie had to recognize her. She witnessed the scene everyday during the summer when Maggie came to feed her. The memory of it had to be etched somewhere in her mind. After a few more painful steps, Maggie finally swished to a halt a few feet from Dixie's head. She patted the pocket in her jacket one more time.

"Dixie, it's me, your friend Maggie," she cooed softly as she did the first day she met Dixie. Dixie stood motionless.   "Come on, girl, follow me home," Maggie begged as she folded her hands in prayer and pressed them to her lips. Dixie didn't budge. She thought that Dixie's head quivered, but she couldn't be sure. The movement was so slight that it could have been the breeze blowing through her mane. "Please, Dixie, just take one step forward and we can go home." Dixie stared blankly while Maggie stood dumbfounded. Paddy said to stall for time, and that's exactly what she was doing. She would stand in place until they dragged her from the corral.

"Time has expired," the bailiff bellowed, shattering the silence. Judge Cowherd reluctantly raised his gavel. It was time to end the proceedings. His deliberation would be short. Based on today's proceedings, he had no choice but to award Dixie to Hudson Hills. Since Dixie had not shown a preference for an owner, the paper trail of Burns had to be viewed as the facts of the case, and the law operated on facts. If the new owner was willing to sell Dixie to the Jolly Jockey, Cowherd was willing to broker the deal.

Maggie paid no attention to the bailiff. She was busy staring into Dixie's eyes, trying to peek through the windows of her soul. "Trust your horse. Trust yourself," she mumbled repeatedly. She was certain that Dixie had moved her head. Any second Dixie would move again. She could feel it in her bones. Another minute was all she needed, and she knew how to get it.

When Maggie bent down and loosened the leather straps on her brace, the crowd gasped in disbelief. "What's she doing?" they asked in hushed tones. Hearing the crowd, Cowherd turned to Maggie and lowered the gavel to his side. Meanwhile, Burns, who had opened his mouth to object, slowly exhaled. His legal curiosity had gotten the best of him. He always appreciated courtroom theatrics, and this was as good as it gets.

After the straps were unfastened, Maggie carefully slipped the brace from her leg. Holding it at arm's length, she dropped it on the ground directly in front of Dixie. "Ride the magic carousel, girl," she whispered softly. She didn't think twice about stalling for more time. It was time to test her faith. Without waiting to see Dixie's reaction, she turned to walk back to the fence where Carolyn and Paddy were waiting. After three short and clumsy steps, she stopped and shifted her weight to her good leg. A look of angry pain creased her face. Walking without the brace was more difficult than expected. For a brief second, she was thought about asking for help, but that would be too embarrassing. No cowgirl worth her weight in buckskin should ever be carried from a corral while still standing. That just didn't happen to real cowgirls. Maggie was going to walk out of the corral under her own power if it took all afternoon.

Maggie grabbed her bad leg and lifted it forward. Very gingerly, she planted her foot to maintain her balance. As she stepped forward with her good leg, the bad one buckled under her full weight. In an instant, she toppled sideways and crumpled to the ground with a dull thud, her cowgirl hat flying from head. The crowd gasped in horror, fearing that Maggie had been seriously injured.

"My leg! I can't move it," she cried out in anguish. Carolyn vaulted over the fence and entered the corral. As she stepped toward Maggie, a shrill whinny blasted her ears, stopping her dead in her tracks. All eyes shifted from Maggie to Dixie. As spectators watched excitedly, Dixie jerked her head from side to side and snorted loudly, yanking the lead line from the officer's hand. Lowering her head to the leg brace, she clenched one of the leather straps in her teeth. Rising up slowly, she stood motionless. The crowd held its breath. In slow-motion, Dixie raised her right foreleg and stepped forward, teetering wildly and almost toppling to the ground. Her ears flicked forward, and her tail stiffened as she fought to regain her balance. Staring straight ahead, she now staggered toward Maggie with the leg brace dangling from her mouth. This time the crowd gasped in terror, fearing that Dixie would accidentally fall on Maggie and crush her to death.

As Carolyn watched, her mind flashed to Bojangles. In a splint second, she replayed the entire scene in the pasture and then cracked a smile of relief. Trusting her horse, she knew exactly what Dixie was going to do. "Stay down, cowgirl. Dixie is coming to the rescue," Carolyn said calmly. Maggie face was still buried in the wet grass.

Dixie halted at Maggie's side and dropped the brace. After a whispered neigh, she lowered her head and gently nudged Maggie's side like a mare nudging a newborn foal. "She's trying to help you stand," Carolyn said excitedly. "Work with her. Let's try a push-up."

Maggie slipped her hands under the chest and pushed. With a loud grunt and a grimace, she raised her body about six inches above the ground. Dixie snorted and squeezed her muzzle underneath Maggie's chest. Slowly, she lifted her head, and Maggie rose like a puppet on a string until she was able to reach out and grab Dixie's neck for support.

"Great job, girl. I knew you could do," Maggie gushed as she kissed Dixie on the forehead. Carolyn and Paddy rushed over to hug Maggie and Dixie. Together they held hands in a small circle and followed Paddy's lead in an Irish jig, their hands and legs flailing the air. Maggie's pain had disappeared. Her leg had never felt better.

"You saved the day, cowgirl. I don't know how I can ever repay this one," Carolyn shouted joyfully as she handed Maggie her hat.

"No need to, pardner. I think we can call it even," Maggie replied with a broad smile. "Just glad that I got the chance to prove that I belong."

"You belong in the Cowgirl Hall of Fame," Carolyn joked. "You're the only cowgirl I've ever seen who can work a horse with her face in the mud."

When the crowd started to applaud, Judge Cowherd erupted. "Order in the court," he shouted angrily as he pounded the gavel against the top of the podium. He didn't stop pounding until the top broke off and sailed towards Burns, landing at his feet. "I believe Miss Dixie has spoken," he bellowed when the crowd had quieted momentarily. "It is the decision of the court that she be awarded to the Jolly Jockey in accordance with all state laws regarding the ownership of property." He then gently tapped the top of the podium with the handle of the gavel. "Court is dismissed," he declared hoarsely before making a hasty retreat to the farmhouse where lunch was waiting.

Burns and his team picked up their briefcases and headed for their rented limousine. Even though victory had been snatched from their hands at the last second, they showed no emotion in defeat. The case was nothing more than a cold and calculated business deal. They were legal guns for hire, ready to do the dirty work for anyone who could afford their bidding. They knew that there would be other showdowns in the future but none in this part of town with a pony named Dixie. By sundown, they would be ridin' out of town.

Carson walked over and picked up the top of the gavel. To his surprise, it was a fifty-cent crab mallet that had been painted dark brown. Judge Cowherd was as Baltimore as the blue crab after all. Carson then wondered if the judge was as Baltimore as a Baltimore Colt. Would he have ruled in favor of the Jolly Jockey if Maggie hadn't saved the day? One day when they were both retired from the legal profession, Carson would ask him.

"Today you're the good guy in the white hat," Carolyn said to Mr. Carson as he finally joined the group.

"I'd like to take credit, but Miss Dixie saved the day," Carson said humbly. "That's an amazing horse you have."

"She was just doing what a woman has to do," Carolyn boasted as she turned to Maggie with a wink of an eye. Maggie winked back, knowing exactly what Carolyn meant. Dixie was the four-legged matriarch of the Jolly Jockey who cared for all of her humans and horses.

"Does this mean we can take Dixie home?" Maggie asked anxiously.

"Just as soon as you can load her up," Carson responded cheerfully. The girls had been waiting to hear those exact words for the last three days. Carolyn looked around for Paddy, but he had headed for the parking lot. A minute later, he pulled up in the pick-up with a grin from ear to ear. He leaned out the window and held up his pipe that had been bitten off at the end. Carolyn chuckled at the sight but wondered about Paddy's behavior. Did he insist on bringing the trailer to boost Carolyn's confidence or did he really intend to kidnap Dixie if they lost the case? That was question for a future trail ride. Right now, she just wanted to get Dixie home.

Before leaving, Carson told Mr. and Mrs. Clark that he would get them an official copy of Cowherd's decision for their business records. From this day forward, Dixie legally belonged to them. Mr. Tuttle, who had watched the hearing from the back of the crowd, stepped forward to offer his congratulations. He was thrilled that Dixie could continue as his mascot. After conferring with

Mrs. Clark, he readily agreed to keep Dixie home for tomorrow's game.

"I'll take care of it with the Colts and the fans," he promised. "We want our stars to be rested and ready." Tuttle saw no reason to rush Carolyn and Dixie back into action. There were still two home games on the schedule. Even though, he couldn't publicize the case due to the court order, there were other ways to turn this incident into a rally cry for the home team. Win or lose on Sunday, he had a strategy planned. Dixie would be the landslide winner in the eyes of the public and her fans.

A loud, joyful whinny sounded from the trailer as the pick-up pulled into the driveway of the Jolly Jockey. Inky Dink came running and barking, following alongside the trailer until it stopped. When the trailer gate was opened, Dixie stuck her head out the back and sniffed the air. She rolled her head and let out another loud whinny that echoed across the farm. She was glad to be home.

Walking down the ramp, Dixie wobbled slightly, but Paddy quickly reassured the girls that it was a mild case of stress. There was no need to make a fuss about his drug theory.

It was time to celebrate, not investigate. He guaranteed them that Dixie would be back on her feet in a couple of days.

As Dixie turned the corner and spotted her stall, she neighed softly and shook her head up and down. Hanging above stall was a blue and white banner that read: "Welcome Home Dixie." She couldn't read, but the brightly colored banner caught her eye. Carolyn's artwork was always good enough for her if not for a grocery store flyer.

The victory party was a low-key affair, filled with a sense of relief instead of celebration. Everyone realized how close they came to losing a member of the family. While the partygoers feasted on pizza and root beer soda, Paddy snuck out to the stable. What Dixie needed was a home-cooked meal, and the master horse chef went right to work in preparing his secret recipe. Paddy quickly whipped up a sweet-smelling concoction of oats, honey, molasses, herbs, and spices. He thought about adding a liberal dose of Irish whiskey but saved that special ingredient for himself. "Ah, girl, it's almost as good as corned beef and cabbage," he boasted as he dipped his finger into the bucket and brought it to his lips. The doughy mixture was so good that Paddy wanted to bake it and sell horse cookies, but Mrs. Clark put the kitchen off-limits after she saw Paddy cook on the trail. He was just too messy in an outdoor kitchen. She could only imagine what a disaster he would be indoors.

After splitting the last piece of pizza and the last root beer, Carolyn and Maggie spent the rest of the day hanging around the stable so they could check on Dixie. After Paddy's meal, she was resting comfortably in her stall with Inky Dink asleep in the corner.

That night, the girls decided to sleep in the stable near Dixie. With Paddy's help, they dragged out the old, musty-smelling, army cots that were used for stable emergencies, such as a sick horse or a pregnant mare. They turned down the itchy, wool army blankets that Paddy offered. Flannel sleeping bags would do just fine for camping indoors. For any emergencies, they had their camp flashlights and a whistle. Except for one light bulb at the far end of the building near the office, the stable was dark.

"Kind of spooky in here," Maggie whispered in the darkness as the dull beam from the light bulb cast a mosaic of shadows near the cots.

"Especially with tonight being Halloween," Carolyn replied in hushed tone. "Any second I expect a headless horseman charge through the stable with his head tucked under his arm and a blood curdling scream upon his lips."

Since Halloween would be spent in a cold, dark stable, the girls decided to celebrate the occasion by swapping ghost stories before going to sleep. Silly and spooky tales about ghost horses, ghost coaches, and ghost riders filled the dank air. Just as Maggie was finishing her yarn about a murdered jockey who returns from the grave every Halloween to search the countryside for his stolen horse, an unearthly shadow fell across the cots. With a raised hand ready to strike out in fury, the creature trudged towards them. The girls shuddered in their sleeping bags. Carolyn fumbled for her whistle. Gasps turned to chuckles as the creature stepped into the light. It was neither human nor demon, but leprechaun. It was Paddy checking on Dixie and the girls. He had removed his cap to scratch his head.

After a quick conversation, Paddy walked back to the office, and Maggie continued her ghoulish tale. To enhance the ghostly mood, she turned on her flashlight and held it under her chin. Outside, the wind gusted, rattling every piece of equipment that wasn't tied or weighted down. Inside, the walls creaked and groaned as if they had come to life. In the darkness of the rafters, a metal object chimed the bewitching hour. Maggie finished her story with a dying gasp, switched off the flashlight, and fell back on her deathbed.

"I'll tell you a scary story," Carolyn said irately, her hot breath hovering like a cloud in the cold darkness. "The real horror story is that we almost lost Dixie this week, and I blame it on Mr. Tuttle and the Baltimore Colts. Because of his publicity stunts, everybody in the world knows about Dixie. It was just a matter of time before something bad happened to her."

"But the story had a happy ending. Me, you and Dixie are together, and that's all that really counts," Maggie replied cheerfully, trying to ease Carolyn's anger.

"Just maybe the story about the Baltimore Colts and their world famous mascots needs some new characters," Carolyn grumbled as she slid under the sleeping bag.

Maggie propped herself on an elbow and looked at Carolyn who was staring at the rafters. She had never seen the happy-go-lucky cowgirl so upset. "Carolyn Clark, Queen of the Cowgirls, and Dixie the Wonder Pony are the perfect characters for this fairy tale," she chuckled, hoping to end the night on a happy note. There was no response from the other cot.

Maggie rolled over and listened to the wind as it increased in fury. It whistled through every crack in the stable with a shrill cry that sounded almost human. Was it calling for her or Carolyn? And why was it calling? After a good night's sleep, her saddle pal would be ready to ride the oval once again. It had been a long day out of the saddle. Tomorrow, it would be time to saddle up and face the world as cowgirls always do.

Chapter 15 – Horses, Heroes and Healers

On Sunday the Colts scored four touchdowns and a field goal and still lost to the Cleveland Browns by a score of 38 to 31. When Carolyn heard the news, she was sorry for the team but glad for Dixie. Her pony was not ready for five trips around the oval. Taking a day off was a good thing, but Carolyn worried about its affect on their reputation. She had a nagging thought that many superstitious fans would blame the team's loss on Dixie's absence. The idea sounded crazy, but most fans did not display a lot of sanity. The first person that came to mind was Uncle Frank. On game days, he woke up at the same time, wore the same clothes if the Colts were on a winning streak, ate the same meals, and left for the stadium at the same time. Breaking the routine was like shattering a mirror; nothing but bad luck would follow, and bad luck ran in streaks. And right now, the Colts could not afford a losing streak. A few more losses would make a repeat championship impossible. No fan would risk that happening.

On Monday morning Carolyn found out just how superstitious the sportswriters were about their team. The inside sports headline of the morning newspaper read: "Colts Lose Without Their Good Luck Charm(s)." In a fictionalized tale, the writer playfully suggested that Dixie's absence was the cause of Sunday's loss. He detailed how Dixie had strained a leg muscle after working out with the football team. As a result, she was placed on the injured list for Sunday's game and forced to stay on the farm. Later in the week, Johnny U delivered a get-well card and a bouquet of flowers that were promptly eaten by Dixie. On Sunday afternoon, she listened to the game on the radio and reared up with a loud whinny when the Colts scored. After the game, she refused to eat her oats and honey, sulking about the loss. Later in the week, she had a doctor's appointment to see when she could suit up again. In the last paragraph of the article, Mr. Tuttle assured fans that Dixie was chomping at the bit to take the field. In two weeks, she would be riding victory laps around the oval.

"Horse manure," Carolyn fumed after reading the article. It may have been cute, but it wasn't funny. Tuttle certainly had taken care of everything alright. He took a defeat by the Colts and turned it into a public relations victory. Gullible fans would be swamping her with get-well cards.

Carolyn was peeved because Tuttle should have told the truth about Dixie. He knew people in powerful places. To get around the gag order, all he had to do was pick up the phone and call his friends at the newspaper. "First, the court hearing, and now this," she grumbled loudly. "So much for truth in advertising." It seemed that nobody was capable of telling the truth anymore, whether swearing on a Bible in a courtroom or talking to a reporter in a locker room. Lawyers and football executives were leaving a bad taste in her mouth.

On Friday afternoon, Mr. Tuttle stopped by the farm to drop off Carolyn's paycheck and three sacks of fan mail.

"But I can't accept this," Carolyn protested when Tuttle handed her the envelope. "I didn't work."

"Carolyn, you're on the payroll just like any other player," he diligently explained. "When a player gets hurt or sick, we don't stop paying them. They're still a part of the team."

"Dixie was sick, but the truth wasn't told," Carolyn said sternly with a scowl. "The fans deserve the truth."

"In public relations, the truth is what people want to hear," Tuttle chortled, unfazed by Carolyn's outburst. "The truth is that no amount of money in the world could have bought the goodwill of fans around the country. And we got it for free."

"Goodwill from fans around the country?" Carolyn asked with a puzzled look.

Tuttle grabbed a mailbag and dumped its contents on the floor. Hundreds of get-well cards, letters and telegrams spilled out. Kneeling down, Carolyn sifted through the pile and read a few of the return addresses. Horse lovers from Florida to Maine were asking about Dixie's health and offering homemade remedies guaranteed to cure man or animal. In another week, there would be bags of mail from west of the Mississippi River as soon as the Pony Express arrived in Baltimore. "You and Dixie are stars. Who would have known?" Tuttle exclaimed proudly as he headed for the door.

"Yeah, who would have known the unknown?" Carolyn groaned as she plopped down on the couch and stared at the mountain of mail. At this point in time, she didn't want to be a star, just a seldom seen cowgirl. She wondered how Dale Evans and Gail Davis coped with their fame and fortune. Did they have to lie to their fans? Did they sell their souls for fortune and fame? The whole story about Dixie's injury was a lot of phony baloney about her pony. Carolyn wondered how she could honestly answer the letters when she knew the story was a

lie. The idea was making her sick to her stomach.
Maybe she needed to explain the cowgirl creed to
Tuttle, but that would be a waste of time. Unless it
involved money or free publicity, he would turn a
deaf ear. A request for a raise surely would get his
attention. But with Dixie being a public relations
gold mine, he would smile, pat Carolyn on the back
and tell her to name her price. Money was the root
of this evil, and Carolyn didn't want to dig any
deeper in the money pit.

Carolyn picked up a handful of letters and
tossed them angrily in the air. She and Maggie
would be busy until the end of the season. At first,
answering fan mail was fun, but now it was hard
work. Carolyn would rather be watching Buddy
Deane and dancing with the Deaners. Four months
ago, she despised the thought of appearing on the
show. But now, gliding across the linoleum tiles of
the television studio seemed like a dream vacation,
a chance to get away from evils of fortune and
fame. She even thought about writing to Dale or
Gail for help, but they'd respond with an
autographed picture and a form letter telling her that
a cowgirl always follows her heart and trusts her
horse. At least, that would be an honest answer.

The Colts split their next two road games.
When they returned home for their final two home
games, fans were in frenzy. The season was
hanging in the balance. The Colts needed to start a
winning streak, and it started with the mascots. Mr.
Tuttle had big plans for Dixie's return. On

Tuesday, normally a quiet day in the sports world, he issued a press release detailing the debut of the "pony mobile." Newspapers around the state immediately picked up the story. Now young fans didn't have to attend a football game to see their heroes. All they had to do was stand along the designated route that led to the stadium.

Sunday followed the usual game-day schedule. During the morning grooming session, Dixie neighed cheerfully, flicking her ears and switching her tail. While Dixie was showing no ill effects of her recent ordeal, Carolyn's spirit was sagging badly due to Tuttle and those newspaper articles. She knew it was a sad state of affairs when her pony was coping with life better than she was.

The only change in the game day routine was the ride to the stadium. Mr. Clark drove the trailer to a parking lot near the stadium where Paddy was waiting with the "pony-mobile." Paddy quickly loaded Dixie into the back of the converted sedan and drove down 33rd Street to the front of the stadium. Fans of all ages, mostly parents with their children, lined the street to see the one-car parade. Dixie stood and Carolyn, sitting on a bale of hay, waved, smiled and occasionally tipped her hat to the crowd. For three blocks, the sidewalk was packed with people. Some of the children held homemade signs in paint and crayon that proclaimed "Welcome Home Dixie."

When Carolyn saw the excited smiles on the faces of the children, her spirit soared. She wanted to jump out the car and hug every person in sight. These were her real fans. They wanted Dixie because she was a beautiful pony who touched their hearts, not because she was a horse who ran around a football field. Every boy and girl standing along the street dreamed of owning a pony. After they went home today, they'd spend hours daydreaming about their pony adventures. They weren't there for football; they were there for friendship. No one knew more about that special bond than Carolyn. As long as she had these fans, she could bear the burden of being a mascot, or at least, she hoped she could.

The Colts beat the 49'ers by a score of 45 to 14. Six touchdowns and a field goal resulted in seven trips around the oval. In the cool weather, Dixie barely broke a sweat. After the lay-off, she was now in the best shape of her life, even better than when she was jumping in competitions. Back at the tunnel, the line stretched halfway around the stadium. Ushers barked orders to keep the crowd under control. With a walkie-talkie pressed to his lips, Tuttle directed the event while riding in a golf cart. Maggie walked the line, handing out souvenir picture cards from a blue, canvas bag with the Colts logo slung over her shoulder. A blue and white bumper sticker plastered across the front of her cowgirl hat read "The Colts Will Shine in '59." The crowd was the largest and loudest yet. The mascot business was expanding like a balloon.

Carolyn wondered how long it would last before it burst. She couldn't wait to get home and find a pin.

The final home game was a repeat of the previous week. The Colts won, and the autograph session was larger and louder. When the Colts won their last two road games, they were conference champions and headed for the championship game to be played in Baltimore. Their opponent was none other than the New York Giants. The game was already being billed as a grudge match with bad blood waiting to be spilled on both sides. With two weeks before the game, the Colts public relations department was working overtime to hype the biggest game of the year.

Carolyn was one of the first people that Tuttle telephoned. He had big plans for the big day. There would be a pony booth where fans could meet the mascots before and after the game. Special championship cards would be distributed, featuring Dixie and Carolyn and the other stars of the team. In addition, there would be concession stands near the booth where fans could buy food, drinks, and souvenirs. And that was only the beginning. Tuttle mentioned bigger plans for next year.

"Next year, I was thinking that maybe we could sell some Carolyn and Dixie souvenirs instead of just giving them away," Tuttle said snidely, referring to the blue and white pompoms that Carolyn had been giving them away for a small donation.

"But the money goes to the riding academy for handicapped kids," Carolyn replied defiantly. She was offended at Tuttle's suggestion that she was profiting unjustly from the job. She didn't like being called a horse thief. Besides, the pompoms didn't feature the team's logo. They were plain blue and white pompoms, paid for out of her pocket. As far as she was concerned, it was none of Tuttle's business what she did with them.

"I'll check with our legal people to see if you can sell souvenirs on stadium property without a permit," Tuttle replied gruffly. From the tone of his voice, Carolyn knew that he didn't like being told what to do by a mascot.

"Mr. Tuttle, do what you have to do, and I'll do what I have to do," Carolyn sighed politely as she hung up the phone.

Tuttle didn't hear the pop, but the public relations balloon had just burst. After the phone call, Carolyn decided that she was retiring as the mascot. The championship game would be her last. She was fed-up with Tuttle and the business side of football. Everything was about money and more money. Next year Tuttle would want Dixie to jump through the goalpost like the pony pictured on the team logo.

She decided to tell Tuttle sometime after the game and then write an official letter of resignation. On Saturday, she'd break the news to Maggie. She was going to do what was best for her and Dixie. There were other ways to raise funds for the academy, and Maggie was the self-proclaimed expert in that field.

As usual on Saturday afternoon, Carolyn and Maggie were sitting in front of the television, watching the Buddy Deane show and sorting through fan mail when Carolyn made the announcement.

"Maggie, I decided to retire after this season," she said casually, waiting for a response.

"Yeah, I'm a little tired myself. A break would do us some good," Maggie replied without a second thought.

Carolyn walked over and turned down the volume of the television. The Deaners whirled and twirled in silence. "I don't think you heard me," Carolyn said. "I'm retiring. I'm quitting as mascot after this season."

Maggie was stunned. She thought back to Halloween night in the stable when Carolyn mentioned retiring, but thought her friend was just venting some anger. "But you can't," she sputtered. "What will happen to the riding academy?"

"There's other ways to make money," Carolyn countered. "Remember, you have the business plan. You're the fund raiser."

"But the business plan depends on you," Maggie politely reminded her.

"No, the business plan depends on Dixie, and I've decided to do what's best for her," Carolyn insisted.

"Well, you're wrong there, pardner," Maggie replied sharply, alarmed at Carolyn's bad attitude. "We can always get another white pony to be the mascot, but there is only one Carolyn Clark, Queen of the Cowgirls. You are the link between the fans and the Dixie. Without you, there is nothing."

"Just maybe, I want to be a cowgirl and not Queen of the Cowgirls," Carolyn huffed.

"It's a little too late for that," Maggie scolded. "You have people depending on you. They deserve better than to have you walk out on them."

"I'm not waking out on them. They're walking all over me. I deserve better from those crazy football people," Carolyn shouted angrily.

"Well then, what about me? Do you think I deserve this?" Maggie said, grabbing her leg brace and glaring at Carolyn.

"Of course not. You're my friend,' Carolyn mumbled sadly. "But I need to get away from all of this. I don't know what people want anymore."

"Some people want to be just like you," Maggie fired back.

"Then let them take riding lessons if they want to be like me," Carolyn snapped.

"They already do," Maggie replied weakly, head lowered to her chin with tears in her eyes.

"But I quit. I just want to be left alone," Carolyn roared as she stomped her foot and threw her hands in the air.

"Well, cowgirls don't quit. I'm not a quitter and I'm not hanging around a quitter," Maggie yelled back as she bolted for the kitchen door.

"You can't quit. You're fired," Carolyn screamed. When she heard the screen door slam, she raced to the porch.

Maggie walked briskly to the stable with her head still down; her face flush with anger. After a few steps, she turned around to take one last look at the farmhouse as tears streamed down her face. "If that's the way you feel, then you can keep your stinky horse to yourself," she shouted at Carolyn who was standing at the rail.

"And you can keep your stinky business plan to yourself," Carolyn shouted back.

Instead of stopping at the parking lot, Maggie walked to the end of the driveway to wait for Walter. When the sedan pulled into the driveway, she yanked open the door and slammed it shut. Walter didn't even have time to unfasten his seatbelt. He simply waited for the dust cloud to settle before stepping on the gas.

Carolyn watched the sedan disappear down the road. "If that's the way you want to be, that's fine with me," she hollered to an empty field. Storming into the living room, she threw herself on the couch and sulked. She tried to watch the rest of the Buddy Deane show, but tears blocked the view. "What in the world have I done?" she muttered to herself sadly, biting her lower lip. A friendly chat had turned into a heated conversation and ended in a

317

fiery argument. Carolyn was angry with herself for getting angry with her best friend. "What a mumbled, jumbled mess I've created," she sighed deeply as she headed for the door. It was time for some serious thinking. It was time to visit the fence.

Chewing on a piece of grass, she leaned against the top rail of the fence and watched Dixie at play with other horses. At least Dixie still had a playmate, she mused. Over and over in her mind, she replayed the last few months of her life to figure out what went wrong. First came Maggie, then the Baltimore Colts, and then the riding academy for the handicapped. Everything was fine until Mr. Tuttle called, but blaming the mascot job for her problems was taking the easy way out. She made the choices. At the time, they were good choices. It's just that they didn't turn out to be the right choices, at least not at the moment. On the bright side, Dixie still enjoyed being a mascot, even if she didn't. But since her latest problem involved the mascot job, maybe that was a good place to start patching the cracks in her friendship. Now she had to figure out how to begin the repair work.

"Some people want to be just like you," Carolyn whispered, echoing Maggie's words. She repeated the sentence a few more times and then frowned. Maggie had been talking about her. Carolyn wondered how she could be so stupid and mean. Her best friend said that she was her hero, and Carolyn replied that she didn't want the job. If growing up was about being a more responsible person, Carolyn had failed the lesson miserably. But on the flip side, she was only twelve years old and still had all of her teenage years to get it right. But right now, that wasn't much consolation.

"Aye, lassie, why so glum?" asked Paddy who stopped to chat during his afternoon walk. He couldn't help but notice the Carolyn's furrowed brow and sullen face.

"I screwed up big time," Carolyn said sadly. "I just lost my best friend because I'm a stupid bonehead."

"Well, from one bonehead to another, I can tell you that it won't be the last time," he chuckled, trying to ease Carolyn's pain. "Good judgment comes from experience, and a lot of experience comes from bad judgment. It's part of life." Paddy inhaled hard on his pipe and blew a cloud of smoke into the air that hung above his head like a halo. That was a signal that he was in a serious talking mood.

"But I don't know what to do," Carolyn sighed. "All I know is that I hurt Maggie badly."

"Some people say that time heals all wounds, but it's love that heals all wounds. It's a magical potion," Paddy said tenderly.

"I still have plenty of that in my heart," Carolyn said meekly.

"It works on the deepest cuts. Just remember, sometimes, it stings a little, but that's when you know it's working," Paddy cautioned. "Just remember to rub gently so it won't leave a scar."

"I guess that I'll just have to apply it in large doses," Carolyn replied thoughtfully. Walking back to the house, she was hopeful that she could somehow patch things up with Maggie. Paddy always had a knack of putting things into perspective whether it was with people or ponies.

After an unusually quiet dinner, Carolyn volunteered to dry dishes. Mrs. Clark recognized the signal immediately. In the Clark household, towel time meant girl-talk time.

"You're going to rub the paint right off the plate if you rub any harder," Mrs. Clark said jokingly, waiting for Carolyn to open up.

"Mom, what's a good friend?" Carolyn asked casually as if nothing was bothering her.

"Let me think for a second," Mrs. Clark mused as she dried off her hands. "A good friend is like a guardian angel because they're always by your side even if you don't see them." Her answer sounded a little corny, but it was the best she do could on the spur of the moment. Hopefully, Carolyn would start talking about her problem, and she could buy time for a better answer.

"Mom, the guardian angel thing was great, but not exactly what I'm looking for," Carolyn said, nodding her head and twirling the towel in her hand.

"You're absolutely right. I'm sounding like Pastor Goodwin," Mrs. Clark chuckled. When the last dish was stacked, she poked around the kitchen counter for eyeglasses. After dinner, nothing was more relaxing for her than a couple of chapters from a western romance novel. But without her glasses, the print on the page was just smudged ink.

"Next to the coffee pot, Mom," Carolyn announced. The search for the eyeglasses was a daily post-dinner ritual.

"That's the answer to your question," Mrs. Clark proclaimed with delight as she waved the glasses in her hand.

"Friends are like eyeglasses?" Carolyn asked jokingly.

"Exactly!" Mrs. Clark stated with gusto. "A good friend is another pair of eyes. They help you to better see yourself and the world around you."

"That's a good start," Carolyn said with a bemused look. "Now that I know what a good friend is, how do I keep a good friend?" Before Mrs. Clark could answer, Carolyn poured out her heart about her tiff with Maggie and her talk with Paddy.

"Sounds like Paddy's on the right track," Mrs. Clark said, taking a seat at the kitchen table. "You have to understand these things happen to everybody. When it happens to people your age, it's hard to understand because it's the first time. Hopefully, you'll learn from this, but there's no guarantee it won't happen again."

"So you're saying as I get older, I'll make fewer mistakes in life?" Carolyn asked hesitantly.

"Something like that," Mrs. Clark laughed. "And when you're Paddy's age, you shouldn't be making any mistakes at all."

"Are you trying to tell me that Paddy is over a hundred years old?" Carolyn kidded.

"Hmm, maybe that's not the best example," Mrs. Clark piped up, placing the eyeglasses on the edge of her nose. "Let's use Grandma Clark instead."

That evening Carolyn thought about her mother's comments. Only an hour later, she was already seeing her life more clearly. The mascot job wasn't the cause of her problems; Carolyn Clark was the cause of her problems. She was so busy trying to do the right things that she couldn't see anything else around her. She needed all the eyes she could get to see where she was going in life, and there were no better eyes than those of a friend. It was time to climb back in the saddle and start searching for Maggie. Now she had to decide when to put her foot in the stirrup.

Paddy knew that broken hearts were like broken bones. The quicker you set them; the sooner they healed. He wasn't going to wait around for either Carolyn or Maggie to make the first move. Two hearts had to be mended by the championship game. When Maggie called him about picking up her gear, he saw his chance. He told her to meet him in the tack room at 10 o'clock tomorrow morning. He'd have her phonograph records and riding clothes boxed and ready to go.

The following morning, Paddy found Carolyn sitting on a bale of straw polishing her saddle. In the background, a rock and roll radio station was playing the Top Ten hits of the week. "Been looking all over for you, lassie," he said as he peered around the doorframe. "Mind if I sit a spell?"

"As long as I can bend your ear for a few minutes. I really need to talk with you," Carolyn said glumly. "I need to start applying the ointment that you mentioned, but I don't know where or when to begin."

"I think this is a good place and a good time as any," Paddy said sincerely. "But I'm not the person that you need to speak with."

When Carolyn looked up, Maggie was standing next to him. "Just came by to pick up my stuff. Didn't think you would mind," Maggie said softly.

Carolyn gulped hard as her mouth went dry. She wanted to jump up and give Maggie the biggest hug in the world but feared her hug wouldn't be returned. She tried to stand, but her legs suddenly felt weak. "Yeah, no problem," she replied weakly. "I can give you a hand if you don't mind."

"Wouldn't mind at all," Maggie replied with a weak smile.

Before Carolyn could stand, Paddy sat down and invited Maggie to sit next to him. It was time for the horse doctor with his diploma from the school of hard-knocks to apply his own healing potion.

"Maggie, you remember at the campout when you asked me about my family," Paddy began in a casual tone. "And I said I was saving the story for the right time. Well, now it's the right time." Paddy leaned forward with hands on top of his knees. "I had a beautiful wife and daughter when I was a young man. One year when I was away from home training horses, the family took sick with a fever. I rushed home, but it was too late. They were already buried behind the church."

Paddy paused and leaned back. He lifted his cap and wiped his brow with a handkerchief that was always kept stashed in his shirt pocket. His voice grew sad as he continued. "I was mad at everybody and everything. I came to America to leave those painful memories behind, but I couldn't escape the past. For years, my heart didn't heal because I didn't love. My heart turned to stone. I blamed the horses for my loss, but in the end they taught me to love again. I learned the hard way that it's love that heals all wounds, not time." With a weary look on his face, he slowly rose to his feet and wiped a tear from each eye with the back of his shirtsleeve. Without another word, he shuffled to the door, hunched over like a man carrying the weight of the world on his shoulders. His soft footsteps faded down the hallway and into the morning light. The secret of Paddy O'Brien had been revealed.

Carolyn and Maggie sat across from each other in stunned silence with their hands in their laps.

Tears welled in their eye. They hung their heads in embarrassment and stole glances at each other. Finally, Carolyn softly cleared her throat.

"I'm sorry about the argument. It was my fault. I was being selfish. From one cowgirl to another, please accept my apology," she said contritely.

"Oh, no. It was all my fault," Maggie insisted. "I'm the one who should be sorry. You and Dixie made my summer dream come true. I'm the one who's selfish."

"But if I was a better businesswoman, the dream of the riding academy would have never ended," Carolyn said.

"But if I was a better horsewoman, the dream would have never started," Maggie joked in a playful twist of Carolyn's words. She knew what Carolyn was trying to say. The argument wasn't anybody's fault, but there was plenty of blame to go around.

"If we put our heads together, we can be better businesswomen and horsewomen. The riding academy would be a sure-fire success. What do you say, pardner. Is it a deal?" Carolyn suggested eagerly, borrowing Maggie's own words to seal the deal.

"Sure, buckaroo. It's a deal," Maggie replied excitedly, realizing that she was on the other end of her own business deal. "It's kind of silly to argue over who is sorrier. Right now, we're a sorry sight for two cowgirls that are supposed to be saddle-pals."

325

"Is it a pinky promise?" Carolyn suggested, remembering her first meeting with Maggie.

"I didn't know the first one had expired," Maggie laughed as she extended her finger.

The girls locked fingers and then hugged. The Pony Power Team was back in business. Stepping back, they wiped their tears. "Okay, pardner, now let's get that business plan updated," Carolyn declared.

Back in the house, the girls poured over Maggie's notebook and talked about funding the riding academy. In a few minutes, they had a list of ten new ways to raise money. The meeting ended with the talk of a long-term business plan. According to Maggie's father, that was the key to success in business and life. Where did they want to be in two or three years other than dancing on the Buddy Deane show? Maggie agreed to give it some thought over the weekend, but Carolyn didn't need to think about it. She already had a plan in mind, but it was short-term rather than long-term. It started and ended with the mascot job.

Chapter 16 – Ride the Magic Carousel

Sunday, December 27th, 1959, was a hard day to be a cowgirl. The weather forecast called for high temperatures in the mid 30's with a likely chance of snow by late afternoon. Remembering her dream ride in the mountains to Sweetwater, Carolyn was ready for the cold. Two pairs of socks, a royal blue turtleneck sweater, and the long underwear that she had received for Christmas would provide enough warmth for a picnic at the North Pole. Even her white leather, uniform gloves finally proved useful. Too heavy to wear for most of the season, they were perfect for frigid

327

conditions. For added insulation, she slipped them over a pair of cotton gloves. To protect her ears, Carolyn decided on a pair of blue earmuffs. A cowgirl hat just wouldn't look right on top of a knit hat. Today was the biggest rodeo in town, and she had to dress her best no matter what the weather.

Maggie was waiting with her parents at the tunnel entrance when the Clark caravan arrived at the stadium. She wasn't hard to spot. Today she was as wide as she was high. In place of the usherette outfit, she wore a blue and white snowsuit. It wasn't the cowgirl look, but it did have the team's colors. In place of her white cowgirl hat, she wore a blue and white knit hat with the Colts logo that was pulled down tightly over her ears. Maggie thought she looked like an Arctic explorer. Carolyn thought Maggie looked more like an overweight snowman. Either way, Carolyn knew that both costumes would work for today's festivities.

While Maggie escorted her parents to their seats, Carolyn walked the oval with Dixie. Despite the recent cold weather, the cinder track was in good shape. Some sections were frozen hard, but there were no dangerous icy spots. A vigorous trot in place of the traditional gallop would be the pace, but that was easier said than done. Dixie loved to run in the cold weather. It was in her genes. Her ancestors had lived in the windy, snow-swept mountains of Wales. While Dixie didn't need protection from the weather, Carolyn wasn't taking any chances. She dressed her in the team's official blue horse blanket, trimmed in white with a white horseshoe on each side and the word "Colts" at the bottom. It was a perfect compliment to the blue and white pompoms.

As Carolyn neared midfield, the players waved. They were glad to see their good luck charms. Johnny U walked over for a brief chat and asked about Dixie with a wink and a nod. It made Carolyn wonder if he knew about the court hearing. "Just remember," he said. "Everybody who steps on this field today is a champion. Win or lose, these games are always fondly remembered. Plus it gives the fans and sportswriters something to talk about in the off season." He chuckled at his words and then headed off the locker room after giving Dixie a good luck pat on the rump.

Turning back to the stands, Carolyn spotted Uncle Frank hanging over the rail, calling her name. As on opening day, he begged for a picture and an autograph in his championship program. Carolyn readily granted him his every wish. After all, today was his Christmas gift from the Colts, only a few days late like last year.

After Uncle Frank departed, Carolyn scanned the crowd near mid-field, hoping to see Mr. and Mrs. Farnsworth. Even thought she couldn't spot them, she was confident that they could see her. From their expensive seats, they should have no trouble seeing Dixie on the run. As she continued to walk, fans crowded near the rail to chat. After a season as the mascot, she was on a first name basis with many of them. It was a good feeling to be so readily accepted. She had no doubt that any Colt mascot would be treated the same.

Back in the corner of the stadium, Carolyn watched the pre-game festivities with Maggie. It was like opening day except the grass was browner, the clouds grayer, and the temperature fifty degrees cooler. Even with her earmuffs, the stadium was loud. Boos for the Giants and cheers for the Colts were thunderous. Now she knew why sportswriters described Memorial Stadium as the world's largest outdoor insane asylum. Today everybody was delirious with Colt fever.

Feeding on the energy of the crowd, the Colts bolted out of the starting gate. In the middle of the first quarter, Johnny U threw a 60-yard touchdown pass to Lenny Moore, the shifty halfback known as Spats for way he taped his cleats. Like a lightening strike, the score was 7 to 0. Mr. Clark didn't even have time to give Carolyn the thumbs-up. As soon as Carolyn heard the rumble of cheers sweeping across the field, she jumped in the saddle. When the cannon boomed, she was off to the races. Pulling hard on the reins, she tried to keep Dixie under a full gallop, but that was impossible. Dixie was feeding off the energy of the crowd, and all Carolyn could do was hold on tight and trust her horse. The feeling was identical to her first trip around the oval on opening day. Only this time, she knew what to expect in the dark and gloomy shadows at the closed end of the stadium.

After the touchdown, the game settled into a replay of opening day. The Colts offense was out of rhythm. Johnny U pulled one way, and the rest of the team pulled in the opposite direction. The offense was stuck in the middle of the field. Johnny U was throwing horseshoes instead of footballs. While the Colts sputtered, the Giants marched up and down the field to score three field goals.

Carolyn spent most of the time out of the saddle, standing with her father and Maggie. Every few minutes, she nudged Maggie with an elbow and grinned. Maggie grinned back, not knowing the mischief that Carolyn had in mind. When the whistle sounded to end the first half, Carolyn grabbed the reins and sprinted towards the tunnel with Maggie on her heels. The moans and groans from the stands told the story. The Giants led 9 to 7. The crowd feared that Johnny U's cold hands might never heat up in the cold weather, but Carolyn knew better. Johnny always had a plan, just like Carolyn.

"Follow me. We don't have much time," Carolyn said urgently as she headed to the trailer under the grandstand that was used as a dressing room for the groundskeepers. Once inside, she immediately unbuttoned her jacket and then her pants.

"You can't go out there not dressed as the mascot," Maggie insisted as she looked around for a change of clothes, certain that Carolyn was going to put on another layer of long underwear.

331

"I'm not going back out there dressed as the mascot," Carolyn replied calmly.

"Then who is?" Maggie asked jokingly.

"You are," Carolyn shouted gleefully.

"I'm going to what?" Maggie squealed with a look of shock.

"Congratulations! You've just been accepted into the Baltimore Colts mascot trainee program," Carolyn crowed. "This is part of our business plan where horsewoman meets businesswoman. Now hurry up, you don't have much time."

"But, but, but I don't know what to," Maggie stuttered in a feeble protest.

"Of course, you know what to do. You've ridden Dixie a hundred times. Just trust your horse," Carolyn replied as she handed Maggie the blue uniform pants.

Since she was a little bigger than Maggie, Maggie had no trouble sliding the pants over her brace. Maggie continued to complain as Carolyn helped her to dress, but her cries for mercy fell on deaf ears. Carolyn was not to be denied. So far, her business plan had worked to perfection.

"Wow, that's a really neat necklace," Carolyn said as she started to unzip Maggie's snow jacket. Reaching in, she carefully lifted the brightly colored, beaded necklace to her face. The centerpiece was a large blue medallion with the white silhouette of a horse and rider that was circled by small yellow stars. Beaded fringes in blue, white and yellow hung from the bottom. The loop of the necklace was as series of smaller medallions in the same pattern as the centerpiece. It had the look and feel of a genuine Indian artifact.

"Mom gave it to me for Christmas. It was given to her at Camp Pocahontas. She said it's now a family heirloom to mark the rite of passage for Farnsworth women," Maggie proudly proclaimed.

"Very impressive. Now let's mark your rite of passage as a Baltimore Colt," Carolyn fired back, buttoning up the uniform jacket that Maggie was now wearing.

"But I'll freeze to death," Maggie whined.

"It's a wool blend suit. Keeps you warm as toast," Carolyn declared as she quickly squeezed into Maggie's snowsuit.

"But the fans are expecting you," Maggie insisted.

"No, the fans are expecting Dixie and a rider in a Colts uniform. Right now that rider is you. And beside, we could pass as sisters," Carolyn replied, handing Maggie the earmuffs and cowgirl hat.

Maggie was resigned to her fate. After all, Carolyn was the boss, and she was just the business manager. "Me and my stupid business plan," she mumbled under her breath as Carolyn chuckled. "I knew it would get me in trouble someday." At the door, Maggie stopped at the full-length mirror. Carolyn was right about one thing. In uniform, they could easily pass as sisters.

Mr. and Mrs. Clark, who were waiting outside, gave Maggie a quick thumbs-up and applauded.

Maggie smiled nervously and returned a limp thumb in the air. At least two more fans thought she looked like the mascot. Now she only had to convince thousands more.

At the entrance to the field, Carolyn went over some last minute instructions and handed the reins to Maggie. "Cowgirl, up," she shouted as she bent down and lifted Maggie into the saddle. "Remember to smile and wave. Look like you're having fun."

"I'll get you for this," Maggie said, feigning anger. "I can't wait to see you on Buddy Deane. I'll make the ticket request personally."

"I can't wait myself,' Carolyn replied smugly. Lately, she had been thinking a lot about the show. She had finally decided to wait until Maggie turned thirteen. Then she'd have a saddle pal to take to the dance.

As Dixie stepped on the field, a blast of cheers sent shivers up and down Maggie's spine. Instantly, she imagined 57,000 pairs of staring eyes wondering who was the stranger riding Dixie. As she gazed the stands, she pictured the fans shouting "We want Carolyn!" To her relief, they were cheering for the players who were lining up on the field for the second half kick-off. Seconds later, the fans in the corner grandstand found something else to cheer about. "Go, Dixie!" and "Get'em, Dixie!" they shouted in unison. It finally dawned on Maggie that she was the mascot. Suddenly, the queasy feeling in her stomach disappeared, but she was still scared to death. For the first time in her life, she was the star in a real horse circus.

Throughout the third quarter, Maggie sat ramrod straight in the saddle with Carolyn at her side. With her bad leg, the Pony Power Team decided that Maggie would remain mounted. But Maggie didn't mind, even when it started to snow. From her leathery loft, she viewed the players on the field like a general watching his troops in battle. Dixie's back was the best seat in the house. Now she knew why Carolyn always gushed about sitting tall in the saddle.

Every few minutes, Maggie glanced at Mr. Clark who was always fidgeting with the earplug on his transistor radio. Since neither team was threatening to score, his technical difficulties weren't a concern. Carolyn would occasionally glance at her with a stupid grin as if the snowsuit was cutting off the circulation to her head. Since both defenses had taken control of the game, all Maggie could do was sit and wait. In a hard fought battle, the game was being played one yard at a time. At the end of the third quarter, the score was still 9 to 7. The Colt offense had been corralled again at mid-field.

Carolyn coaxed Maggie into riding Dixie around their end of the stadium during the break between quarters. At the rate the Colts were scoring, it might her only ride of the day. Fans cheered as Dixie headed their way. Feeling more comfortable as the mascot, Maggie waved and smiled. A wide grin creased Carolyn's face at the sight. It reminded her of her first ride when she was too scared to even look at the crowd. Only two hours on the job, Maggie was already performing like a seasoned professional.

At the start of the fourth quarter, the Pony Power Team took their usual positions. Only this time, Carolyn brushed up against Dixie, ready to alert Maggie when the Colts scored. She knew that Johnny U would score at least one more touchdown. During the game, he would figure out a couple of special plays and then save them until they were needed. And with time running out, they were needed in a hurry.

"Please, Johnny, just one more score. I know you can do it," Carolyn whispered to herself. Even if the Colts lost, Carolyn wanted Maggie to have the ride of a lifetime, one lap around the oval. That would ease the pain for her and the thousands of die-hard fans who would solemnly file out of the stadium and wait another seven months for summer training camp to begin.

Mr. Clark, who had spent most to the second half tinkering with his radio, looked up suddenly and stared downfield. Something was happening at the closed end of the stadium. The fans were on their feet and cheering. Mr. Clark tuned up the volume on his radio. The earth trembled, and a wave of noise slowly rumbled across the field like prairie thunder. In the distance, players chased each other across the field while being knocked to the ground. From the chaos, a lone player in a blue jersey emerged with the football tightly tucked under his arm. A Colt defender had intercepted a pass and was sprinting for the end zone where they were standing. The race was on. Only a few steps behind the Colt, a Giant was chasing madly, gaining ground with each step.

"Run! Run! Run!" Carolyn screamed at the top of her lungs with her hands cupped to her mouth. Next to her, Mr. Clark was jumping up and down, punching the air with his fists. At the ten yard line, the Giant's lineman dove forward in a last ditch attempt to grab the leg of the ball carrier. He slid face forward in the loose dirt and skidded to a halt, empty-handed. The Colt galloped across the goal line and dropped the ball on the ground. Carolyn and Mr. Clark threw their arms straight up in the air to signal the score. Touchdown Baltimore Colts! The cannon boomed, and the fans exploded into another round of wild applause.

Maggie froze in the saddle at the sight. One second, she could barely see the players. Seconds later, the team was celebrating a few steps in front of her. She looked at Mr. Clark for a signal, but he was still jumping up and down. There was no need for a thumbs-up. It was obvious to anyone living in Baltimore what had happened. While thinking about her next move, Maggie felt a hard tug on her pants leg. She leaned towards Carolyn until they touched heads.

"Ride the magic carousel," Carolyn whispered in her ear with a beaming smile, knowing exactly how Maggie was feeling.

"Ride the magic pony, cowgirl," Maggie responded with a wink. She pulled on the reins and turned Dixie toward the oval, ready for her ride into football history. Reaching down, she patted her pocket. The plastic lump was missing. She panicked for a brief second and then remembered that she had switched jackets with Carolyn. Too late to turn around, she reached up and pulled out her necklace, rubbing the large blue medallion with her fingers. A cowgirl never had too much good luck.

On the track, Maggie gently tossed the reins and pressed her heels. Dixie quickly found her stride and settled into an easy gallop. The crowd was still on its feet and cheering even louder as the extra point sailed through the goalposts. Fans leaned over the rail to touch Dixie. As Maggie smiled, a gentle warmth bathed her body, washing away the years of pain. At last, she was finally free from her crippled body. At last, she finally realized that she had been preparing for this day since her arrival at the Jolly Jockey. For the rest of her life, she would always have this magical moment to remember, and whenever she remembered, the pain would melt to joy.

Mrs. Farnsworth was busy gossiping with her friends when the Colts scored their first touchdown. Much to her disappointment, she had missed

Dixie's first trip around the oval. For the rest of the game, she sat with her husband's binoculars in her lap, ready for the next score. As Dixie passed in front of her section about thirty rows from the field, she peered through the lens. "Oh, my gosh! It's our Maggie aboard that pony," she shouted hysterically.

Mr. Farnsworth quickly grabbed the binoculars. His wife couldn't tell the players apart with a program, how she could recognize mascots so easily, he wondered. He quickly zoomed in on the rider, but the oversized cowgirl hat shaded the girl's face. He then tilted the binoculars downward. "It's Maggie! It's Maggie," he screamed with delight. The blue medallion flapping outside the girl's jacket was all the proof that he needed.

"How in the world did she pull it off?" Mrs. Farnsworth asked calmly as she wrenched back the binoculars to watch Maggie finish her ride.

"Just a cowgirl's rite of passage," Mr. Farnsworth joked as he squeezed his wife's hand.

"Who would have thought that our daughter would grow up to be a cowgirl?" Mrs. Farnsworth replied, beaming with pride. She had come to the game looking for a champion on the field. To her heart's delight, she didn't have to wait until the end of the game to find one. In a loud voice, she let everyone in her section know the identity of the girl who was riding the white pony. Then she turned her full attention to the field, rooting for the Colts to score again and again.

Carolyn was waiting with two thumbs up when Maggie returned. Her short-term business plan had been an overwhelming success. It was going to take a long time to wipe the grin from that cowgirl's face. When Dixie pulled up, Maggie leaned out of the saddle to thank her saddle pal. "That's the best carousel in the world, and Dixie's the best pony in the world," Maggie gushed. "Where's the ticket booth? I think I'd like to ride again," she joked.

"Then you better find Johnny U because he's selling the tickets. It's up to him whether you ride or hide," Carolyn chuckled.

A minute later, Maggie took her second ride around oval. Johnny U was hotter than a desert rattlesnake in a wool suit. The Colts scored two more touchdowns and a field goal to turn a nail-biter into a lopsided 31 to 16 victory. When the final gun sounded, thousands of jubilant fans streamed onto the field and surrounded their helmeted heroes to celebrate. Somewhere in the sea of madness, Uncle Frank was busy scooping up pieces of the field. He had carefully calculated that a clump of turf could produce enough grass seed to eventually cover his lawn. Even Uncle Frank had a long-range business plan.

Carolyn glanced over to the tunnel grandstand where a large crowd was waiting to greet the mascots. Uncle Frank was standing in line with pen and program in hand and a chunk of sod hanging from his coat pocket. "Let's go cowgirl. It's time to meet your fans before we get trampled to death," she trumpeted.

"Thanks, pardner. I'll never forget this day," Maggie said sincerely.

"Think nothing of it, buckaroo," Carolyn replied in her best Texas drawl. "Just doing what a cowgirl has to do."

Carolyn grabbed the reins and walked Dixie to the tunnel. As she stepped forward and swung her arms, a hard object poked her side. She first noticed it when she switched jackets with Maggie, but didn't give it any thought. Reaching into the coat pocket, she pulled out the freshly painted, spittin' images of her and Dixie in their mascot outfits.

Touched by the display of affection, all she could do was smile and shake her head. Looking over her shoulder at Maggie, she gently stuffed the figures in the pocket. She opened her mouth to speak but turned her head in silence. Maggie was busy smiling and waving to her fans. It made no sense to ruin the moment with some mushy words. Cowgirls didn't get that kind of emotional in public. Cowgirl secrets of the heart were treasures to be shared at a late night campfire under a starry sky.

With each step, Carolyn's thoughts drifted farther back in time. "Horses, heroes, healers, and heartache," she whispered under her breath. She chuckled at the thought of her own 4-H club. Those four words summed up the year. It had been quite a ride in and out of the saddle. With its ups and downs, the magic carousel seemed more like a roller coaster ride at times, but that was simply part of life. If being a pre-teen was this dramatic and traumatic, Carolyn cringed at the thought of her teenage years. On the bright side, she had learned a few valuable lessons about growing up that might guarantee survival as a teenager. What more could a cowgirl ask for, she thought. In good times and bad, she had Dixie, Maggie, Paddy, her parents, and even Johnny U. Next year, there would be the riding academy and more horses, heroes, and healers. Only this time, she would be a little more prepared for the heartache.

At the edge of the track, Carolyn stopped for one last look at the field. Some fans were jogging on the cinder track, waving a Baltimore Colts flag. She knew just how they felt. They were riding their own magic carousel, not wanting the moment to end. "Yes, siree, step right up for another year and another ride on the magic carousel," she muttered as she glanced up at Maggie. Even though Maggie wouldn't be in the ticket booth, Carolyn was ready to climb aboard a painted pony and reach for the brass ring.

A sudden click and a brilliant flash of light jolted her back to reality. A wandering newspaper photographer thought he had just captured the picture of the year, a snapshot of Carolyn, Maggie and Dixie staring into the stands and gazing into the future. Carolyn reached forward and put her hand in front of her face, temporarily blinded by the camera's flashbulb. Through the white orbs that seared her eyeballs, she saw the outline of the photographer dressed in a trench coat with a press pass clipped to the lapel and a knit hat pulled tightly over his head. There was nothing unusual about the man until she looked at his feet. Not too many photographers wore black high top shoes with cleats.

"I didn't mean to startle you," Johnny U apologized. "But I just had to get my own souvenir. I'm not big on trophies and that kind of stuff, but a picture is something to cherish forever."

"No problem, Johnny. Just make a copy for me and my teammate," Carolyn replied casually, pointing to Maggie. She had found the perfect picture for the last page in Maggie's scrapbook.

"It's a deal, cowgirl. Until we meet again," Johnny said with his trademark crooked grin. He shook hands with Carolyn and headed back to the locker room, hunched forward and unnoticed by the fans who lingered on the field.

"Good old Johnny U! What a cowboy! He certainly plays for the right team," Carolyn said to herself. As she continued her walk, she mused about Johnny's comment. "Cowgirls and the Colts," she exclaimed softly and smiled. Those words had a nice ring to them. It would be a great title for Maggie's classical concerto.

By the end of the game, a soft, white blanket of snow covered the edges of the field. Carolyn gazed at the ground and noticed the prints in the snow. She and Dixie were blazing a well-marked trail that led from the end zone to home. Carolyn sighed longingly. The impressions would melt with tomorrow's sun, but the memories would remain forever in her heart. No matter what happened in the future, 1959 would be one of the greatest years in her life.

ABOUT THE AUTHOR

Paul Travers grew up a long touchdown pass from Memorial Stadium, home of the Baltimore Colts. As a young boy, he idolized his helmeted heroes in blue and white, but there was one unforgettable Colt who had him spellbound. Her name was Carolyn Clark, and she had the greatest job in football, mascot for the Baltimore Colts. Decades later, a book was born when the ghostly image of Carolyn and her pony, Dixie, raced across his mind. Rekindled memories became the chance to saddle up with Carolyn and Dixie and ride the magic carousel of dreams one more time. Paul received a B.A. from the University of Maryland and an M.A. from Pepperdine University. He served in the United States Marine Corps and later worked with the Maryland Park Service as a park ranger and historian. In addition to writing, he lectures on American history and conducts workshops for young writers. Visit him at www.paultravers.com.

Other Books By Helm Publishing

Tutor
by Tom Te Wu Ma

Memories Trail
Promises to Keep
by DL Larson

Cabbage Requiem
by RL Paul

Northern Escape
by RL Coffield

Sigourney's Quest
The Separatist
by Gordon Snider

A Gift of Dreams
by Robert A. Benjamin

Lord Emberstone's Quest
by Michael E. Hill

An Unlikely Duke
by Debra Killeen

The Beach Club
by Richard Paloma

Inside Out
by Gerald Zipper

Ghost Whispers
by William Gorman

The Griffin's Gauntlet
The Coven's Initiates
The Royal Quests
by Wesley Lowe

Double Identity
by Margaret Clay

Incident at Pittston Crossing
by CB Nelson

Thicker Than Water
by Benjamin Frazier

In Pursuit of Pat O'Brien
by Tami Hotard

Curse the Darkness
by Phillip J. Medley

The Third Condition
by Richard Gilbert

Available at Barnes & Noble, Border's and
Amazon.com
Visit www.publishersdrive.com

Printed in the United States
200814BV00001B/1-51/A